ALIEN BIZ

Jozeph Picasso's Alien Trilogy
Act 2
Filmmaking Adventures

Karl J. Niemiec

ALIEN BIZ

ISBN 978-0-9833663-1-7

LapTopPublishing.com

Carmel, Indiana 46033

For him who went unnamed,
for his family who knew not why,
the truth is within these pages,
of how this little man died.

ALIEN BIZ

Two blows to the face. Two shotgun blasts. Thespian, barman, victim, policemen, it was a conspiracy thing. The truth, the reality of the crime goes unsolved. No dignity, just an all out cover-up and the life of a seemingly innocent man vanishes from the face of this planet – left to haunt me in my sleep. That's how it goes down. At least that's how it appears to me. No integrity, no excuse, my blunder, and all the shame of hiding my past from my future. What starts as a nightmare only gets surreal as the truth unfolds. We are not alone. There are worse upon this Earth. My apartment building, Mystery Towers, is visible proof.

Jozeph Picasso

Drowning

At Tujunga Wash I, Jozeph Picasso, hang an involuntary stage right, heading south. Then all bazooka hits me. I'm awash in roaring sewer rapids. Rolling head over heels like a turkey pinwheel. Things are bouncing off me. Trash, cans, cigarette butts, ironically my beloved LA Times, and who knows what other kind of gutter tossed, ocean bound trash. In between these twirls of doom, I'm sucking sewer enhanced stench through my armpit. For some self preserving reason, I've elected to cover my face from the San Fernando Valley grit trying to ooze between my teeth with my left forearm. It's not working, so I'm fighting the gag reflex and moving excessively fast. The Colfax Bridge is coming up quick. I'm still breathing but I'm bobbing, sucking what life I can savor between mouthfuls of gutter runoff.

At the top of the converging waters, I end up facing skyward heading headfirst. I'm rudderless though. Much like my life. A metaphor I'll die reflecting because the torrent trying to suck me under is so much like my past it's almost funny, even though the lark's on me alone.

What a floater I am. Claire Davis, the shining starlet, will give my dog, Bubba, a good home and a showbiz career. Before long, a better man will come into her life, getting the opportunity of a lifetime that I messed up. Even Bubba will forget all about this waterlogged Dogman.

One thing is for sure, I'm not looking forward to pounding my noggin on the Colfax Bridge. With all my strength I use my arms to rudder me blindly around so that I'm going feet first.

Big mistake! Immediately, the backwash of water on the bridge support drags my boots under, and TWANG! My right oil resistant Elk Wood boot is stuck in something I can't see. I don't have to; I'm stuck in a submerged shopping cart.

I'm flung momentarily skyward out of the water and quickly face down into the murkiness. The river is streaming over me with its entire wrath, and I have no recourse to right myself. I'm just another aquatic reed in the stream of brown yuckiness.

Then it happens. I can actually feel my hip socket shatter with a sharp lightening blast of pain. I roll over, knowing that I've just snapped my upper leg in two, if not at the socket itself. There's no bone holding me to the cart now, just butt muscle and other gooey human fibrous tissue.

This doesn't do me any good either. Now I'll drown in even more pain. Much, much more! As if, three or four broken ribs weren't bad enough, and a lung full of backwash. However, after one or two good twirls of upper leg tissue, I'm facing the boisterous sky again. Damn, I'm a half arm's length under water and in so much pain my eyes rivet shut. "Mooky!"

Where is the Mook man when I need him? Isn't he the alien way ahead of these kinds of mindless games? "Mooky!" Didn't he say he'd be around if I needed him? Well, I'm drowning like a human cockroach flushed down the toilet of humanity. I have maybe twenty seconds of bubbles left, and from there it's just a matter of letting the river run its course. By the time it recedes to its normal trickle of greenish-black, oily yuck, I'll be nothing more than an unrecognizable lump of human protoplasm sporting a bad hair day.

Why does it all have to end this way?

1

(The Nightmare Began Three Years Ago While Bartending in Beverly Hills)

The normally slow Monday night at Charlie's starts to go south when I watch a well known drunken actor sucker punch a happy little nobody for zero reasons other than they are both drunk and the little guy is defenseless. By the time the little guy comes back for an apology, the actor is gone, but the bar manager, who is high on Beverly Hills coke, kicks him out by literally kicking him in the butt. Not kidding.

So once outside, the little guy opens the driver's side door of a 70's Mercury Marquis woody station wagon and reaches inside. I'm now watching him from the upscale hot spot's stoop.

At the same time, Skip, the darkly handsome bar manager, seems to be losing his mind, because he is in full stride on the sidewalk, and goes airborne to plant his black dress shoe into the little guy's passenger-side front door, leaving a very large dent. I've seen a lot of dumbass stuff go down already but this is above and beyond.

Thinking that's the end, Skip turns his back on the little guy as he steadies himself from his heroic deed. He's got a big triumphant smile on his coked up face. The Spanish busboy standing between us isn't so sure it's over. But Skip ignores the busboy's expression of disbelief and checks Charlie's patron filled windows to see who is watching him be so gallant.

What a moron, is all I can think of. Because I'm actually watching this all in split screen. As though I saw the results of this scene happen already. The racking of the first shell, the attempt to aim, me only getting out the words: "He's got a...." Bam! The shotgun goes off as the little guy comes down onto the roof of the station wagon with his twelve gauge pump, fully intending to take the back of Skip's gallant head off.

But the little guy is too short to reach over the top to get a bead on Skip. So his first blast whizzes up just inches past my face. I don't have time to move. I'm frozen in time and space. If the pellets have passed through me I don't register pain. As the initial concussion fades, all I hear are the pellets striking anything metal and wood behind me. By this time he's already pumping a shell back into his chamber. The freaked out busboy and the now less than gallant Skip are sprawling on the sidewalk crawling towards me. I see their silent cries for help on their faces, but only those four muscles holding my eyes in my head, controlling their movement in the four cardinal directions, are free to move.

There just isn't time to even help myself.

And it gets worse, fast. The little guy turns toward Third Street. His front door is open, so he's got to step around it. He now knows he's too short to go over top again so he's heading around the car to finish the botched up murder-revenge job.

Skip and the busboy that had stupidly followed him out of the restaurant are still bellies down, crawling, seemingly stuck in quicksand toward me. None of us three have time to make a safe move. The first one he plans on killing is dead, but the second one's got a chance if he's lucky enough to run in the right direction. But the third one is just an idiot if he's still there after two more shots.

I know I should be scared, but I feel no fear. In my peripheral view off my left shoulder no one's left in the windows. Except for the silent cast iron statue of a man with the menu who started all this mayhem and a strange Goth looking chick that can't take her eyes off what is taking place. I can hear screaming and tables being pushed out of the way as the rest of the patrons smartly scatter back into the restaurant. Yet, there this one girl kneels, eyes just above the window ledge, taking it all in, a voyeur getting off on the scene.

The little guy has pulled the trigger and he's going to prison. He's got that determination on his face that he might as well get the satisfaction of killing someone.

My eyes rack focus on movement from the street behind the little guy. Heading right towards us, on West 3rd Street, is an Wilshire Division squad car. Weird second act plot twist if there ever was one. Never is there a cop around when I really need one. Yet here these two guys are. This is just too convenient.

The squad car speeds up, screeching to a stop. There's not even time for the two surprised young cops to turn on their lights. The passenger is short and chubby and the driver is tall and stocky, both in uniform blues. Had someone called the police from inside? I really don't know. Having them here this quick is so surreal. Regardless, here they are, making the little guy turn toward them at the sound of their screeching tires.

He's sideways to me now, looking north. The shock on this side of his face will be with me for the rest of my life. All he wanted was a happy moment. All he wanted was for life to register that he existed and that he had a reaction to a stupid statue holding a menu. The cops pulling their guns don't know any of this.

I do. I do! In my mind it is imprinted in 3D. It'll haunt my sleep forever because he'll always be denied that happy moment of pure wonderment of thinking a statue to be real. It was stolen by Jetty, a drunken actor.

And now this: Instead of killing Skip for throwing him out of the restaurant and kicking him and his car, he suddenly finds cops with guns on him. I swear the guy is so startled to see them there that he pulls the trigger of the shotgun again by accident. It pushes him back against his open car door, blowing out the window of the medical high-rise across the street.

Immediately, the two cops unload the stroke of death on the little guy, blasting through his head, chest, and stomach.

I still haven't moved to save myself after coming outside to get Skip and the busboy back inside. Like the statue sitting inside, I'm frozen, looking down on the end of a life. Skip and the busboy are now facing the cement. They see none of what I see. But the impact of the bullets spins the little guy to face me, eyes barely above the car top, face half ripped open. He sees me. I know that, an instant of awareness. I'm the last face he sees in his unfulfilled life. Then he's gone, as though someone, something, his soul, I don't know what, but something left him behind to suffer the consequences of his actions on his own.

He has no idea of who I am. I'm no longer his buddy, the old Cappy that he had oddly called me, the generous bartender who bought him coffee and a drink. I'm a stranger. He is now just a befuddled little weird person with no idea of why he is there or why this is happening to him.

This is my confession to myself. The stroke of death has passed through him. These cop bullets were a complete and utter surprise to this poor guy. Yet, there he is, shot to pieces, holding a twice-fired shotgun.

As he fights to understand, I know I'm the last living person he will see. It's a responsibility I do not want to bear. Even though I'm just a flash of light before the dark, and he drops down behind the station wagon's door.

Am I the only one who sees this?

Who has time to think? Something is still moving in the station wagon so the cops speed load and start firing into it until a voice from some actor I can't remember but recognize his face yells: "It's a dog." At least ten shots went into the station wagon but the beagle still lives.

Good old Skip must've been thinking overtime. He gets up, taking the busboy by the arm and moves to me at the top of the stoop. He says the words that will forever wake me up at night that will forever scar the vision of my self-respect. "If anyone mentions Jett DiGarbo's name, you're fired."

But truth be known, we're all sad humans for the lies we'll tell about what just happened here tonight. Lies that hide inside us, binding us, rotting in dark recesses of our tainted souls.

Yet, this little guy's death has ultimately led me here, to own my apartment building. For the Goth chick watching in the window ended up being my agent for a spell and sold my first script that paid for this Magical Mystery Towers Tour.

2

(The Morning I Drowned)

Usually I wake up at the gun blast and don't see him die. This morning I'm fully awake as these guilty memories flow through my head. I never mentioned Jett's DiGarbo's name to anyone. No one did, although we all spent the night at the police station being questioned about what had happened. No one there really wanted to know. This guy was just a crazy nobody. And nobody but me really knew what had happened. I'm the craziest nobody of the bunch for keeping my mouth shut.

Yes, I should've sent him home, yes I should've known. In fact, I did. I just didn't act on my intuition in the right manor. I made a choice, the wrong choice. Now this little guy is dead. It's easier to see in hindsight in my dreams and late night regrets. Maybe it's the only true way. But this guy got put in a deadly position. He got pushed to the brink by heartless others, until he did not fear to be dead any longer. But when the moment of death came to him, something left him behind. What I do not know. He had no idea why he was there. I saw this. I will carry that knowledge with me for the rest of my nights because I sadly said nothing about the truth of that night.

The LA papers didn't even mention his name. I still do not know it. It was left as a random shooting outside of a Beverly Hills establishment. No mention of the violent scuffle inside. No names, just: "Two Wilshire Division officers mortally wounded a shotgun wielding man during a shootout in front of a bar on West 3rd Street. The gunman, who had earlier been thrown out of Charlie's Restaurant, fired one blast at three restaurant employees as they left the building. Police said, the two officers were waiting at a red light in their patrol car and saw the incident. When they moved in and identified themselves, a gunfight ensured."

I saved a copy. This guy is dead, and Jett has his name in a star on the Walk of Fame, forever validating him as a someone. He is now actually coproducing Claire Davis' new TV series where my ex-girlfriend's dog, my best friend, Bubba, happily works as her dog Friday. And this is my guess for why these dreams have returned so vividly. Jetty is back in my life. Or even worse, I'm back in his.

The two cops, the lucky heroes, I assume went on with their rising careers. I don't know what happened to Skip and the busboy. I had finished out the week, filling in for the other bartenders who went home for the holidays. Before my next shift, I got a terse phone message left by the day manager. He said my cash bank was thirty dollars short and I was no longer trusted, so don't show up to work for my shift on Monday.

Despite knowing it was a lie, a setup, a way to distance me from the situation, I didn't even fight it. It being Christmas Eve, I was actually relieved not to have to go back there. I didn't fit in. Never would. The experience had left me as cold to that crowd as the statue holding the menu. My illustrious Beverly Hills bartending days were over.

But because Jetty punched out this little guy, he is dead. Because I said nothing, there is no apology, and for me, again on this night, no sleep. Bam! The blast flashes before my eyes like an unfinished thought working its way back into my present day, looking for answers. What really happened that night? What left him? What am I missing? And how do I make it stop?

3

El Nino is here. The rain comes down in wheelbarrows. I can only hope that the Quick Seal I used on the front steps at the base of the new facade is working and my lobby isn't flooding again. It doesn't happen all the time, usually only when the rain comes in from the east and runs down the facing of the building. It's not just the perplexing water but the awful stink that follows while I wait for the carpet guy to come.

I sit up in bed. I've had this same nightmare many times. Bubba, my ex-girlfriend's poodle lifts his curly white head, seeing it's just me again."Go to sleep, Dogman." He sighs and closes his eyes. I gave him a bath yesterday, so he gets to sleep in my bed in exchange for me getting soap in his poodle eyes.

I'm trying not to recall anything. But details to the dream are as vivid as though I was there and it was still happening. Sometimes the dream disappears for months. As of yesterday though, it's back with a vengeance. It's so real. I mean it really happened, just like the dream. Man, it's freaky. It's so like right now, leaving me in a funky bluesy way. Maybe I should pick up the tenor sax, stand on a street corner somewhere lonely and lament my dark tones to passersby.

Instead, I just sit here in bed, listening to the power of the rain. I put my feet on the floor trying to forget. The sound of the rain helps

Bubba's so cute. My ex who named him is from Texas. I give him a kiss. He looks at me. "I'm sleeping here, Dogman."

Alien Biz

I look in the mirror of my dresser as I get out of bed. Damn, my name is still Jozeph Picasso. I'm past thirty now, six-feet even, not counting my genius bump, pushing one-ninety-five after eleven months of not smoking. Please, no applause, just buy me bigger pants. Regrettably, I have no relations to the late great artist, although my last live-in girlfriend, who will forever go nameless, may beg to differ. The past few years, after dropping out of UCLA Film School, I've kicked around Los Angeles trying to make a living as a practically unknown and now unwanted screenwriter/director. This only means, like thousands of other wannabe filmmakers, I spend long lonely hours in front of my computer.

Oddly, my very first agent was in Charlie's that same night the little guy came to visit and die. She was the one hanging on to every bit of the true life violent behavior from the window over my shoulder. She even signed me because of it, and sold my very first screenplay, appropriately titled Violent Behavior.

Somehow it represented her image of me based on what she witnessed. When she saw my script title she found it fitting to begin our business relationship. She literally got off three times watching how close I had come to dying without flinching. I assured her it wasn't from being brave. I was petrified.

Was making me money on my script a payback for her enjoyment? I didn't ask. Ann and I never sat down and really discussed the whys or how she came to call me. Though I've wondered if she saw what I saw, the moment of the little man's death. Did she see the something that left him behind? I met her a few weeks before not knowing she was an agent the way she dressed in all black. She was with a group of others dressed just like her waiting to eat.

I was told that Ann had asked about me a few weeks later. She looked me up because she heard from Tina, one of the waitresses at Charlie's, I had been screwed with and let go. When we first met in her office she was dressed differently, business like. I could tell there was a morbid fascination there.

She introduced me as the writer who cheated death. Telling her underlings in the office I had come within an eyelash to being murdered right before her very eyes while she came in her pants. In her view, it was a sexy marketing tool. In mine, it was a stain on my soul. She saw me more as a living ghost, a freak perhaps, a human who had cheated death, than a filmmaker. I'd find her looking at me funny sometimes but she never once asked me about the truth of that night or came on to me. She had her own image of it to play with, and didn't want the truth to spoil it perhaps.

Shortly after a production company based at Paramount bought the script, her personal life unraveled with drugs, girlfriends, and a monkey on the backseat of a taxi in Bahamas. She now works at *Go Magazine*. It's a New York based free lesbian publication. Unfortunately, my script is now eternally hidden on death row on some secret shelf in the back archives of some unnamed production office. It's stuck, probably destined to never-ever to see the key light of a working set. Like thousands of other scripts bought before and after it. Somehow, during some weird break in what I believed to be my reality, it has all pointed me to this, an isolated life trapped within the walls of what has become a living nightmare, my own Magical Mystery Towers Tour.

I had hoped I had gotten off scot-free from wrongly being accused of murder when I walked out of that cell, dumping sodas on MacAroy's and Tucker's cop car seats. I claimed ownership of a new life as I drove off into the sunset grooving to the Moody Blues. However, that was the subtext to this adventure as often it turns out in Hollywood. As I found, the new life one gets isn't always the new life one wants.

Because as it turns out, I'm free of legal charges but in the eyes of those that will never ever hire me, I'm still the lowly apartment manager and sometimes writer/director who got away with murdering four of my tenants. No matter what I say or do to refute it, that is who I've become. The bad taste remnants left on screenplay buyers' tongues only turn to staler, older jokes behind my back the more I pound the streets trying to sell my work.

Much like the Elephant Man, I've become my own personal freak show, a one man traveling carnival in the eyes of the showbiz silverspooners. Nobody that is anybody dares ask for my autograph on a picture deal. But most everyone likes to stop and gawk at me for the privilege of being able to say they saw me loose on the streets. As in many of Hollywood's unsolved murdered careers, truth isn't what sells news rags on either coasts, or any of those resting spots in between.

So by the time the Mystery Towers' murder stories finally faded out of print, the Essinola's were the salt of the Earth. They were simply working hard to make a living, after losing their home in a Peruvian mudslide, to send their two honor roll children to a better American school. While me, the sordid Jozeph Picasso of Mystery Towers, melted into a greedy, murdering landlord. I'm now a troublemaking, untalented college dropout, masquerading as a wannabe filmmaker. In other words, it was as though my filmmaking career had died out in that desert with the Essinolas, shot once in the head, my creative ideas left to feed the wild life.

This has all been brought on because of an element of my new life that I'm not at full liberty to discuss in public. I had the displeasure of falling into the acquaintance of an alien underworld. Since then, I've been known to speak more often to my chiropractor than to my closest of Facebook friends. This is partly due to the fact that my two closest friends are already dead. Michael and Roger, taken by human diseases neither of them saw coming at so young of an age. Leaving me to suffer their demise alone and practically friendless forevermore. Sadly, I am the last of the three amigos.

The second to go, Roger, actually died in my arms right here in my building while I was remolding it. Only to have me revive him and then watch Roger die slowly six months later from a brain tumor just above his ear. We all die, I understand that. It never gets any easier watching it in living color. The rag-tag papers wrote nothing of me extending his life by reviving him in my lap while sitting in a pool of his blood. I still don't like to answer my cell phone thinking of what it's doing to me. Roger was always on his cell phone trying to feed his young family. His family always came first. They knew that. Above all the searching for camera operator jobs, Roger was a family man.

It's part of a long story, but I got this white Jeep Grand Cherokee, and a lump of tax-free cash, after surviving nearly being executed for not killing four of my deadbeat tenants. Plus, another dead guy's head ended up in my refrigerator's crisper. Never mind, it's a long sordid story involving other worldly healing stones and different alien factions trying to get them from me. None of which made it into any of the stories written about the unsolved murders.

Like the little man in my nightmares, it's a part of my life that I must bear alone. Who would believe me anyway? Those I have shared some of it with, regardless of how close they are to me, just look at me blankly like I'm even weirder than what everyone says. Like many things about Mystery Towers I try my best to keep my thoughts, anger, and fears internal. This is not good I know. At times it makes me feel as if I'll implode until I burst into some human big bang theory and end up an emotionally wasted inkblot on a faded page of my wasted life.

It's these truths of what has happened here that are eating at me from the inside out. They chew at my image of myself every day, every waking moment. Now in my sleep the more I suppress them. The anger I hold is from how untrue all this is about me. The pain I suffer is for how unwanted they make me feel in the critical eyes of the life I so much want to be a part of – the Hollywood filmmaking community. It's eating me alive in every step I take to make things right again.

To make matters worse, the Jeep started out as a civilized upgrade to my lifestyle, but slowly turned into a pain mechanically. I have no real recourse on the matter because an Alien Mob guy called Mooky gave me the Jeep. He may or may not be one of many black clones not from this planet. Thus far, I have not heard from him since getting out of jail. Frankly, I don't want to hear from him again. Every day I tell myself that it's all not real. There are no aliens. They're not breeding us like dogs, using, and eating us.

But every day, I know it's a lie. We are not alone. Knowing it first hand is maddening. I can actually feel myself being pushed closer and closer to the edge of what I perceive as rational behavior. My feet are now firmly stuck in the grains of hope, digging my toes deep as I can into my one chance to survive all this. That I'll never hear from them again and any memory of what has happened to me will somehow dissolve into a filtered pool of forgotten washed out muted images.

I sit here, knowing the truth about me. A good sign that indicates it's time for therapy is when you stop noticing other people noticing that you're weird. So far I'm still fully aware, and so is my dog.

"Right, Bubba?"

"Come back to sleep, Dogman."

"I can't, I can't."

"Then shut up."

4

I'm talking to myself because Bubba looks up at me like he wants me to beat it. I look at the clock. I must be nuts. But I'm wide-awake. So, I pull on my gray sweatshirt matching the sweats I'm sleeping in. I already have socks on. Yes, as unromantic as it sounds, I sleep in my socks when sleeping alone. Clean ones.

Without disturbing Bubba any further, the real master of this apartment, I make my way down to the front door. The carpet's still dry. It's three am. I'm not even close to yawning. I open the right front glass door. The cool wet air feels good. I think Mother Nature is lost or just teed off. The houses of Los Angles are washing out of the hills and off the coasts. Maybe it will take me with them.

Thunder rips off to the west, rolling towards me like a drum, washing over my building with a vibrating rumble. Then the flash of faraway lightning hits a switch in my memory bank. The face from long ago turns to me, his eyes filled with death. The little guy, he's back. He'd been away but I've been sleeping deeply on borrowed prescription drugs lately. My mind has been free to visit my past.

The answers are all in there, written on the walls of my mind's cave. The little guy comes to me, knowing that I alone can atone for his unexpected death. I should've manned up back then. I should've grown some hair. I should've spoken up by telling the whole truth of the punching and the shooting when I had the chance. But no, instead, I hid behind the fear of not having a job. I thought only of my own well being. Fearing what they would do to me if I talked. So I let this guy die for nothing. For what little tip money I made back then.

I came home that morning not having said a word of truth to the cops. I didn't outright lie, I just held stuff back. I was in bed and by seven a.m. when my phone started ringing. I knew who it was. Or at least I feared who it might be, the dark crisp voice of Leonie DiGarbo, the older brother of the actor who caused this nightmare, making it perfectly clear. That if I were to mention names, I would get my legs broken. I didn't answer yea or nay, I just hung up the phone. My time to tell the truth had passed. I thought, or I hoped that the shooting officers would do their job and investigate what had happened. However, I'm not so sure they did. Not even the little guy's name made it to the papers. Who was he? What was he really doing there? Why is he back? How was this brushed under the carpet? Worse, what does he want from me now?

As I watch the rain, a sudden flash from a light within a black Lincoln Town Car parked out front in the overflowing gutter drain catches my sleep deprived eyes. I didn't even see it parked there. Was it parked there all this time? Of all the foolish places for anyone to park, the water is nearly coming over its trunk and hood. Could it be? Could he be back? The Mook? Please no, anyone but the Mook.

5

I stand there trying to see inside, but the vehicle's dark tinted windows make it impossible. And the water streams down the drooping pine trees that buffer Mystery Towers from the street. The rain nearly drowns out any light from the old lampposts. Wait a minute. Is that possible? Or, are they just dimmer? The rest of the block seems fine.

A minute or two goes by as I stare into the lampposts light before the Town Car's passenger door opens. A lean, naked leg steps down to the gutter, the water streaming over it. It doesn't matter because the leg has no shoe on it. I follow the leg way up high on the thigh, looking for a hint of panties. The leg belongs to a young woman in the shortest black leather skirt in the history of cowhide, going all the way back to the Stone Age. This woman/child stands up out of the car, looking at me through the pine trees and streaming water. In seconds, she is completely drenched.

"Pardon me. Any vacancies in this building? She asks with a soft English accent.

"Excuse me?"

She steps away from the gutter, nearly matching my six-foot even. She moves to the south steps and scampers up them with the grace of a gazelle. Her blouse of white satin sticks to her slim body. It shows clearly her tiny, though round beautifully shaped breast and scant erect nipples. The curls in her cropped black hair spin down beside her ears, pinned ever so artfully by the rain. She smiles, her teeth perfect, holding out an elegant pale hand with dark reddish painted nails, apparently all real.

If I'm still sleeping, this is obviously the wet part of my dream. I look at her, not taking her hand, but moving aside so she can get out of the rain under the overhang.

"It's a little late to be apartment hunting."

"Yes, sorry. We just arrived in LA. We weren't supposed to stay. But we met some people, and well, we decided to make a go of it."

"We?"

"Yes. My friends and I. They are in the car. We've traveled for such a long time. I'm sorry, I'm Amanda. My friends and I, and well.... Do you have a vacancy?"

"Not at three a.m."

"But you are the manager?"

"I unfortunately own the place."

"You mind if we have a look?"

"Yes."

"It's not as if we got you out of bed, now is it?"

"Okay, enough is enough. Tell Mooky to get out of the car."

"Who?"

"Do I look stupid?"

"I don't know. I don't have my glasses on. We've just been traveling at sea for so long. Please, we'd be very peaceful and appreciative."She touches my forearm with the weight of a snowflake."Price doesn't matter, as long as it's tranquil and large. With two full baths. Does it have two full baths?

"Yes. But...."

"Great!" She runs back out into the rain and to the car. I'm in mind to close the door and go back up stairs when from the other side of the car steps out another woman. Not quite as tall as Amanda, but prettier, with flowing white-blond hair. It cascades nearly down to her knees as she comes around the back of the car. The rain didn't seem to bother her any more than it bothered Amanda. This one has much larger breast, but not overly done to make them look unreal. I'm a guy. We notice these things. They come back up the stairs, holding hands, like young girls do.

"This is Brenda. I didn't catch yours."

"Jozeph. Look, ladies...."

"Please, Jozeph."Brenda takes my hand, heavy Russian accent. "We've got all our things in the car, and we desperately need a place to stay... we're soooo tired and... wet."

"Try a hotel."

"All right, I'll level with you, mister, Brenda says, "we're entertainers, we travel with a guy, a magic man. He's in the car, and we don't want to stay in a hotel because the press is constantly hanging out and well...."

"This is a quiet building, I don't need...."

"That's what we want. Privacy. Please."

"We'll pay three months in advance. We promise no drugs, or noise. We sleep all day and rehearse at night. We're taping a TV special, so we'll be here for only the three months. But we'll pay for the whole lease. Six months. Even a year."

"So rent a house."

"The show members. See, if we have a place where we can't have them over, then we're not being snobs, you are. So we won't have to deal with anyone but ourselves, and that's what we want. To be alone."

"The three of you?"

"Yes, you know... alone but together. Come on, you've heard of such things."

"I can't think of one reason why I should say yes."

"How about cash? What's the rent?"

"Nineteen twenty-five, but...."

Just then the driver's car door opens and out steps a six-four Adonis of a man. Clad in a long black duster over a dark green and red kilt, no shirt. Big black brim hat. His solid red hair hangs down past his shoulders. He stands there in the rain as though it's parting for him, just looking at us, without somehow looking drenched. I must say, he looks peaceful, not the druggie kind, but a kid who's come from a long line of deep pocket money. About late twenties, and though younger, he's much manlier than I'll ever be or ever dream of becoming. He reaches into the pocket of his duster and takes out a wad of bills.

I know I have to say no, even with three vacancies. I'm hoping for better clientele then what I've attracted in the past. Looking at these three, the rain and the time, I don't want them in here. I try to express just that, but instead find myself saying, "Okay, three months plus security." I can't believe I just said that. I didn't want to say that, but I did. I know because my lips moved. I can see them in the glass doors.

Amanda hugs me, pulling me to her and up against Brenda and both of them get me wet. Both are skin and bone, but it feels nice since all I've slept with lately is my French poodle, Bubba. Bubba's got more meat on him, though he's not a tall showgirl. The young Adonis moves towards us, up the stairs so smoothly I had to look twice to see if his feet were moving. He just swoops up the steps, opening his coat to take the girls under his wings as he moves. They fit in perfectly under his armpits. He holds them there. They must be freezing, out in this rain, but neither of them seemed to notice if they are.

"Gray. Call me Gray." He smiles at me as if he's known me for twenty years.

"Jozeph Picasso."

"Pleasure. Thanks for helping us out of the rain. Things got a little out of hand at the hotel so I grabbed up my girls and got out of there, before it involved us. Is this a nice area?"

"Spectacular Sherman Oaks. Everything you need within walking distance. Ralphs, three blocks up, closes at 2 a.m."

"That's fine. I'll have a trunk delivered in the morning. Could you let them in for us? If you don't mind, we'd like to spend the night. Where do I park my car?"

I look into the rain. I'm not about to go in it to let them in the garage. "Why don't you go wait in your car? I'll go get keys and paperwork, and we can get things worked out. I'll let you in the garage."

"Whatever you say, Cappy."

With that he turns, the girls still under his coat, and drifts back down the steps as smoothly as he had swooped up them. I don't think I've ever met a cooler guy. Listen to me, I sound like a schoolgirl. But, the guy's cool.

For the life of me, I don't know why I'm doing this without a credit check. Maybe it's the nightmare, hounding me for not doing enough to help my fellow man. Or maybe it's the women or his even easygoing smile. Maybe it's the thought of having a threesome in the mist of my building, like I'll get some groove thing vicariously through these three sexy people. Maybe they have friends who dig murderous directors. Maybe it's none of the above. Maybe it's something I am totally unaware of. Maybe that's what scares me the most.

"Did he call me Cappy?"

6

Cappy. He called me Cappy. There's no denying it. I stare at him while he signs the paperwork in the kitchen. He glances up at me with a knowing smile. Charming bastard, with money, talent, looks, bisexual women who want him and all he wants is a quiet place to sleep. At least we have one thing in common.

"You have ID?"

His hand unfolds. The largest hand I've ever seen, with ong nimble fingers, with perfect manicured nails. In the massive palm is a passport."Gray McGuiness?"

"Born on a cloudy day."

"Scottish? You don't sound Scottish."

"I'm a child of the world. I speak fifteen languages fluently. But McGuiness Castle will forever be my home."

"Really, at twenty-seven? That's impressive."

"Not really, I can understand close to fifty. Born with it."

"I can type in one. Grade school."

"You got me beat, then."He smiles.

I smile back. I don't want to like him, but I do. "You called me Cappy."

"Did I?"

"I thought you did."

"When?"

"Just... never mind. Is there anything else I can do for you?"

"We'll manage."

"Great. Talk to you, then." I go out into the living room and from back in the master bath I can hear the water running and the girls giggling. I look back at Gray and he's standing at the kitchen door watching me. He smiles again. Lucky bastard. I already need to masturbate.

"Would you like to take one of them up with you?"

"What?"

"The girls, one of them, for a few hours? Take your pick. We owe you."

"Oh, ah, yes, but I'll pass. My dog's asleep. He's got an early call tomorrow." I turn towards the hall door. My dog's asleep. I just passed on one of his girls with the excuse of not waking my dog. Just then Amanda bounds out of the hall leading to the master bedroom, sands any clothing, minus all body hair. She eyes me with an amused giggle and saddles up under Grays arm and pulls him back across the room. She gives me one last deep sexy look, beckoning me to come hither. My feet almost move involuntarily.

"Lock the door, ay, Cappy."

I just watch them go. He called me Cappy again. I lock the door behind me. I have a master key, so I do both dead bolts. He called me Cappy. I may not have thought anything of it but my vision is still vivid in my mind's eye. Cappy? The little guy called me Cappy. With the same familiarity as though he and I were old time friends, like my pop did when I was a kid on his boats. "Cast off, Cappy." Now Gray, this Adonis of a man calling me Cappy with that same glad to see you again charm. I need to shake this off.

I'm feeling sad. Why do I feel so sad? It may just be the rain. It may be my loneliness. It may be the thought that my poodle is getting further in his acting career than I am at both my writing and directing.

I'm actually driving him to Claire Davis' dressing room tomorrow. Check that, in a few hours. The same Claire Davis Show shot inside Stage 12 at CBS Studio Center on Radford Avenue that Jetty DiGarbo coproduces. Bubba got discovered sitting in my shot up Corvair in the Studio's parking lot and brought onto Claire's show as her dog. About a month later the nightmares returned more frequently than ever before. Bubba and Claire fell in love while I was trying to save my life and avoiding tossed salads in jail. By the time I went back to pick him up, they wrote him into the show. It's a very long story, more of that stuff involving Mooky and his friends. Maybe someday I'll relive it further, but regardless, Bubba is due on the set by seven, and makeup by eight.

They actually put makeup on him and primp his curly white head. Part of Bubba's charm is that his nose is brown, not black, with big round dark eyes and fluffy white curly hair, a little barking sheep. To know him is to love him. How corny is that? But it's true. I love that little bugger.

I don't know if Bubba knows what's going on, but he actually likes all the attention, and gets to lick Claire's neck and squirm in her arms at will. The lucky dog. The good news is I cash his checks. I'd rather let him cash the checks and me lick her neck. But it's not to be, yet. Thus far, I've kept Claire at arm's length. She is an actress and after my last fling with one, Bubba's mother, I am skeptical of getting my heart tromped on again by an egomaniac thespian. Apparently Bubba, the hairy ham, has no such worries, even though he was dumped by my ex as well. So he spends nights with Claire up in her new Wilshire condo. Unfortunately, he can't lick and tell. After all he's the original Ladies Dog.

I'm relegated to sitting around the set taking notes, hoping to avoid running into Jetty. But Bubba's such a natural at it. He sits, barks, rolls, smiles, licks, runs. I'm sure they'd give him dialogue if they could. When this all finally hits the air, there will be no living with him. I can only hope his mother won't come back looking for him demanding her share of his paycheck. It's just a matter of time.

Of course, now that I'm known as the murdering landlord, sometimes writer/director, I'm hailed with all the respect of an eight ball on an opening break. It's always yes Mr. Picasso, no

Mr. Picasso, park anywhere you want, Mr. Picasso, just stay away from me, Mr. Picasso. In the meantime, not an agent in town will touch my work. Though everyone has this morbid curiosity and wants to meet me. Just never during a public lunch. That would indicate a possible deal and no one wants to be the first to cross the line and take me seriously enough to employ my unofficial blacklisted butt. Every time I setup a pitch meeting I'm never left in the room alone with them. It seems that there's always a hulking figure waiting around the lobby just in case I go on a murdering shorthanded rampage again.

While I wait in lobbies, secretaries are constantly coming in for no apparent reason other than to ask the receptionist a stupid question. My favorite is 'What time is it?' followed by the resetting of their gilded timepieces. I'm probably the cause of synchronizing all of Hollywood's secretarial pool. I'm a live pinup doll at a piñata convention on the Rio Grande. Everyone wants a whack at busting my chops but no one wants to pick up my pieces and take me home because of the tainted dirt I've landed in. It may be my own paranoia, but I know I'm followed off most lots. Maybe they're afraid I'll steal a parking spot. On the other hand, everyone knows my name, loves my work, and plans to get back to me on it very soon. Twofaced bastards.

Back upstairs, I find Bubba waiting for me at the door. "Where ya been, Dogman?" It's barely five in the morning but he's decided he needs to go out in the rain. I don't know about him, but I need a shower and a shave.

I take him downstairs into the dungeon like garage and past the garden studio apartment I let an actor, J.J., live in for free as long as he keeps the laundry room clean.

He's a good guy, a little scary, and breathing much better after recently having his nose fixed on my tab. He had his face kicked in and ear torn nearly off by a redhead who was trying to kidnap Bubba over the alien healing stones we found in dog poop in apartment 101.They may or may not have been cuts from the original Hope Diamond stolen during the French Revolution. Some two hundred years later they were discovered in South America on one of Mooky's dead clones. I can hear how absurd this all sounds. How can I tell anyone and not sound crazier than I already do to Follywood? Anyway, J.J.'s good to have around. However, I only know he's from Alaska, been in prison and used to live on the needle but now a working actor. He was suppose to clean up the studio but so far has just managed to fill it up with set and prop junk.

But everything looks hunky-dory down here, so I take Bubba through the laundry room and let him scamper up the stone steps. I stay in the doorway watching the water flood in. There are massive pines back here so Bubba can do his doody dance without getting too wet. His feet get a little muddy, but for some reason he prefers the muddy pine scented feet to a wet brow. Maybe it's because he can lick his feet, and is getting high off the pine tar. Actors.

Bubba sneaks out under the tree, doing his doggy thing. "BUBBA!" Bubba moves away from the plant and pees on the fence. He looks up at me, annoyed."What, Dogman, I'm a dog, we pee on things. We're not particular."

There is a sudden silent dark movement up in the trees. I look, trying to see through the rain. I didn't notice it at first because I was trying to see the pool overflowing. But a great big crow is in the tree just above Bubba's head.

Bubba barks halfheartedly, not liking it shaking the wet branches above him. The giant black bird ruffles his feathers and glides down to the railing right beside me. I cover up like some great big sissy. So what, this is a great big bird. I open my eyes expecting to get pecked to death by this thing. But no, he's sitting there intensely looking at me. I haven't seen a crow this big. I've heard of Jungle Crows in Japan that actually stalk people, and chase down pets, seeking revenge if you try to harm them, but the chances of one flying all the way here on its own is remote. Could be a fly away.

Bubba runs back to me, staying clear of the bird. He looks at me then back to the bird, raindrops making him blink. So he goes back into the laundry room and sits in the doorway just out of the stream of water making it to the drain, watching us. "Screw the bird, Dogman, let's go."

How weird, the bird just sits there watching us back, then spreads his wings up over his head as if to block the onslaught of rain.

"What do you think, Bubba?"

Bubba barks. "Your call, Dogman, but I found him so he's mine if we keep him."

So I hold out my arm. The crow hops onto it and sidewalks his way up to my shoulder. He sits there for a second. I step back out of the rain. The crow ruffles its feathers, spreading its massive wings. It shakes off the wet, filling my ear with used raindrops.

What am I supposed to do? I wait for it to fly away. But he only lets go of a large glob of white mess that splatters in the drain just outside the rain swollen door. I look down at Bubba. He turns away. He's not a fan of falling things. He heads into the garage, looking back like, "Pull the trigger, Dogman, I'm due on the set for my close up." He's paying the bills, so we, the bird and I, follow him.

Once I get inside the elevator, the crow jumps on top of my head to peck at the light. Like that we make our way up to the third floor. I'm adopted I guess. He's a fully grown crow. He must belong to somebody. Until that somebody makes himself or herself known, that somebody is Bubba Dog and I. He looks down at me, meeting me full face, as if to say, "Aye-aye, Cappy. To the crow's nest wit' us."

"What's your name?"

"Caw!" he yells. Then he goes into this weird cackle that crows do, and I swear he's trying to talk to me. I mean crows are smart. I look down at Bubba. He's heard it all before.

Everyone's a star in Hollywood, and fighting for their share of the best dialogue.

Upstairs I move to the terrace door and open it. I take Caw off my head and put him on a black iron baker's rack were I have cacti growing. He grabs a hold of the shelving with his massive feet and turns around, "Thanks, Cappy, how about some monkey chow?"

I go into the kitchen and find one of Bubba's old bowls, and open a can of Bubba's dog food. Bubba materializes right there below me. Whimpering. "Relax, Bubba, you'll get doggy treats all day."

Bubba doesn't care. All he knows is that I'm not giving him his food and that I appear to be giving it to that bird. To be fair, I plop Bubba's share into his dish. I take them both over to the terrace, and put Bubba's beside his water bowl, just out of the rain, and place the other up on the shelf were Caw can reach it. He picks at it, shaking his head, flicking cold, slimy dog food bits right into my face. "Thank you."

Bubba looks away from us trying to hold back his poodle twitter by gobbling his food in Olympic record setting time.

7

By six-thirty a.m., after letting two young stagehands haul Gray's magical trunk up to his room, Bubba and I are in my White Jeep Grand Cherokee making our way east on Moorpark heading toward CBS Studio Center. It's raining so hard that if I were driving my Corvair I might have to paddle. No one will be driving my shot up, sixty-six red and black ragtop Corsa anytime soon. So I plow along, windshield wipers at full tilt, in the luxury of a 4x4 through the knee-high streams that cross the intersections. I'm a kid on spring break. I almost feel like getting out and jumping in the puddles it's so much fun. This is a lot of water.

At Laurel Canyon I'm forced to wait in traffic because some teenage lummox in a black four door BMW couldn't tell the water is nearly up to his driver's window. He's attempting to push his car out of the torrent crossing the intersection. In my opinion, the BMW is nearly sitting on the cement as it is, but these kids like to lower the suspension until the tailpipe systems spark on the pavement right under the gas tank.

It's finally my turn to get around him. I have a front brush guard on my Jeep so this kid starts waving me into the intersection to give him a push. Bubba looks at me, then over to the dash like he's checking the time. "Relax, Bubba."

"Hey, I've got eye-boogies, Dogman. Get me to the makeup girl, quick." He starts rubbing his eyes with his paws. Poodles have this nasty earwax colored gooey stuff that seeps from their tear ducts. It turns their paws orange from rubbing if I don't keep on top of it. It has something to do with breeding. At home, I use Peroxide and a Q-Tip to keep it under control and out of my carpeting. But Bubba wipes at his face, licking his feet, another self-centered little actor these days.

"Stop it Bubba, we're almost there." He starts licking the seat. "Bubba." "What? I'm a dog. We lick. Get over it."

I pull up alongside the kid. He's got his head shaved. Rain is running down the back of his neck, into his T-shirt. It's flowing into the crack of his bottom smiling out the back of his baggy knee high shorts. He looks ten days out of junior high, standing there nearly hip hop deep in runoff, oily saturated rainwater. I power down my window an inch, not wanting to get my tan leather seats wet. It doesn't work.

"How about a four wheeler to safety, Batman?"

"You've got it too low. I'd crush your trunk."

"Pull me then."

At this point, I wouldn't mind dragging his baggy butt across the street just to get him out of the way. He opens his trunk hood and pulls out a snow chain. I steer around the traffic building up behind us. Horns honk, eyes glare and fingers flip me off as I back up to his car. A Toyota Four Runner zooms through, pulling around me. It throws a wake to its sides, completely drenching this kid in feigned innocence. The jerk laughs as he passes me. He puts his finger to his tongue and scores one for the insensitive butt holes everywhere on his foggy window. "Thank you."

The stupid kid stands there, fist in the air, holding the chain, newspaper stuck to the side of his skinned head. The rain is coming down in cement trucks at this point. I'll be damned if I'm getting out in the middle of Moorpark and Laurel Canyon while a river runs through it to make sure this kid doesn't damage my Jeep. So, I crawl in the back, open the hatch door, and watch him hook the chain to my tow bar.

"Which way you want to go?" Thunder drowns out my words.

"What?"

"Which..." I look up and another truck is taking aim at us, so I close my hatch. Splash! The kid takes it full on the back, knocking him down on his knees, getting the torrent full face now. I reach and grab the seat of his pants before he washes into traffic. A tennis shoe washes away. He gets back up on his knees using my bumper.

"You see that? Was that cool or what?"

"Better hurry."

"Just get me across the river, dude," he says.

"How about into the gas station?"

He looks. "That's cool-d-adequate, man." Somehow it hadn't occurred to him.

So, despite all the cars piling up behind us, I turn hard right and pull the BMW across traffic and into the Mobil Station. We stop under the overhang. It isn't doing a whole lot of good in keeping anything dry with the wind driving the rain down in a nasty southerly angle.

It's at this point I venture to get out to make sure my bumper is still intact. When I look up, I see that Caw is zeroing in on my Jeep and thumps on my roof rack. "Caw, caw, caw!" I look at the kid again. Maybe he's about eighteen after all. Not Chicano or Blood, but perhaps middle eastern dark and seems to wish he was either. He stands chain in hand, rain blanketing him, eyes lit up.

"Damn! You see that?"

"Yeah." I hold out my arm. Caw jumps from the truck rack to my arm in one easy move. The kid covers up again just as I did the first time.

"Get it away, get it away!"

"Relax kid, Caw's harmless."

The kid moves away from us."That your bird, man?"

"I'm his human."

"They're carnivorous dinos, man? From way back."

"I know what you mean." Bubba starts barking. I give him a look. He has his feet up on the window, impatiently tapping his nails. "Let's go, Dogman. This rain is ruining my curls!"He's not fooling me. We're about to see Claire and he can't wait. I know the feeling, but first things first. I must help my fellow man.

"What's wrong with this portrait?" The kid asks.

I'm standing under torrential rain in a long black slicker, a giant Japanese Jungle Crow on my arm, with my leading white French poodle barking orders at me. What's wrong with that? "He's got to be on set in a minute. Will you be all right?"

"Sure, I'll call Daddy. He loves to hear from me in times of embarrassment. Makes him feel smarter. What's your name, Tarzan?"

"Jozeph Picasso. You?"

"Ernie. Ernie Burnstein, Junior. You're that Picasso?"

"The painter? No, he's dead."

"No, aren't you that murdering landlord Picasso guy? That crazy mother who's like offing his poor tenants? That stump they found in my dad's parking spot with some crying redheaded bimbo? About six or seven months ago? Remember? That was you, the one with the shot up piece of Ralphed up Nader baiter?"

"Have we met?"

"This is so whack."

"It's tempting, yes."

"Get this. I've got one of your scripts on my desk. Wait, I thought the poodle was Claire's."

"No, I'm his. You're a movie producer?"

"Mail clerk. But I'm practicing to be a reader right now. I should be directing any day. Once the funds set in, and I get a script written. Couple of weeks or so, max. I got this killer, can't miss high concept idea. It's practically writing itself. All the studios are creaming over it, man. I'm like, being offered their stepchildren and mistresses. I got so many chicks wanting cast in this thing, my balls are sore. I haven't been home in five days. You ever get blown by three hot babes?"

"All the time. So how's my script fairing through all this degradation?"

"Huh? Oh. Where'd you learn to spell, man?"

"In a boat on Lake Michigan. How's the story doing?"

"Oh, you know, it's valued, not high concept white powder keg enough for my taste buds. But, I've seen way too much in my life already. Life is so much further out there, dude."

"Where?"

"Out there. There's this whole way different out there life out there, man. Your story, it's cute, it's safe, but it... has no morphine trisexual midgets or anything rad like that squeezing out someone's butt cheeks to get me hard, you know."

"Every great script needs at least one, I guess."

"But the dialogue's not half bad for a practically dead guy. Only genuine peeps don't speak that PG substance anymore."

"Not enough cuss words? Let me write this down."

"No, your characters use real words. Big words. I mean, your peeps must read stuff, man. Care about each other and think. Normal peeps, peeps I know, don't really read, give a stitch, or sound like your peeps do anymore. Real peeps are walkin' idiots in fools for gold triangles, man. Ya know what I'm sayin'?"

"I'm trying to."

"Depravity is what today peeps want to witness. If they wanted normal everyday life, they'd go sit in a park."

"Yeah, which park is that?"

"The park of norm, man. Hell in a box is what today's peeps are about. So they don't have to go outside and have a life of their own. It's all out there, man. You just have to get out from behind your desk and go see it to see it. I know you dig that."

Great, he's stoned. "You have to see it to see it. Got it."

"It's a twenty four seven wild on orgy of craziness right next door to Happiness Ville, dude. Life's a mockery of itself, man. Not just a thirty-two inch blinking bedroom TV no more. Peeps do crazy things, man. Make things happen overnight."

"Like driving through rivers and flood their rides."

"Yeah, real peeps are mental. Tormented, microwaveable psychotic potatoes. Digital to the way max, dude. If you haven't been Youtubed by twelve, you're probably asexual. If you got scripts about them kinds of real screwed up peeps, I can make it fly for really, man. I got the power. I'm hot."

"All the way from the mailroom?"

"Do you know who my dad is?"

"Let me guess, your dad, Ernie Burnstein Senior, gave you my script to practice wiping yourself on."

"Yeah, he's training me to think for him. He's an a-hole, but I'm doin' his coverage to tame him so I can direct my flick."

"But your dad has no intention of buying my script."

"Hell no. He hates you. But if you want, I'll mail you a copy of my coverage printed on my personal letterhead."

"Ernie, have you ever written anything down other than a postcard home from band camp?"

"Who writes postcards, man? I'll tweet you my pass."

"I'd be thrilled, Ernie. In the meantime, would you mind if I strangle you to death right here in the rain?"

"What?"

"Someday you'll multiply, and put forth an Ernie the Third. I want to put an end to that threat on Hollywood Kind right now. Would you mind? Come here?" I reach out to him. Caw starts to cackle as if he gets the inside joke. Only I'm not joking. Snapping this kid's neck would be the humane thing to do.

Ernie senses I'm serious."Get away from me, man!"

"Come here, Ernie. I won't make it a drawn out thing. I'll just snap the airflow to your Lilliputian brain!"

Ernie is back in his car before another drop hits my face. I'm beside myself. Dripping wet after coming to his help. From the look in his eyes, Ernie is either calling 911 or Daddy. Bubba has seen enough and he wants to go to work. So I put Caw back into the air and get behind the wheel. Water running down the back of my slicker sops my leather seats. This is what I get for trying to be a good person on such a shitty day.

8

I'm thinking back to when I was in Ernie Burnstein Senior's office over a month ago. He didn't give a darn about my script, or anything else I had to pitch. All he wanted to know about was what happened to the redhead screaming in his studio parking space and what happened to my car. He didn't actually ask me if I killed anyone, but made it very clear that the real inside story would make a great green lighted MOW.

I told him and the two thugs he had sitting behind me that there wasn't an inside story to be told. He said that was too bad, got up, refusing to shake hands. Said he'd read the script because Claire wanted him to, and dismissed me into the hands of his two so called consultants. Now his son is using my script as a sample on why not to hire a writer. Well screw them both.

I pull into the lot at CBS Studio Center just North of Ventura Boulevard. The same one I hid in from an alien named Mooky not long ago. That's the real inside story I couldn't tell Burnstein about. The guard knows who I am. It's raining, so I don't bother to lower the window. I can imagine what he thinks about the look on my face because I'm thinking about the look on his. He's pointing to the roof of my truck like Godzilla is up there. Most likely Caw has grabbed a ride. As I pull away, I see him cowering back into his tollbooth, fighting to get the door closed. Caw must have left the truck and flown his way.

To be good I pull up to soundstage 12 to let his majesty, Bubba out. The snooty Production Assistant, who I sort of met the first time I had lunch with Claire Davis, is waiting with an enormous pink umbrella. I still don't know her name. Until she introduces herself politely we're strangers. At first, I think I'm seeing a thick mustache but another glance proves it to be a misplaced chinstrap from her rain hat. She opens the door without a welcoming smile to me and picks up Bubba. I open my mouth and she shuts the door in my face. The butch little bitch in her Khaki shorts and hiking boots wants me. I can tell, because I like her, too.

I'm forced to pull all the way across the lot to the visitor's parking lot because a new black Land Rover is parked in Bubba's parking spot. In Hollywood, show dogs get parking spots if he's important enough. I, on the other hand, am not, and have the four or five story parking lot all to my lonesome. Who else would be this crazy to park so far away? But at least I'm temporarily out of the rain.

I get out of my Jeep and Caw isn't there. Maybe he's in the pine trees at the lot entrance. I'm about two hundred yards from soundstage 12. I have boots on and a long slicker, but no hat so I grab up my umbrella and wade my way to the stage. I'm singing in the rain. I start a little soft shoe. Why not, I have the feeling that I'm about to be arrested anyway.

Because, at stage 12's door are two guys I don't want to know any better. Big guys. It's too late they know me all too well. They're Ernie Senior's two tax consultants moonlighting as bodyguards. They may have come out of the Israeli army, or off the Beverly Hills High School action debate team. Who really knows? Ernie Senior has a production company on this lot, and executive produces Claire's sitcom. That is how I got into his office in the first place, to negotiate Bubba's contract.

Actually, he sent for me because he didn't want Bubba or me on his set. He begrudgingly lost that fight with his new budding star, Claire Davis. Apparently he is sending for me again to give me his second opinion and bust my balls about hassling his only kid in the rain.

"Mr. Burnstein would like to take a quick meeting with you, Mr. Picasso," the bigger of the two says. He's got an earphone plugged into the side of his head like some kind of android. He's got a big thick east coast accent, perfect teeth, handsome in beefcake cartoonish ways. A carry a gun kind of fellow.

"Have him call my office to schedule."

"He's got time right now."

"I'm happy for him but I haven't had my coffee or newspaper yet." I try to push through them to the door and out of the rain, but they converge on me like a gay bar tag team. If their pecks where any larger a pig could suckle them. I bounce back into the rain. The shorter one has an ugly jagged scar running from his chin to the back of his ear. It's very scary. I hadn't noticed before. Maybe a gunshot wound or knife.

"It would be simpler if you just came with us, so we don't have to involve anyone else in this meeting."

"Are you two guys packing?"

"Not at the moment," Android says.

"Come back when you are. Otherwise don't try to muscle me again. And tell that little insulting schmuck that both he and his mail boy son can kiss my hard drive."

"What are you talking about?"

"You heard me."

"He's got a job for you."

"What, baby sitting?"

"You're a writer aren't you?"

I look them over. Could this be on the level? I'm skeptical about anyone wanting to know me beyond morbid curiosity these days. "Yes, sometimes."

"Sometime is about now, if you're smart," Scare Face talks for the first time. Android looks at him like he's surprised that his friend has a voice.

What the heck.

9

So I'm standing in Ernie Senior's inner office after receiving a lousy reception. Ernie Burnstein Senior is one of those gift spooned, New York chosen boys, born knowing all the right answers just because he got lucky and latched onto the right actor. He signed Jetty DiGarbo when Jetty was just a bum thug on and off the streets of New Jersey.

He's Harvard Law, once an agent, now a full-fledged TV and film production company with a studio deal, Burn Productions. Jetty is now his less than silent partner. Meaning the Mob owns him and his bones.

Rich guys like Ernie Senior don't gleefully anticipate the fruitfulness of original ideas from low end writers like me. He's convinced that his own painfully pedestrian thoughts are what the world wants to see. So, he hires peons to bring them to life. In the big picture of things, it just creates more writing jobs because of all the drafts it will take to put it back into the original writer's words. So here I am taking my turn in Burn World expecting my own mental fruits to be freeze dried into powdered thoughts. But no.

"So, what do you think?"

I just look at him. I'm at a loss for words.

"This is your lucky day, Picasso, so what do you think?"

"I think you're both out of your gourds."

I'm a little surprised, I didn't know my late night tenant, Gray McGuiness, was The Magical Man, and so bankable. Or that renting to him would put me here in front of the Burn holding the bag of worms. They don't need to know this.

"We know he's staying at your place."

"What makes you think so?"

"We just do."

"If Gray McGuiness is staying at my place, what makes you think he'll want to be in your kid's flick?"

"I can guaranty you he won't. But that never stopped the Colonel from making Elvis movies."

"Then, from where Elvis and I sit, I can guarantee you that you're wasting my time with this sure to be a dump of an idea."

"That's why I'm on this side of the desk and you're pushing cars out of drainage ditches, Picasso. You have no vision for what sells in this town. This McGuiness guy sells. Claire Davis sells. You tell someone you got this guy and that girl, and the green lights start blinking from here to Amsterdam."

"You and your little mailroom boy have told people you have them? A tad sparse on the truth. Even for a producer like you."

"Junior, get in here!"

Behind me, I hear the private bathroom door open and close. Ernie Junior passes beside me and stands in front of his daddy's desk wiping his hands on his pants. He's now dry as a bone. I'm wet as a boner. So who's the cold prick here? I look at him. He's still mad at me. So, he's got my vote.

"Read anything good lately?"

"Kiss off, you bird walker."

"He found that attitude at Harvard School of Meatheads?"

"Sit down, Junior. You've met, I've heard."

"This is the thanks I get?"

"Mr. Picasso, may I call you Jozeph?"

"No."

"Fine, my son here has a mega international idea and we'd like you to ghostwrite with him on it."

"You want me to be his babysitting secretary so you can get at Gray through me."

"I don't type, I text. I'm a creative thinker."

"How hard were you thinking when you hit all that water?"

"I was lighting a joint."

"I rest my case. You're brilliant. It shows."

"Let's stop this arguing."

"Are we finished here?" I ask.

"How much do you want?" Because Ernie Senior went to Harvard he doesn't have to hear drop dead for an answer.

"I've got two scripts for sale. You want Claire to act in one, make an offer, but I direct, not him. In the meantime, you and your mailroom prodigy can kiss off."

"Picasso, I'm offering you a Writer's Guild job! Where the hell is all this bullshit animosity coming from?"

I get up, turning to make sure, Scare-Face and Android aren't making a black belt or ballerina move on me. Mailroom boy cowers as if I'm going for his throat again.

"Do you really want to know where this is coming from, Ernie? I'll tell you just once. Take notes so Junior will get it, too. I've kicked around this heartless town for years. Not once has anyone attempted to green light one of my scripts, reflect my vision on their wall, or ask me how I'm doing today. But now this knucklehead comes along right out of Beverly Hills High School and says he hates my work. Supposedly he's got some kind of drug induced high concept idea involving one of my tenants. And, because he's your sorry mental offspring, you want to fast track it. But unfortunately, you need someone like me. A born-again looser in both your eyes, to make Junior's one clever thought come to fruition. Nice and easy and without credit. So you can hide the fact that he didn't write it on his own. Well, Ernie, I'm sorry you and your better half birthed a skateboarding-x-gaming-dimwit, but drop dead."

"Am I missing something here? Isn't that what you writers do? You write. You're a hack for hire like all the rest. What in hell's the matter with you?"

"He's what's the matter with me. High concept boy, here. He wouldn't know a real story structure if he lived in it and it spoke to him. I wouldn't ghostwrite for him if I were dead!"

"I ain't workin' with this dinosaur lover. Get me a fresh mind, someone who thinks like me!"

"See, we both agree, let him do lunch with a Twinkie."I head for the door. Burnstein's two goons part the carpet, but don't open the door. I wait. Android finally reaches for it.

I go out into the outer offices. A whole set of new secretaries are now there to take a morbid look at me, and set their wristwatches. T-minus crazy writer and counting.

Burnstein's standing behind his desk now. "Picasso! Jozeph! Picasso, you foolish bastard. You'll write this script! And you're getting me Gray McGuiness. Nobody else in this frigging town will touch you if you don't! You hear me, Picasso? This is your last chance in this town! I'll have your dog fired!"

"Kiss off, Ernie."

Eyes are diverting all round me. But they can't hide their smirks. The notorious murdering landlord has just told their boss to kiss off.

"Shut the door," Ernie Senior yells behind me. It slams on my deal. Tomorrow's Hollywood Reporter will read, 'Killer Kills Killer Killing.' What a deadbeat.

At the exit to the production bungalow, I turn back to all the production head hopefuls."Sorry, I couldn't kill him today."

They just look at me blankly, until finally a little pixy of a nub says. "Could you come back and try again tomorrow?"

"Sure."

I leave them in a snickering room. Why not, if I kill Ernie someone has to take his place, right, like a rock into pond scum, more of the same rushes in to fill the unexpected void. Why not one of them? You go, production girls.

10

Coffee please. A cup? Anybody? A caffeine laced syringe? I need it badly, and the blissful lonely refuge of my beloved LA Times.

If I were somebody, it would've been here by now. On the surface, I'm not sure why I feel so much anger towards Ernie Burnstein and his son. Maybe it's because Ernie signs Bubba's weekly check. Maybe it's because he resents Bubba being on his show of shows when it wasn't his idea, and me being on his set, so close to his bread and butter.

Maybe I resent making a living off my ex's French Poodle, while I can only muster getting arrested in this town. Or babysit dimwitted namesakes as a ghost knucklehead writer.

But most likely it's because Ernie's a pompous gray matter sucking pimp who used my heartfelt writing effort, *Crazy Kind Of Love,* to properly potty train his brainless offspring.

On the other hand, maybe I'm angry because I just left my umbrella in Ernie's office. And can't go back in to retrieve it now and ruin a perfectly good kiss off and lose face in the synchronized secretarial pool.

In all truth, thinking out here in this downpour washes away the self imposed clouds of doubt. Deep down, I do know why I'm so agree. I don't want to admit it to myself. Jetty's winning. And it's getting to me off that I'm still losing sleep over it. Worse, there's not much I can do about it.

Because, after all these years, I'm desperate again, keeping my mouth shut, collecting chump change off the bar from the likes of Jetty DiGarbo, in exchange for keeping my dog working, so that we can pay the bills and stay close to Claire Davis.

I, still on the outside of this biz, watching Jetty pick her up for dinner. Watching Jetty escort her to movie premieres. Reading their names linked in the trade papers. Seeing their happy pictures on the boob tube. Knowing full well she doesn't care for him. Knowing that she, and a non alien tormented I are better suited for each other. Knowing she's just playing the Hollywood game. Staying employed. Just like my dog and I.

Now Gray McGuiness has entered the picture. "Why? Why? Why?" It's the drowning question of the moment. Why did Gray McGuiness come to live at Mystery Towers? Who in hell is he really? Why haven't I heard of him if everybody wants him?

He's The Magical Man. Is it ironic that the Burnsteins, Jetty's partners, are so interested in him? Now I'm the go between guy to their green-lit deal. How high will I have to get before the perspective of all this peaks above the clouds?

Am I the only one having this nightmare? Or is Jetty having them too? So far, I've managed to avoid him. However, today he'll be on the set. Damn. Perhaps I'm still asleep and this is just the tragic part of the dream where the Mob finally realizes I'm still a viable threat and they do something about it.

Maybe I'm just nuts and this is all a shell game.

Maybe it's all true, but since the five murders involving my apartments, only the morbid spectator has toured the building. They were either so weird, I couldn't rent to them, or just a story hound in search of a gruesome tale to tell.

Perhaps Gray thought the evil spirits would ward off the throngs of evil fans. Maybe the murder mystery intrigued him.

I kick at a pinecone, and I slip down on the muddy grass. Great. Now I'm real sloppy-muddy and walking through a hard rain toward my dog's dream job.

11

I finally reach Stage 12's door. Of course the do not enter red light is on. I try the door to stand in the small service entry, but it's locked. The unfriendly Production Assistant comes to mind, since she knows I was due to enter. So I wait in the rain thinking this would've been a good place for an awning. At this point there's no place to hide, so I wait it out.

By the time I'm inside Stage 12, I might as well be standing naked behind the running engine of a swamp boat. I'm so wet and muddy my boots slosh inside from the goop that's run down my legs. But within seconds of entering the Nordic soundstage air I'm in hugging heaven, groping five gallons of shiny canister of the gods. Hot coffee is bringing me back to my morbid self. Who needs a syringe when you can suck caffeine in by the gallons through osmosis?

"Excuse me."

I turn to find the unfriendly pudgy Production Assistant standing impatiently behind me. She sports choppy, poorly colored blond hair, hacked and moosed to smithereens, on purpose no less. "Can I help you?"

"Can I help you?" she asks back in her little 'how did you get in' tone. She wrinkles her nose like I stink.

"No thanks, I've taken all the bull I need today."

"You're getting the floor wet."

"Mr. Burnstein stole my umbrella. Would you mind fetching it for me?"

"Right. Would you mind moving so I can get Mr. DiGarbo his cup of coffee?"

I step aside. I ran across Jetty only once since that night of the killing, the one in my dreams, the little Keebler elf, while crashing one of his production parties at the Director's Guild. He didn't seem to recognize me then. I'm not so sure he'd recognize me now, because we never were formally introduced. Three years are plenty of days to forget a face. It was only a matter of time before we ran into each other again on this set. Of course, I knew he coproduced the show before I agreed to let Bubba become Claire's Poodle Door Bell. I have no one else to blame for the spot I'm in. Maybe that's really why I dislike Burnstein so much. He's in bed with Jetty DiGarbo and not with me.

Well, here you are, Picasso. The sour moment you've been waiting for. Knowing the arrogant little prick, Jetty might not even remember my name, if he was ever made aware of it. I know his "We'll break your legs" brother Leonie will remember. Considering the explicit characteristics of my violent dreams involving Jetty of late, the ironic nature of him being on this very set right now is fitting. Perhaps confronting him will make the dream go away. This would be a good time to leave. Too late. Here he comes. Damn. Move feet move!

"Who do I have to sleep with around here to get a hot cup of coffee?" The PA looks at me. Even she knows he's a bigger jerk than all of us. Jetty shuffles over in his stage slippers, way too impatient of a person to acknowledge the fact that a muddy nobody is practically dripping on him. He squints up at me though. Like "Back off, can't you see I'm talking to the lady?" But I don't move. I was here first. I just look over his head like I can't see him. So he shares another hateful look before turns, sucking the little PA away in his jet stream of fame and power of signing the checks. "Who is that?"

"Nobody. The Dogman."

"I thought that little fur ball was Claire's dog."

"No, it's Mr. Picasso's."

"Picasso? Jozeph Picasso? That's Jozeph Picasso?"

Isn't it touching? He remembers me."She doesn't even own that stupid dog? We're nearly rewriting every scene over his dog?" He looks back at me again. I'm enjoying his money way too much to care. It's killing him. Suddenly, I'm winning. It feels good.

"Yeah, can you believe it, we're stuck with him. Look at him. He's practically crazy." What does she mean practically? It took all morning to look this crazed.

Jetty glances back over his shoulder at me again. Like I can't hear them trash me in public. "Tell that crazy bastard he owes me a pair of genuine Gucci."

"Oh, my god, did he drip on them?"

"No, that little dog of his peed on them when I stopped in to show Claire my new dialogue changes."

"Bubba? Are you sure?"

"I know dog pee when I smell it."

The PA looks back at me as if I'd done it myself. I smile politely. Tip my cup. "Eat me, and the Jet you flew away on," I say through my Roman smile. All right Bubba, chalk one up for us Dogmen everywhere. Let Jetty find out the truth on his own. Claire Davis is Bubba's woman, and I'm just here for the ride home. In the meantime, let the little punching bag stew.

12

Suddenly the shadows of my mind are pushed away by a golden light at the mouth of Plato's tunnel accompanied by a soft soulful voice. That voice that melts me from my dripping Mt. Hooded head to my muddy Mississippi toes.

"Jozeph, why are you standing here dripping?"

"Ah..."I turn around to find Claire standing there in her customary lavender terrycloth. Man.

"I see you've met, Jett."

"Did I?"

"Jetty's guest starring on the next five episodes."

"Too, bad. What is he, your father?"

"My boss."

"Your editor?"

"Yes. I'm afraid Bubba had an accident on his shoes."

"I assure you that was no accident."

She looks at me with a twinkle in her eyes. Just a little hint of an upturn curl on her lips that she gives me once in awhile. Letting me know she's aware that I'm still the mysterious man she first met. Her natural blond hair is pulled back in an Ivy League ponytail. She's killing me softly with her smell. I lean on the table awkwardly. This is good because I swoon for the first moment of her presence every time. She knows this happens. She reaches out to touch me ever so daintily on the hand, steadying me, making me whole again. It draws me in, a willing prisoner of her allure. Like a minor leaguer brought up to the Show. What a gas. It's the golden moments like this I'll someday wake up in a smelly home for the stupidly poor, wishing I were man enough to have taken advantage of such riches.

"I was being polite," she says.

"So was Bubba. He would've pooped, if he meant to be rude."

She laughs aloud, a great big belly laugh. I'm being funny, so charming in my umbrella less aqua suit. Her laughter fills the whole soundstage to its catwalks. Every set of devilish stagehand eyes peer around obstructions to take in the utter from which all their bread is buttered. Only to sadly find her laughing with this walking talking unsolved crime wave.

She's so eatable. I'm so clever. I glance over to find Jett dawn patrolling us with the hateful eyes of a Flying Tiger. Why would he be pleased? Someone else has actually made the Queen Mary of the sound stage laugh aloud in front of everyone. How could he possibly top that to redeem his status as the most charming lout on the lot? Personally, I can't wait to start the rumor that he was the butt of my doggy trick joke. But somehow I don't think it could make him dislike me more than he does at this very moment.

To all others on this stage, his look may read just contempt for another hapless man. To me, I'm the one person he'd most like to see vanish from the annals of mankind. I'm the one soul who can bust his public good guy bubble by tarnishing his Hollywood Walk of Fame Star. I'm the lowly bartender who fibbed through his teeth. Who ran and hid for three years. The guardian of his dark secret that he and his mob friends have so artfully hidden. Wait until he finds out that I wrote our fateful saga down.

Unfortunately, he has the unreciprocated hots for Claire and I just walked in front of his afterburners. Suddenly, I don't feel so cold. I'm a glow with happy, revengeful thoughts. To pin the killing on him after all this time. What a truly well written third act that would turn out to be.

I don't kid myself in any way here. I've entered Jetty's jet stream of wrath. It won't take long for him to contact his hunt and destroy kinsmen. They'll compute that I am the same bartender that is plagued by the brutality of my past and the weakness of my character. Who at this very moment, would love to confess his sins to the most exquisite rocky Irish shore on the face of this doomed planet. And I would, if I were half the mortal I crave to be. Or, I would if I even came remotely close to my potential as a decent human being. But nay, I'm but a silent Dogman after all. I let the moment of true confessions pass. I just snivel my nostrils over a safe steaming cup of coffee, trying to stay charming in her oceanic blues.

"What's the matter, Jozeph?"

"What?"My hooded eyes betray me again.

"You went away, again. I could almost hear your visions."

"Oh that. Burnstein turned down *Crazy Kind Of Love.*"

"But I've already told him to make you a fair offer."

"Fair to him was drop dead, I guess. He offered a babysit job, though." Everyone's still watching so I don't want Claire to get upset out here in the open, and risk any misconstruing to the nature of her unhappiness. That could get me pounded into pulp porridge by some Neanderthal grip who sees his child's one and only chance of private school slip down river. "Maybe we should talk about this later. The Ids of March are upon us."

Claire looks around at the snooping observations. "Right. Go to wardrobe. Get something dry. Have lunch with me. You've got one half hour. I'll give Ernie a call."

"Claire. Don't. Wait until we talk. Okay?"

"I'm too mad to wait." She storms off. Leaving me in the void of a hundred abominable eyes wondering what I said that got her so exasperated that they may have to redo her makeup.

13

I shove my hands in failure into my slicker and jam my knuckles into my cell phone. Damn! I pull it out fully expecting it to be non-functional. But not all is ruined when with a simple push the light turns on. I look down to the craft table full of donuts and muffins to find a box of plastic Ziploc bags. Mooky had given me this phone with the Jeep. Thinking of the umbrella less trek back to my Jeep, I'm not giving Mother Nature another shot at ruining my alien enhanced cell phone. So I grab up two bags and double Ziploc the phone before putting it back into my side pocket.

Just then, people start running around, screaming, ducking for cover, and pointing at something moving up in the air! "Caw, Caw, Caw!" rains down from high up in the rafters as I run out into the middle of the Claire set. I'm suddenly the madman in a black slicker, drenched from head to toe, leaving a trail of sloppy denial behind me. I look up, seeing nothing, but sensing Caw up there. I hold out my arm and amongst frantic screams of "Shoot it" and "Oh my God." Caw swoops down, in all his five-foot wingspan glory, onto my wet arm, and lands effortlessly. Ruffling his coal black feathers to dissipate the damp, and cackles that weird crow talk. He comes so close to forming frustrated human words that I can't help but answer him.

"They're supposed to lock the doors, Caw," I answer him.

He cackles again, giving my ear a loving nip.

"Ouch! To keep vicious birds and murdering writer/directors off their set."

Caw poops right in Claire's pretend living room. Caw and I think this is very funny. But somehow not another soul even remotely thinks we are being humorous. So our laughter falls upon sullen ears. We're two crazy birds cackling about dumb stuff. Mindless twitter of mad cows and daffy ducks. He poops again and we can't keep ourselves from cackling with laughter about it.

Suddenly, the working director's voice from the booth booms down on us. "Mr. Picasso, would you mind removing your bird from our hot set?"

I stick my finger in Caw's mouth. He likes this and makes the sound infant birds do when their parents feed them bugs high up in the trees. It's kind of a birdish gargle.

"Someone get him off the set."

No one makes a move.

"Picasso! Get off my set!"

"Okay, okay. He's just a bird. I've seen worse droppings taking place on this stage."

"Get out!"

14

Minutes later, we're banished. I'm reading the LA Times under the dripping overhang of a set loading dock, drinking coffee, when Claire comes out looking for me. She's not happy to find me still wet and muddy. "What are you doing out here?"

"Waiting for my dog to get off work. Reading an article on human myoglobin laced coprolite."

"Dare I ask?"

"Coprolite's what archeologist call prehistoric human dung."

"Interesting topic before lunch."

"It's the final evidence of cannibalism here in America in about AD 1150. Proving my theory that Hollywood wasn't the first to eat their babies."

"You're going to catch pneumonia."

"They threw us off the set."

"Why?"

"Because I gave them all the bird."

"You're being silly. Leave your bird and come in for lunch."

"But...."

"I mean it. We need to talk."

Just then Caw swoops down from a power pole and lands on my head. For a big bird, he's very gentle. Claire doesn't flinch a muscle.

"I see. He's rather attached to you, isn't he?"

"He's harmless."

Caw jumps to the ground, waddles his birdlike way over to Claire, and pecks at the beads on her shoes.

"He likes you."

"Ernie tells me that Gray McGuiness is staying in your building."

"It's just an unsubstantiated rumor going around."

"Is it true?"

"Why?"

"I want to meet him."

"Why?"

"Wouldn't you want him in *Crazy Kind Of Love?*"

"It's not good casting."

"It is if everyone on the face of this planet goes to see it. Think of the backend."

"Believe me I am. The entire view of the script would need rewriting. The whole integrity of the story would be defaced. The.... You made Ernie say yes to my script?"

"Almost."

"How close is almost?"

She hesitates. It's the first time I ever heard her hesitate for anything. "Ernie Junior is to direct if I'm in it."

I jump off the dock into the open air ramp, the rain pouring down on me once again. The one person I honestly thought never would, has betrayed me. The one person in this business that I hoped I could trust to be real. The one person that has kept me in this bone marrow sucking business.

"Jozeph, don't overreact."

"Would you mind taking Bubba home with you tonight?"

"This isn't a done deal."

"Not by a long shot."

"We can pull this off. Without Ernie Junior involved."

I keep walking. I'm feeling more foolish with every step. I have nothing to squander but my self-respect. Even that isn't worth the brain wave it's thought on.

"Just get Gray McGuiness to pass on the project if Ernie's kid's involved."

I stop, but don't turn around. "He's not right for the part you want him to play. He's...."

"If not Gray, then Ernie wants Jetty DiGarbo to play the ex baseball player. You know what he'll do to your script."

A chill sweeps up my spine freezing away my self-pitying tears. I face her, about forty yards into the packed parking lot. It's then that I recognize the new Land Rover parked in Bubba's parking space has Ern Burn on the plate. Bastard. "Jetty will rewrite it. Or Ern the Burn will have it done."

"Until the whole story is about what Jetty wants viewers to think of him. You've read what he's done to our show. He's written Bubba out of the show three times. He's a...."

"A one note blunder. He'll change the dialogue to fit his New Jersey street DiGarble. A writer's ultimate nightmare." At least mine of late.

"All your jokes will disappear into his vision of humor. It's horrible working with him. He changes every line. Not an authentic ad-lib cell in his body."

"Then why are you working with him?"

"I told you. He pushed Burnstein into doing this show. He's got a creative cut. He saw me at the Improv. You know all this so don't make me explain it to you again."

I don't want her to explain anything. Burnstein managed Jetty during his first hit sitcom show, way before I worked at Charlie's. Then they produced his second but failed show together while I busted my hump finishing my building. Now Ernie's on his own, but Jetty and his New Jersey boys have a piece of everything. And I'm standing in their way. Knowing much more than what's good for my health. I look at her, wishing this would all go away. Wishing I could tell her the truth, about the little guy, the shooting, threats and the cover up. All about my lying to the police to keep my job, everything.

"You've cashed all of Bubba's paychecks. You know they are signed by Burnstein/DiGarbo. They own me, Jozeph. They are why I'm here today. Otherwise, my time could've come and gone. I could've been last year's guest star and probably be back on the one night standup circuit. It's not all about me. All these other people have jobs because of this show. Even Bubba."

"So you used Jetty for the good of all."

"A gentleman wouldn't put it like that."

"A gentleman didn't. I did. The writer/director you're trying to get them into bed with next. Were you two ever a real item?"

"He wishes."

I just look at her. I'm not being coy. I literally have no idea how to get from here to there without literally stepping on my tongue. This guy has a jealous bone as big as a Brontosaurus' clavicle. I surely don't want it stuck in my throat, nor Claire out of my life.

"No, I haven't slept with him. Satisfied?"

"There's still HBO."

"Not without this show."

"Claire...."I come this close to telling her everything, but stop. Shit!

"Just get Gray to say yes to the script, and wave the little prick off your picture."

"I'd still have to rewrite."

"At least you'd be doing the rewriting. Come on, Jozeph, we're friends. We understand each other. We're both outsiders. I'm only inside now because someone already within thinks they can make a buck off me. So work with me here. I'm trying to open a door for you to feed a bigger fish. It's the only way they'll let you eat at their table. You know that."

"Damn." I'm not so sure I want in. Not like this. Not with them. I'm already feeling creatively raped and nothings even happened yet.

"Come back inside and get cleaned up. Ernie wants you in his office as soon as you can manage."

"I seem to have time about the middle of next January."

"Please, Jozeph, for me. Do this one thing for me. It's one script. I'm not asking for a first born or next of kin, for Christ's sake, it's a story. A script, a good script, but only a blue print of a movie. Things will change no matter who's in it."

"Fine, throw screenwriting 101 at me. But, I direct. Not that little mindless twit."

"Trust me, if you get Gray McGuiness to say yes on your script with you directing it, every green-light from here to Amsterdam will start blinking."

I don't know why I don't just turn around and start running to my truck right now. The woman I'd love to be in love with, if she wasn't an actress, has just quoted Ern the Burn Burnstein, and my feet aren't retracting me from this scene. I can't believe I'm even contemplating this thing. It's like I'm standing over a pit of wolves. Knowing full well that the tainted meat I want, but don't need, is at the bottom of their dirt caked feet. I'm completely aware that I can surely live richly without it. Yet I still stubbornly want to throw myself onto the mercy of these wolves so badly I can taste my own hot blood.

"Jozeph!"

"What?"

"You're bleeding."

"I am?"

"Yes, your lip."

"You see? This is a coyote ugly idea. Subconsciously I would actually rather chew off my own mouth then say yes to this."

"Fine. Forget it. Come get Bubba when you can."

"Claire."

"Don't ask me to help if you're not willing to help yourself."

"I didn't say...." Why can't I just tell her? Because, then she'd know the truth, and we would both be in danger of Jetty and his friends.

She's back inside the inner door to the stage, leaving me out in the cold, a rotting iceberg, tossed in the gutter. Why are there always compromises?

Caw looks at me. Even he has enough sense to stay out of the rain. "It's your call, Birdman, where to next?"

Hell, I don't know. I really don't know.

I'm as wet as I can ever be, so I just turn back toward the parking structure. I don't have to come to any conclusions right this instance. Do I? Life isn't that simple. Is it? If anyone's life on this studio lot were perfect, they wouldn't be here right now. Would they? I'm actually hoping lightning will strike me and put an end to my misery, but no luck in the heavenly direction either. All I get is a pounding thunder so heavy and so directly above the concussion pushes me down in my sopping boots. Run, Picasso, run!

I don't want to talk to Ernie about his son directing my script. This is the part of life where I need some kind of lawful advice, a lawyer, manager, or an agent even, but so far not a one has answered my calls for representation. ICM actually had a scrub attorney call me back to inform me that I am not to contact them or any of their clients ever again, for any reason on the face of this planet. If I should ever leave Earth, I'll call. I didn't have the heart to tell him about my alien escape clause, Mooky, aka William the Clone, Payne Washington.

I sing out, "What do you do when you're alien branded and you know you're a human?" I get no answer.

15

The rain is coming down so hard that there is actually a refreshing waterfall cascading down from the top of the parking structure. I'm forced to either walk through it or climb in from the side like some alley cat. Caw has flown up to somewhere so I can't ask his advice. What do I have to lose? I'm thick with mud anyway. Why not wash off? The water is at least cleaner than I am. So I scrub all the mud and sod from my knees and boots. I don't want to get my Jeep all wet and muddy. Suddenly I realize I can't get into my Jeep like this regardless of how clean I get. Damn it! It's the little things. I have leather seats. And I already got them wet once today. I wasn't nearly as wet and muddy as I am now. In fact, I kind of smell like fertilizer. Did I smell like this in there? "I hope so."I get a mouthful of roof runoff. "Why not?"

"Keep your mouth shut, Dogman."

"What?"Ahhh shoot, I step out of the water into the parking lot. I clear my eyes to find that my Jeep is no longer the only vehicle there. Did I hear that? "Mook?"

I look around while my mind is going through my inventory of reserve clothing articles hanging in the Jeep's cargo area. No Mook, and dang, no dry pants.

But an indigo blue Chevy Suburban is parked right next to my Jeep. The kind you see government agents drive in all the suspense and action drug moves. Only, it's got no plates, so my expectations aren't high on a friendly visit.

I look around, this whole empty four or five story parking structure and they rudely park this close to my vehicle. I'm not sure what the plan is but this could not be by accident. I turn to make a run for it and find two men in black suits and trench coats standing behind me with handguns and matching mustachios. How fey is that? But that's not the odd part. The odd part is that the handguns they hold have professional grade silencers on them. Any legit government agent who just wants to talk doesn't usually display this kind of hardware. Unless, of course, they're not government agents. And belong to some otherworldly organization like the New Jersey Mob. Maybe the good news is that this is where the negotiation on the backend of my movie deal begins. If it is, this is going to be one killer movie.

"You Jozeph Picasso?"

I look back, not even surprised to find a third guy standing beside my Jeep. He's lean, clean, and mean... and just above my height but fills a suit in a way I could only in my dreams. I've seen this guy before. Heard his voice. But it's coming to me slowly.

"No." I'm a natural fall guy but I'm not that stupid. "He sent me out to get his cell phone. I'm Buddy Wisenheimer, a Production Assistant on the...."

"Shut up, Picasso. We got a message for you."

"You from UPS? FedEx? Reader's Digest maybe? I take my deliveries at the home office." It's hard keeping my eyes on both approaching parties when they stand front and back like this. I turn sideways to give them a smaller target, and brace myself for an unhealthy run of bad luck. If I ever find myself facing one of these types of Hollywood deals again, I'll remember to wear tennis shoes. I'm starting to see my cast approval slip away. I'll be forced to run for my share any second.

"You listening?"

"I got a choice?"

"You do whatever you're told to do from this point on and we'll make this nice and painless for you. Step forward."

"Wait. Can I know who's producing this scene?"

"Shut up."

"How about multiple choice?" I'm dancing here, my mind calculating how to get out of this mess."You two guys might want to free up your fingers," I say over my shoulder to the mustachio twins. "Okay let's see, there's Ernie one and two, there's Jetty and his east coast affiliates, and there's CBS and their local product placement subscribers. I've got my money on that this message is from Jetty DiGarbo himself and you three are his flunky affiliates." Then it hits me. The voice on the other end of the break my leg wakeup call. "And that would make you his big bad brother, Leonie DiGarbo." I can't believe it took this long to come to me. I smile and hold out my hand. "How are you, Leonie? We've never actually met. And it's been a while since you've threatened me. Do I win any door prizes?" I retract my un-shook hand.

"Yeah you do." Leonie raises his gun to kill me.

I look up and beyond Leonie's gun shoulder. His eyes follow. Just then, Caw swoops down on his hand and I'm off to the races. Caw gives it to Leonie good. He's going for the face with both claws and beak. I look back to see Leonie try to shoot Caw, only to put a slug into his own temple as I look away.

Ah geez, why am I forced to see these kinds of things?

The two other goons with the matching mustachios are still behind me and have me cutoff at the civilized exit. So I'm forced to run up hill even further into the parking structure. It's exhausting, but I don't care. At the second level, shots are bouncing around the cement walls like a pinball game.

By the way, in real life there aren't those neat little sparks like in all the movies and bad TV. But red laser tracking beams are putting on one hell of a live action show.

"Oh, shiiiit!" A laser has me red tagged for destruction. So I leap backwards over a divider wall, hitting the concrete flooring hard with my shoulders. I roll over and crawl through probably the only slimy oil spot in the whole parking structure. Damn, that's gonna stain.

At the North wall the structure overlooks the Tujunga Wash. It's about thirteen-miles long, a tributary of the Los Angeles River, filled nearly to its capacity with disgusting valley runoff water because it drains about 225 square miles. Right now, anything and everything is flowing in it. I get up and look back to find the mustachio twins are crouched over their dead friend who acrimoniously shot himself in the head. Maybe I'll cry twice today because I know how he feels. Caw has flown the coop. The twins look up at me as if I killed their mother. I'm a dead filmmaker who won't live long enough to ever write again in their eyes. Running left is as bad as running right. Crud, how would a pigeon get out of this birdcage?

I look at the beckoning river below. Damn it. I'm not so good at astrophysics but my mind does a quick and comprehensive calculation of how much human thrust I'll need to make the river. Not over, but in. Halfway through surmising "No flying way," red-lasers and bullets start bouncing off the walls again.

I've been shot before, four or five times in fact by alien laser guns, and it's not pleasant. Even though what should've been a permanent bald spot was healed by aliens. So, I take nine steps back behind a retainer wall and burst past the twins as fast as my wet slicker will allow me. At the cement railing, while they take new aim at me, I leap up on it, using one last foot of extra thrust from it to help propel myself. I dive out about twenty yards, arms and coat spread like dodo wings. I just make the chain link fence below with a horrific jarring to my navel anatomy. The wind bursting from my lungs with all the painful sound I could muster hoping someone other than my assailants will hear it!

But I don't stop to count witnesses or broken ribs. I flip myself over the fence and roll into a moment of mind shocking blackout before hitting feet first into the rushing brown river.

Oh, Bubba. I'm instantaneously flushed away under the Radford Bridge that divides the old stages from the new stages. Talk about your unscripted reality shows. In another instant I'm down river far enough to avoid their shots. Coming out from under the bridge, I look up and over to find the twins watching me from the railing of the parking structure. They put away their guns. Apparently, they don't want me bad enough to jump in after me. I guess I win by default.

I sink as a swimmer, but my slicker has enough air pockets in it to keep me floating on my back for now. I look up and Caw is directly overhead. "Caw-caw, Caw-caw-caw." He can say that again. "Caw-caw, Caw-caw-caw!" Okay, he's trying to tell me something. I manage to painfully turn around, the air already sucked out of me, and see that I'm coming to a fork in the canal. From the north is the onslaught of water from the Tujunga Wash in the middle of a nasty spin cycle. Up about fifty yards where the two rivers collide is a tremendous upsurge of turbulent water. If I want to live beyond the next twelve seconds, I need to remove myself from this river right now. I can't see a thing to grab a hold onto though. The next bridge isn't until beyond the studio lot at Colfax just before it dead ends at Ventura Boulevard. Well beyond where I'll enter the Tujunga Wash and my ability to hold my breath. I'm a goner. Yesterday's passed-on screenplay. Goodbye cruel Hollyworld, I'm off to join Marine Land.

16

That is how I got here, washing out in a sea of pain, a twisting lump of drowning flesh. With my boot stuck in a shopping cart just below the surface of the Tujunga Wash. MOOOOOOOKY!

It's now, in all this pain, that I remember the phone! What the hell? *7-911, or was it 911*7? Damn, I can't remember! But I reach into my pocket and pull out the phone, still in its double Ziploc-baggy.

Mooky gave me this phone for a reason. I mean, he is the Mook, the mystery alien, who's everywhere we want him to be.

So I stick the phone out of the water and try to use my thumb to dial. I'm not having much luck. I think I got it turned on, though.

Suddenly, my hand is seized by the staunch grip of Caw and I swear to all the Pagan Gods of the Universe that this Japanese jungle crow is dialing my phone. I can feel him pecking at the keypad. This is some bird. I mean, crows are smart, and this crow is beyond anything I've ever come across. But maybe just maybe, he knows how to call Ms. Big Brother Blair, the woman Mooky had me dial to help us out of our last grave. Sadly, saving Mooky and returning the stones only ended up getting me made by an alien mob and shunned by humankind. If this is all too hard to swallow, imagine my gag reflexes. Ah, forget it, I'm out of oxygen. Too little, too late. My inner voice is going silent. Damn. I'm onto whatever the flipside turns out to be.

17

The world stays silent and black, only I'm breathing, I think. I'm on my back, I'm feeling nothing, but it's very black. Black-black, blacker then you can ever imagine. There's no bright light to stay away from. Is this purgatory? "Where am I?" I don't sense my lips move.

"You don't want to know, Picasso."

"Mook?"

"You cut it real close. Next time call before you leap."

"Where am I?"

"If I told you, I'd have to part you out like an old Ford."

"Why is everything so dark?"

"You're unconscious."

"I'm... what?"

"Don't worry, we're reattaching a leg."

"A leg? What leg?"

"The right leg. There was a minor unforeseen snag when we brought you out. But things seem to be under control so don't freak out. We got lucky."

"Did I die?"

"A little. It's a good thing Caw likes you."

"He's your bird?"

"No, he's your bird. I just trained him."

"But...."

"You're welcome. I don't have time for him, so I gave him to you because you're so weird who'd even notice him."

"Thanks."

"The good news is we were able to save your balls. I've got a couple extra big hairy ones here, if you want them."

"My.... no!"

"Give us a minute, we're almost done. When you wake up, just go home."

"How long have I been here?"

"An hour or two."

"But my leg...."

"Will be good as new. Better even."

"I don't want it better. I just want it back. Mook? Mooky?"

"Didn't I tell you to be careful of whom you rented to?

"You know Gray McGuiness?"

"Go home, Picasso. Just go home and lock your doors."

18

Who can tell how long I was wherever in hell I was? But just like that, I'm walking back through the torrent of water coming down the CBS Studio Center parking structure like nothing had happened. Only I'm limping. I'm not in pain of any kind, which is unusual even for me. But I'm definitely limping, almost teetering. I almost don't want to look down because I'm too scared of what I'm about to find. I do anyway, and a wash of sticky relief drifts over me like Mountain Dew. Both my feet are there, and they haven't left me with a wooden peg. Only, I'm missing my right Elk Wood boot and sock. Damn, that's half a hundred bucks to Sears down the Tujunga Wash drain. The best news is that the Indigo Chevy Suburban is also gone. Plus the mustachio twins are nowhere in sight. No bodies of any kind are left behind, at least any that I can see. After having been framed for a handful of murders, and seemingly gotten away with them, my mind never overlooks the reasonable possibility that I'm always the perfect fall guy.

I go for my keys only to find that my entire pant leg, pocket, keys and all are no longer under my slicker. Dang, a good pair of Dungarees. Buddy Lee will be so disappointed to find he lost. Screw it, I'm alive and that ain't half bad. I'm not sure what the chances of getting a taxi are in this kind of rain, but what the hell, I might as well give it a try.

So, I attempt to call Yellow Cab on my Hefty One Zipped cell phone but it's nowhere on my body. Damn it! What now? I have no coins to use the pay phone near the staircase, so I head towards the front gate.

In route, I start thinking about Mooky and Caw and how I hoped beyond hope that he and all his outer limit space-kind were just my messed up writer's imagination. But no, now it's my unquestionably screwed up writer's reality. Mooky and his space travelers are out there, looking after me, piecing me back together like some 21st century Frankenstein. I'm a made man by a cannibalistic alien mob with universal health benefits.

How many Hollywood filmmakers can put that on their jacket sleeves? I should've asked about dental. I can't help but worry how they fit into all these things that are happening to me. Or wonder if this alien healthcare extravaganza is just a random death intervention to preserve me for something else down the road.

Reality sets in as I see Stage 12 in the distance. Still, like it or not, I'm living off my ex-girlfriend's poodle's weekly sitcom paychecks. I'm stuck fighting for the creative control of my life. Wishing the girl I want to love wasn't who she was so I could trust her with my heart.

I'm standing at the abyss of my reality, overlooking the fabric of my very soul, knowing that I'm nothing more than the byproduct of my environment. Despite what I might have thought of myself over the years, I'm the total sum of human collective experiences. I'm apartment dwelling man, bred by aliens from the bloodlines of my ancestors, tree and cave dwelling man, to be better domesticated, healthier looking and extra tasty to a secret society of space travelers. Worse, I can't tell anyone. I am, the meek and pitiful, Jozeph Picasso, the equivalent of an alien's dog in the eyes of the real world.

"We are not alone," I hear myself yelling again into the pouring rain and cracking thunder! My despair seeps out of me into the tempest, dispersing into nature as if I didn't exist beyond the sound of my voice. If a man screams into the storm and no one hears him, is he still an idiot?

Alien Biz

"I don't see anyone but us two dipshits."

I look over and standing under the awning of one of the closed casting bungalows is Ernie Junior. He's smoking. "You want some of this?"

I walk over to him. He's looking at me like I'm insane. Am I not? He doesn't look so sane himself, standing way out here just to smoke. I know it's just pot but the smoke still makes me pang for a cig. "This the smoking room?"

"This is some killer glowworm. Daddy's stash, and from the looks of you, you can use it. "

I move up under the overhang. "Smells strong."

"Take a hit."

"No thanks, I'm nuts enough as it is."

"Yeah, what the hell happened to you? You look like a truck scraped you off the curb and threw you into a ditch."

"You get the number?" I wave off the joint again.

"It's not heroin. It's pot. Just take a hit. It'll relax you, you crazy bastard. If anyone needs a hit, it's you."

"My bird and I have had our share of hits today, thank you."

"Yeah. Where is that freaky bird of yours?"

"Caw? Somewhere. I don't know."

"That bird is unreal, man. The way it looks at me. Where'd you get that thing?"

I look closely at the joint. "You roll well."

"High school wasn't a total waste, dude"

"I guess not, dude."

"You headed over to talk to Daddy? That double crossing prick bastard."

"Yeah, I don't know if I'm up for talking to sweet old dad."

"Can you believe he's selling his own kid down the river? His only kid, his namesake? He's going after Gray McGuiness himself. To act in your script, no less. That slice of stale bread love story I used to wipe my butt? This stinking business."

"You should smell it from my position."

"It stinks no matter whose yard they dump in."

69

"I thought you signed on to direct *Crazy Kind Of Love* with Claire Davis?"

"I hate your script. I don't even want to relate to it. But Claire Davis wants to shoot it with McGuiness. Now Daddy, the back stabbing bastard, bags my idea and expects me to climb on board yours, like a good little sport."

"Do your script next."

"I'll get one shot at McGuiness. Without him, my concept's just another sleeping turtle peakin' out. Don't worry, this story isn't over."

"Seems to me McGuiness isn't even in the picture."

"He'll sign. Or else. He's a walking time bomb. You had to have been there, man. The guy's out there, way out crazy stuff."

"You've got something on him?"

"Yeah, a real disappearing dead girl. I got her last picture."

"That's sick."

"Not on me, like I'm into her. It's all very hush-hush. But she was found with no blood in her. Nothin'. Not one drop. She was as brittle as a cracker, but intact like a bloodless zombie. I'm not lying. One picture got out by cell phone, taken in a field of flowers by some stoner who tripped over her."

"And you got it?"

"Things gets done when you can afford it."

"So, she was...."

"A vampire's cocktail whore to the last drop. Why do you think I freaked when that big black bird of yours swooped at me? I'm not afraid of birds. Believe me. I'm afraid of him."

"You're afraid of vampires?"

"Gray McGuiness. They let him go on a weird technicality in Germany two months ago. Things about the girl, dropped, all charges, vanished into thin air, no corpse to speak of, nothing. Except for the one picture I scanned and e-mailed to myself that nobody but you and I know about. Hell, she's probably a vampire herself by now. The original shot was gone from my backpack by nightfall. Not the flowers or the actual picture, just her body from the picture. As far as I know, I hadn't encountered anyone the whole day, so switching it wouldn't have happened. No one else knows about this. The dude I bought the picture from recalls nothing. Not even meeting me, man. It never reached the press like he said he was gonna do. I called him. Gray's an untouchable or something. He has some kind of a diplomatic bullshit protection from somewhere. I don't know what but no one messes with him. Except now I got him locked in cyberspace. I can produce the goods. He'll do my movie. Trust me.

Are we talking governments?

Aren't you listening? Vampires, man. The guy's gigantic in Europe's magic world. People go crazy over him. Drawn like moths. I got a whiff of the scandal when I was packing through Amsterdam's hill country, scoring some righteous bud from the dude who discovered her body. He was on the way to meet me and hadn't told anyone else yet. So I made him prove it and bought the photo from him. People tell you the weirdest stuff when you're flyin' high."

"I hadn't noticed."

"I'm not pulling your hamster. Nobody really knows why, but freaky stuff like this dead girl happens all the time over there. This guy told me as much before goin' blank on me. It's been going on for a long-long time, too. Stuff people don't have answers for or remember the details. Nothing's being done about it. It sounded like a movie scoop to me, but it hadn't hit me on how, until McGuiness headed for the States."

"Sounds like you've seen too many vampire movies to me."

"Vampire movies sell though, man. So, I followed him back here. I've got him pinned down at your place, of all places, with those two broads. You see them? Jesus, the guy's got all that munch just dripping off him. I can't tell you how many times I whacked off just watching them from my car."

"Don't bother."

71

"While following him across the Atlantic I was nearly struck dumb with the perfect idea. The ultimate vampire flick. And a surefire way to make McGuiness tell us his own sordid bloodsucking story. Now this slap with your sucky script. Claire has my daddy by the contractual agreements. If he makes a movie during hiatus, she's in it. And if she makes a movie, he produces it. One flick a year, for the next five years. Or for as long as the show stays in production. That prick Jetty made both Claire and Daddy sign it because he gets a piece off the top. The humpin' thug's got it bad for her too, in case you got any dumb romantic ideas. He's doin' all this to stay close to her. So don't. He wasn't cheerful to find out Bubba belongs to you and not her, believe me. I can't believe nobody told him."

"Yeah, it wasn't good news to me either. Actresses are off my love menu anyway. So if you speak with Jetty, tell him to leave me alone. Claire had your daddy step in the way of your big for sure green-lit idea with my sucky script because she wants to work with Gray McGuiness. Not because she wants to work with me."

"Daddy's steaming about you not showing up at his office. He thinks you're a fruitcake. He's also thinking about maybe having you whacked. To keep you away from Claire."

"Did he?"

"What?"

"Attempt to have me whacked."

"Yeah, right. She doesn't want to do my vampire idea. She wants a romantic comedy. She actually likes your sucky script. *Crazy Kind Of Bullshit*. But they're a crapshoot at best. A good vampire movie will sell from here to Amsterdam. It's a no-brainer."

"Must be contagious on this lot."

"What the hell happened to your shoe, dude?"

"I lost it swimming in the Tujunga Wash, dude."

"I always wondered how idiots got down in there."

"They jump."

"Shit, you try to kill yourself?"

"Not on purpose, but almost."

He holds out his wrist and sure enough he's got slits up and down both arms, elbow to palm. "I was twelve, and Mummy and Daddy kept at me about school. Screw all that brainwash stuff. I got my dough the natural way.

"You earned it?"

"You bet. Kissed Grandma's flabby old bottom my whole life until the day she up and croaked. Called her every Sunday night and talked to her for hours, no matter where she was. Dedicated my Bar Mitzvah to her. Even did it in New York so she wouldn't have to fly. She was a great old broad though, man. Made me laugh, the things she'd tell me about my dad and mom. Stupid stuff they'd fight about. The mean things they'd say about me when I was a kid. I guess I was an accident or something so they got stuck with each other over it. Conceived me inside a N.J. synagogue, if you can buy that. Grandma says it's so, so I say it's fact. Towards the end, I'd call Grandma and leave long loving messages for her to wake up to in Yiddish. Sometimes she'd think it was Gramps and play them back to my father. I got her Manhattan apartment, the Malibu beach house and every dime she had. Mommy's not speaking to me right now, hasn't for about a year. Daddy hates me to death for it. I miss Grandma, but I'm happy and I'm stinkin' rich, dude."

I step back out into the rain. Better leave before his good fortune rubs off on me and ruins my perfectly dour day. "Well good luck with that, see ya."

"Hey, where ya off to? I still want to talk about my vampire movie. You wanna go shoot some pool? I know a place where the chicks shoot topless, and will do us on the tables for a hundred bucks each. My treat."

"No, gotta catch a cab. If you got so much dough, why don't you just go out and hire a bankable writer? Nobody will touch my work anyway. Even my friends take my name off my work."

"Yeah, at first I thought that. Then I'm out here tokin', you know? And I start brainstorming until it hits me."

"Can I hit you next?" I get back out of the rain.

He backs away just in case."See, man? You're perfect for this piece. Dude, if Middle America hears the hype I build up on hiring you to write my script of blood sucking true Magical Man horror, and they find out that he's staying in that freaky place of yours, they'll flock like bats at the theaters. I'll even tell how you wanted to strangle me in the rain, man, and give them all your scary bird. It's so friggin' cool. Man, you're a walkin' talkin' media hype waitin' to take a colossal dump on America's psyche and beyond."

"You have no idea. But look, you don't even like my work."

"I just hate it because it's not mine. So what? Everybody in this town feels that way. There's no real money in it unless your name is on it. To you, my idea sucks. Right?"

"Only because you want me to write it."

"You're missing the point."

"No, I get the point. Forget it, Ernie. I'm not your go-to guy." I'm back in the rain again.

"What about your Jeep?"

I pull back my slicker to show Junior my lack of pant leg. "No pocket, no keys."

"Far walkin', man. You want a lift then?"

"I'm gonna get in your car while you're stoned?"

"Hell no, my dad's got a Land Rover. Just keep the freaky crow away from me and I'll door to door ya."

"Does Daddy still want to speak with me?"

"Yeah, Daddy sent me out in the rain looking for you. But frankly, Mr. Picasso, I don't want to direct your stinkin' script. I got my own visions."

"Don't we all. And let's drop the mister stuff. Jozeph or just Picasso suits me fine. I get tense if I'm shown too much respect in this town."

"You know, you're not nearly as big an asshole as everyone makes you out to be. We could work good together."

"Who says I'm an asshole?"

"Everyone."

"Why?"

"Hell, I don't know. Maybe it's because you go around killing people and getting away with it. You're the Fresh Squeeze of the writing world."

"But I...."

"Look, I don't blame you on that home front. There's a few studs in Beverly High I'm havin' crushed in the ocean next time they reach Cancun."

"You the man."

"I'm the very rich-mother man. Things rise when you can put enough heat under the dough."

"Really, I wouldn't know." I continue walking away from him. Amsterdam? Everyone seems to know about that groovy place today. Good old Ernie Junior jumps in step with me, opening up an umbrella. It takes me but a moment to realize that it's mine.

So, huddled under it, we head back towards the parking spot I once left Bubba and my Corvair in. Somehow I get the feeling that I've come full circle with me helping Junior out of the water and now he's helping me get back home. Only now that I'm back, life is a much more messed up, uncivilized place than it's ever been. Amsterdam, full of drugged out rumors of dead girls and vampires. Now Mook's second caution about what I let take The Mystery Towers Magical Messed up Tour. Since I've regained both my feet, I should run far-far away to never-never filmmaker's land.

So then, why don't I?

19

I'm actually smiling because I'm getting Burnstein's leather wet and not mine. My mind keeps pace with the windshield. Wipe, swipe, wipe, swipe, over and over, maddening when the thoughts are useless. We're moving down Ventura Boulevard, heading West near Coldwater Canyon. Traffic has stopped up at the light and we stand still in front of Sportsmen's Lodge. There's a great little Patio Café in there. The chicken soup is to die for on a good day. I wouldn't mind choking to death on a bowl right now. We were just past Laurel Canyon when I told Junior to shut up and drive, hurting his feelings and I feel bad. "So, tell me your vampire idea?"

"I'm driving."

"You were weaving through traffic."

"People drive like chicken headed idiots in the rain."

"You drive like you're stoned."

"You whine like my mummy, stinky."

"Does she hit you?"

"Why?"

"Because I want to make you feel right at home."

"Shut up. It's not my fault you smell like Tujunga Wash."

"Then tell me more about Gray McGuiness and this real live bloodless dead girl."

"She was a wannabe super model from North London. No one took notice that she was being slowly bled to death because they just figured she was some crazy anorexic nightmare. Or didn't care enough to see it as long as she kept working."

"Is this your half-witted theory? Or am I to assume that all overly skinny women are being sucked to death?"

"This is how I heard it. You saw the two he's with now?"

"Yes. Up front and personal."

"Tag team. He offer you some yet?"

"Why?"

"That's how it starts. Him sucking you in with sex."

"People have diverse taste."

"With supernatural flavor."

"What are you saying, Ernie?"

"I'm saying the guy lives the life of a real vampire, and is a sexual freak of nature."

"Give me a break."

"I am. Write the script for me."

"Tell me the story and I'll think about it."

"We sign a nondisclosure contract, then I tell you the story."

"How about pinkies swear?"

"Forget it then."

"How much are you proposing?"

"How about six figures? That romantic enough for you?"

"Which six? I'm not bending over for you."

"Mid six. You ain't good lookin' enough to me, so shut up."

"Okay, we're talking the same language. Daddy knows the real story?"

"That lying, back stabbing thief? Are you kidding?"

"No."

"There's one more thing."

"You want to meet McGuiness first."

"I pitch it to him. He says aye, you're in. If he says nay, we don't need to talk any further. You thinkin' yet?"

"I'll let you know."

He's making the right turn onto Mystery Avenue like I've given him directions. I look at him."I followed him to your place late last night."

"So that's why you got into the runoff on Moorpark?"

"I was trying to beat you back to the studio."

"Because you didn't want me talking to Daddy without you."

"Is there a spot for me down under?"

"I don't even know this McGuiness guy."

"Come on, I'll order pizza, and we'll pound out some kind of agreement between us."

"I don't know, Junior."

"I could eat an elephant's leg, I got the munchies so bad."

"Look, I think there's more to this than you think."

"You're not kidding. This guy's really screwed up. So don't be in the room with him when he goes into one of his sexual frenzies. I heard no one's safe, if you catch my back story."

"Good to know."

"Believe me. Everyone thinks he's this prince of magical cool. This international Don Juan of elusion. But he's a sleaze ball, bloodsucking, lady killer. So if you know something...."

"I can't tell you."

"Come on, I almost told you everything I know."

"There are people out there who might be aware of what's going on. Mysterious people that you don't want to know."

"Jetty's people? Forget him. I'm not afraid of his people as much as Daddy is."

We're sitting in front of the driveway. I stop listening to him because I'm looking up at the rain rushing down the face of my building. The lobby has to be wet by now. But that's not what I'm looking at. Under the short overhang with street numbers at the top of my steps are five scantily clad, wet kids huddled together. One of them searches the intercom before punching a number. Someone lets them in.

"They found him."

"They're kids."

"Teens follow him everywhere."He pounds on his daddy's steering wheel.

"He's a public figure."

"I'm telling you, he feeds on them. Picking from the adoring crowd of fools the ones nobody will miss right off. Only he messed up and that's why he's hiding here."

"Lucky me."

"She had a good agent who was secretly groping her."

"Hey, if you want that killer job you need a groping agent."

"Man, that's tasteless, dude. Even for a mass murdering landlord slash sometimes filmmaker like you. So, we got a deal or what?"

"Or what. Stay here."There's two thousand unidentified remains stored in the county morgues on a daily bases, about one hundred and fifty of them children. I'm not looking to let number two thousand and one end up in Mystery Towers. So, I get out into the rain, run up the steps, clop-slap, clop-slap, the Cyclops-shoed idiot. I grab the door just before it closes all the way, pinching the hell out of my fingers in the process. "Ouchy-momma!" I go into the lobby. The carpet is sopped. In two days, it'll stink like dead cats. If I dry in this river stained apparel, so will I. I one-shoe-limp to the elevator. Someone's got it shut off. "Bastards."

I click it on, and drop down into the dungeon like garage. I move to the dumpster and elevator motor room to retrieve my spare set of keys and gate opener from my new hiding place. Not a very pleasant idea considering I'm one shoed. I mean, it's a garbage room doubling as an elevator machinery room. There's excess oil at the base pan of the old elevator machinery, broken glass, pizza crust, chicken bones, vegetable yuck, and stuff from the overshooting of the trash chute that I have to sweep up still. I turn on the light and hop in and out like a wounded kangaroo, planning to clean it up again some other time. The dim light reveals that a pizza box and a stack of newspapers are jamming the garbage chute, with gooey, funky trash bags piled up behind them. Apparently, signs indicating "No Boxes, Small Bags Only Please" still carry little weight in this uncivilized place. Another body or two shoved down the chute and maybe things will change. I reach up with a hoe I keep for this problem and down rains a half dumpster of trash all over my arms, but worse dirty kitty litter! "Bastards!"

I open the dungeon gate and Ernie Junior drives down. I wave him in one of 101's empty parking spots. He gets out, and looks about the almost empty flooding parking lot. "How many vacancies do you have?"

"Not enough believe me."

"From the looks of this place you'll need Noah's Ark soon."

"There are sump pumps that should kick on shortly." I look around. Even J.J.'s red Toyota pickup is gone. He's the actor from Alaska I let stay in my garden studio free in exchange for fixing up the studio and keeping the laundry room clean. I'm a little befogged given the weather myself, it being mid-afternoon when most normal people work. So, it's more than odd that my building of abnormal tenants is nearly void of life, particularly since the rain is making driving prohibited at best.

The only cars not mine are the black Continental from last night and Felicia's smashed white Toyota. She lives up in 304 with her husband and two children. The other is my partially dismantled red 66 ragtop Corvair Corsa.

There's sad things I don't like talking much about, but needless to say, I managed to clean most of the glass out of the Corvair's interior without ruining it after an alien named Victor Castro was shot to pieces in it and dissipated. No, I didn't kill him. Mooky accidently did. He was trying to kill me for poking him in the eyes. We were all arguing over alien healing stones found in apartment 101 and getting my dog back. Anyway, the Corvair's windshield is still shattered and the taillights and back bumper are on order. I have no plans on driving it soon, now that I have the Jeep. So I drained the oil and will do a complete renovation when my ship sails in.

Unfortunately, my Queen Mary's haunted by me right now and probably holding my poodle for ransom of a groveling apology. But maybe I can con Junior into seeing reality for ten minutes and siphon a check out of him to write his fanatical screwed up vampire idea. Only it may end up being more real than both of us can handle. Because at this point, I'm not so sure he's not on to immeasurable trouble with Gray McGuiness. The fact that Mooky gave me a second warning about my choice of tenants, and... I don't know. I really don't. Things are so complicated from a warbling inside perspective.

The only thing I do know is that there are kids wondering around my building that don't belong here. I plan to joyfully kick them out. Something I've done many times since the murders of my pig family tenants in 101 four months ago. There was also an art collector specializing in ancient jewels named Val Simpkins with his head stuck in my fridge's crisper, too. I found him with his brains all over my kitchen wall. But don't get me started on them, because despite what everyone in this town thinks about me, I didn't drive anyone out to the desert or shove any deadheads into my crisper. Yet.

Then the lights go out. Great.

20

"Uh-oh."

"What happened?"

"What do you think happened?"

"The rest of the block's still lit."

"I see that, Junior."

"Where's the main power?"

"Right there in front of us."

"Then turn it back on. I don't like the dark."

"There isn't a boogieman, Ernie."

"That's what you think. You rent to him."

"Listen."

Ernie shuts up and the unmistakable sound of running feet permeates the cement above us. They're followed shortly by human screams that you can only imagine in your wildest nightmares when they come from inside your life savings.

Ernie is on me like a polar bear in heat, hugging the breath out of me. "Get off me."

"He's killing them!"

"Shut up!" I put my hand over his mouth, to stop his heavy breathing. His nose whistles. I clamp it. The running footsteps above split up. A door slam follows. Then the screaming starts up again, closer this time. Ernie bites me! He runs to the truck. The staircase door on Graystone bangs open and the screaming runs out of the gate and onto the sidewalk. Young bodies trip over each other. There are only four of them now, picking themselves up, and looking back towards the door. I can only see their legs through the black iron bars.

"Where's Brad?" one of the young females yells over heavy frantic breathing!

"Oh my god, where is he?"Another one yells.

"Come on!"A boy in boots comes back and grabs her.

"I'm not leaving him!"

"He must've gotten out the other way."

"He was right behind us!"

"Come on, the guy who owns this place is crazy!"

"He's still in there."

"Come on, we'll call the cops!"

At this point, I don't need cops. "Hey," I yell through the iron barred open arches. There are shrubs blocking view of me. Not to mention the lights are out. So I'm probably not what they want to hear.

"Did you hear that?"

"He's coming!"

"It might be Brad. He might be killing Brad!"

"No one's killing anyone," I yell. "Just...."

But it's too late. They're running down Graystone, slashing through the torrential rain filled gutters. They stop traffic as they cross, screaming at passing cars about Brad being murdered by crazy Jozeph Picasso. Obviously, I don't need this. It's stupid kids like these that have kept this mystical of mayhem myth about my gray stone, twenty-four units of bad news, alive.

Junior starts up his daddy's truck, pulling out of the parking spot. Apparently, he plans on leaving. I got bitter news for him. He wanted in. Well, he's in until the power comes back on. He waits in front of the dead in the rainstorm dungeon gate. I tap on his window and he looks at me as if I'm the bride of Frankenstein. Considering I've been probed and had my right leg reattached by cannibalistic aliens recently, I might just be. I tap on his window again.

"Open the window, Othello."

"Open the gate."

"I can't."

"Then I ain't openin' this window."

"What the hell's the matter with you?"

"McGuiness, man. He's feeding."

"Those were just kids scared off by the dark."

"Wake up, Picasso. The guys a monster. Why do you think the lights went out?"

"The storm?"

"Feeding frenzy. This same thing happened on the ship. The power went out. The ship was dead in the water. People were screaming and running everywhere. It was total mayhem. A young French kitchen helper was never accounted for. No one said a single word about it to the press. Now open the gate!"

"It's electric, Ernie. You want out of this building, you'll have to walk."

"I'm calling the cops, then."

"Think of your movie deal."

Ernie stops. I can tell he's still thinking it over because his lips are moving if not just by quivering."Okay, I'll stay. But you got to promise me you'll keep close. I don't want to be blamed for any of this."

"Ernie, I'm known as an infamous mass murderer of four of my tenants. I wouldn't even make a legitimate alibi. Now park the truck and give me back my umbrella.

"Why?"

"Because we have to go outside to get back inside."

21

I pull a flashlight out of my still dead Corvair and check the circuit breaker just outside the laundry room door. It's right next to the phone's binding post panel. Ernie stands so close he's touching me."Back off, Ernie."

"Turn them back on."

"There's nothing popped."

"Damn."

"It's probably the transformer just outside the laundry."

"Can you fix it?"

"What I can do is strike you with this flashlight if you don't stop gasping down my neck."

He steps back. Lightning flashes and he's on me again in the middle of the flooded laundry room. So I butt him with the flashlight. He strikes me back with my umbrella. Outside, I take back my umbrella and he huddles close as we make our way up the river flowing down my laundry room's steps where I found Caw. It's not so dark out here by the pool, but the pines sagging overhead funnel the rain down in droves. I can just make out the transformer through the branches. Who knows what's going on with it? There's no smoke.

"What do you think?"

"I think we go inside and up to my place and wait it out."

"Do we have to?"

"We don't. But I've got to use the head."

The pool area is still overflowing with rainwater. Nothing I can do about it now. But the pool furniture is pulled to the side again. What the hell? Who keeps doing this? Without the sump pumps the elevator shaft will eventually flood. And expenditure I don't want, but will nonetheless endure if the lights don't come back on in time. We go up the back stairs like this. Both worried but for different reasons. There's a locked door at the first floor landing. I use my spare key set to let us into the backdoor. The hall is pitch black. Not even the newly installed emergency lights are on. A matter I don't bring up to Ernie as I turn around and put the light on his morose, scared to death face. "One foot after the other, Ernie."

"What floor is he on?"

"He's in 102."

"Are we walking past it?"

"There may be another kid hiding in here. So yes, while we're looking around."

"Do we have to?"

"Coming home with me was your idea, Ernie."

"Not in the dark, it wasn't."

We go past the witch's apartment in 105 overlooking the pool, another story, and 104, where Erin and Janet live. This leaves us outside the first fire door in front of 106. This is where Serina and her mother still live with her now fifteen year-old brother. They're two weeks behind on their rent, so I haven't seen any of them around of late. After all, I am a psycho killer landlord. So why should any of my tenants trust me? By the time we get past 103 on the left and through the next fire door we are approaching apartment 102. A service hall is there and runs to a staircase emptying out onto Graystone. Ernie grabs my right hand and points the flashlight down at the lower half of 102's double doors. A small bloody luminous handprint is smeared across the base of the door. Great!

"Is that...?"

"Sssssshhhh... you hear anything?"

"Just my heartbeat."

"I'm hearing heavy breathing."

"From in there?"

"No, from over there." I point down the side service hall that heads north behind 103 and past 102's dining room to the back door leading into the apartment's kitchen. It also provides access to the North exit onto Graystone where the kids ran out. We're in complete darkness beyond the flashlight, but the labored breathing is getting stronger as we make the turn. I let the light fill the short hall as much as I can. At the end of it is more blood.

The staircase door clicks shut! We both almost faint away. There's smeared bloody footprints on the lower half. Like someone crawled along, pushed the door open with their barefoot, and tried to get away.

"Please tell me it's only a movie," Junior says.

"More blood."

"The breathing is coming from the other side of this door or that door?" He points at Gray's kitchen door.

"I can't tell."

"Whose blood is it?"

"My guess is Brad's." I carefully push the staircase door open over the top of a pool of even more blood. It reflects hideous reddish hews from my flashlight's beam onto the cut stone walls and stairs leading to the two upper floors.

"Jesus, this person is running on empty."

"You see anyone?"

"I ain't lookin'."

"Listen."

"What?"

"I don't hear the breathing anymore."

"I never heard it above my own heartbeat in the first place," he says. "In the second place, I don't want to, and in the third place, let's get the hell out of here."

I let the flashlight follow the trail of blood. Someone's bleeding badly. It trails away from the upper staircase down the four gray stone steps to the north side exit door. I can't tell if the person was dragged up the steps or crawled down, or both. Outside the door is a small stoop where I sometimes find Serina from 106 smoking cigarettes. She's the moody model slash troubled teen who usually sits out here late at night. There's an ornate iron gate with a busted lock beyond that and a once gas lamppost. I'm hoping she's not out there now.

"Whoever it is might still be outside."

"Good, let's stay inside."

"If it's Brad he may need help."

"If Gray is with him, he'll need more than that."

"Give me a break."

"Look if you want, but I'm staying right here."

"In the dark?"

"Okay, I'm coming."

22

We go down the steps, making sure we don't slip in the blood. Man this victim's a bleeder. I push the door open to find the flood of body fluid ends at the door. What might have been outside is now fully saturated by rain and runoff water from flooded roof gutters. "You see anyone?"

"No. You?"

"Not yet. I don't know how but I think it's raining harder."

"Impossible. Let me look." Ernie sticks his head out and opens the umbrella. "Damn. That truck is floating."

"What a mess, aye, Cappy."

Huh? Ernie and I look at each other. Realizing we are not alone. A long elegant hand cups a shoulder on each of us. Like Jack in the Boxes, we spring out into the rain. We're ankle deep in runoff water that streams around the truck, over the curb and onto the sidewalk. The rain is hitting our faces so hard we can barely keep our eyes open, let alone see back into the door. I put the light on the door and Gray McGuiness is standing there in his duster. He stays just out of the natural storm cloud filtered light. He's sans his Scottish kilt underneath. His skin is an eerie white. It's sort of a soft enchanted fluorescent. Damn, he's hung like St. Petersburg!

Ernie tries to run away. I grab him and hold him back. He's wrestling my fingers but I got his belt good. I don't know why I'm doing this. If he wants to run away, let him. But I find myself compelled to pull him back to me with more power in my arm then I know I possess.

Gray just looks at us with a steady hypnotic marble stare worthy of the ancient mythological lover of Aphrodite. There's a slight grin on his Adonis face. I step toward the door, dragging Junior with me. Not until he turns and faces Gray McGuiness does he stop struggling. We stand there facing him, childlike in our adoration. This guy's so cool, with his thick red hair cascading over his shoulders. The blood runs down the steps between his long slender exposed feet, like some great vanquishing warrior. It dissipates into the pouring rain. Run, Picasso, run. I can't. I don't want to. Even though I know I should.

"Perhaps we should clean this up, Cappy. Less some mortal fool gets a wrong notion of us."

"We wouldn't want notions?"

"Notions of this tiding could cause confusion on what undeniably took place here."

"Nothing happened. Nothing took place."

"Nothing close to what it looks like, Cappy."

"Just kids."

"Yes, kids were playing inside your scary Mystery Towers. Without a doubt one cut himself on your front door."

"Must've run into it in the dark."

"It would seem to be the case."

"But he's gone now. No one's bled to death."

"I'm sure he's fine." McGuiness gives us a reassuring smile.

"Right. So, we'll clean it up."

"Yes. Before tenants come home from wandering about."

It seems so simple. I didn't hear glass crashing but that doesn't mean a thing. I head for the door, Ernie right behind me. When we both get inside, Gray McGuiness is back into apartment 102, entering the kitchen door. He's left us to deal with enough blood to kill a kid. I feel so calm. Ernie has let go of me. We look at each other. Everything is okay.

"I'll go get a mop."

"I'll stay out here."

So, I leave Junior there in the dark. No remnant of the overwhelming fear that petrified him moments before. Has our Mr. Cool, the Magical Man, Gray McGuiness opened the door into a unabashed serenity filled world of sordid death? Or is there an almighty evil lurking beneath that masculine charismatic beauty that deemed us his two fools, worthy of his most vile deeds: The cleaning of young Brad's blood from the steps to my Mystery Towers?

Just what this spooky place needs, another ghost.

Cappy. Somehow it all seems so groovy.

23

Back upstairs, I head for the restroom. Afterwards, I give Junior something to change into. I light candles. We both take showers. In separate bathrooms. I have three of them, and two bedrooms plus the south side step-up into a tower I call my office.

While showering the river stink from my crevasses after having such a bazaar filled day, I find myself washing my reattached leg without even taking into account that just a few hours back I had nearly lost it and drowned in the Tujunga Wash. Once this grotesque thought bricks me upside the head I stand up in the shower so quick and rigid my back actually cracks. I'm somewhat surprised, if not mystified, to be actually alive and standing on my own two feet. So, I turn to let the water strike me on the back of the head and try to stop thinking about it.

But I don't. The evening before started out filled with a long running nightmare. It led into the mad early morning renting of apartment 102 to Gray McGuiness, the Magical Man, and his two overly hot young women. Plus, there's been a whole lot of near record setting rain. Then I'm adopted by what is presumably a Japanese Jungle Crow. Caw turns out to be trained by an alien named Mooky and sent by him to look after me. At this point, any normal person would've called it a much too screwed-up day and gone back to bed.

But not I, ohhhhh no, for I am Stage Dogman. A Jozeph Fetch-It for my ex's French poodle, Bubba. Bubba managed to get the new Hollywood blonde starlet in town, Claire Davis, to fall in love with him. While me, demon filmmaker, simply managed to get all of past and future Hollywoodland to loath my presence with all their callous hearts.

Thinking about it in these terms, overseeing Bubba's career as I do, this is exactly what I found myself doing with Bubba's mother. I spent all my free time making her acting career work. Only Bubba's paying the bills at least. With her it was always my money paying for her headshots, acting, combat classes, and clothing, plus countless nights out with her thespian friends. The whole time, my career floundered upon the brink of never happening. Finally, after both Bubba and I couldn't take the lack of writing, the emotional neglect, and her stuff strewn all over the apartment any longer, we convinced her it was okay to rejoin a musical on the road without us.

In reality she wasn't being forced back on the open road of Off-Broadway plays by us. She wanted to hit the open road. She was bored with us both and didn't like not living at the beach. We haven't heard about her since we were told she was seeing a young tech person by one of her in touch girlfriends. Not one word from her through all my murdering troubles and Bubba's acting success. Not even on Facebook. It's been an utter abandonment, a crushing of spirit and soul.

Of course I know what show she's starring in and where. But I don't let on to Bubba that her show's a big hit and Broadway bound. He's found someone else to sleep with, and is now on a hit show of his own. So he doesn't need her.

As we sad sap writers often do, I found myself turning all the pain and trauma she caused us into a new script. My first script in over two years, called *Crazy Kind Of Love*. The very same painful story that Ernie Burnstein Junior, the rich mail boy turned Hollywood mogul, prefers to wipe his bottom with. However, Claire Davis, Bubba's new girlfriend and costar, wants to star in it with Gray McGuiness of all people. She's forcing the deal down her producer, Ernie Burnstein Senior's, throat. I can only hope he chokes on the first plot point.

If that's not weird enough for one day in movie land, I might get a chance to direct it if Gray does act in it. But with a much more unfortunate if attached... and that's if Jetty DiGarbo and his New Jersey mob friends let me live that long. He's crazed about me because I know who he really is. He should be crazed at himself. He's a violent cad, a no good, overacting drunk who has already caused me countless nightmares over the years. Just today, he caused me to have my right leg reattached by alien surgeons, after flinging myself into the Tujunga Wash to get away from his brother and friends.

Think about it. I'm made by an alien mob with the best health insurance plan in the universe. They may have already whacked Jetty's brother by having the alien trained Japanese jungle crow grab his gun hand so he couldn't kill me. Worse, I can't tell anyone. Not even my best friends, Erin and J.J., nor Claire or Bubba. The whole truth to why I'm so weird, angry, and sad is one big secret. It just sits inside eating at me.

At the end of the day, in the eyes of everyone else, I've only managed to anger Claire but good, leaving the door open for more self flogging. Next week I'll work on East Coast loathing. One crowded coast at a time. Otherwise I'll end up over loathed, and the United Paparazzi will become jaded. The rest of it, the possible vampire stuff and the body-sized blood we just cleaned up in the hallway, is beyond my comprehension of how it could happen without either of us freaking out. I'm just hoping I wake up from this bloody nightmare quick enough to keep it all from becoming the bloody truth.

The candlelight wavers, the wick is drowning in liquid wax, leaving shadows of light to bounce about the tile walls. Just beautiful.... and phiff, the smell of cherry candle wax, and I'm showering in the dark.

"Son of a bitch."

What next? I rest my head against the cool tiles. Turn up the heat on the water. No peace here. It ain't over until the filmmaker's last frame is cut and in the can. No doubt the mustachio twins, Jetty's friends, will be back to make sure I make that cut. The only truth I know is that I'm not admitting to any of this. In case anyone attempts to prove it, or wants to put me away for knowing it's all true.

Sadly, the lowest part of my day is that I managed to alienate myself from the one creature on Earth who truly and unconditionally loves me for who I am. Bubba Dog.

So, I stand here, in my steamy dark shower, with not a shred of light to reveal what's happened to me. In examining my midsection with my fingers, I feel no apparent scarring or pain to prove that I'm not completely out of my mind.

Another ten minutes go by, an eternity to the sanity impaired and water boiler time. So, I shut off the water because it's getting cold. Hard thunder rolls far off in the distance, coming my way. Good things will not come out of being an alien made bagman, except maybe, and I'm not complaining, my out of this world medical plan.

24

Gray McGuiness' use of mind power is personal magnetism at its worst. Great, this person is one sick magical charismatic mother. Is he a real vampire as Junior proclaims? If he's capable of turning us into his housemaids, cleaning up his bloodletting, why is he here in Mystery Towers, and what does he have in store for me?

Does he know that Junior followed him across the Atlantic Ocean in hope of blackmailing him into starring in his own autobiographical, real life vampire movie? This and less is running through my mind while I'm considering how to prolong my exit back to reality. My concentration wanders when the candle magically comes back to life while I'm toweling off, throwing a pale light onto my right leg.

Am I imagining this? Could it be? I look at my body in the mirror and the reattached leg seems to have a lot more hair on it than my left leg.

"What the hell does this mean? Am I having some weird hormonal alien side effect?"

Since I'm alone and neither leg answers, I'll have to ask the Mook.

25

My dining room is filled with a purple felt pool table and four barstools. That's where I find Junior. I'm dressed in ratty gray sweats and a clean white t-shirt. The rich bastard is au natural, drinking my last Rolling Rock.

"The Chinos didn't fit?"

"I like to air it out a little before I cage it back up, man. It keeps the ball sack from stinking. Hey, you're out of beer."

I take his cue stick. "Put your pants on, Fast Ernie."

"Rack it up, then."

Wouldn't I like to. He goes into the workout room slash spare bedroom and comes out shortly with the pants I gave him. He likes them baggy with no Looms. So he can keep them.

I'm still racking." What'd you do with your other pants?"

"In the shower. There was so much nasty, gooey, sticky, god awful blood. Can you believe we cleaned that stuff up? And we're still not freaking out? It was like...."

"Like something came over us, a compelling to get it done."

"Yeah, I don't know about you but I was feeling...."

"Groovy?"

"Yeah! And he kept calling you Cappy. You notice that?"

"Yes. You still want him in your movie?"

"He is the movie."

"Great. You hungry?"

"Are you kidding?" He holds up a box of chowder crackers.

"Make yourself right at home. How about a tuna sandwich? And tomato soup or potato salad to go with those?"

"How about a couple sixers and a delivered cheese pizzas?"

"No one's delivering in this rain."

He goes over and opens my refrigerator like maybe I made a mistake and there's really a pizza guy in there.

"What good is fifteen million dollars before you're twenty if you can't get a sticky cheese pizza in a stupid rain storm?"

"Life's full of little tragedies, Ernie. You'll get used to them as you grow up. Would you like tuna on rye with sprouts or not?"

"Tuna with sprouts? Are you sure you're not my mommy?"

"Does she hit you?"

"That wasn't funny the first time. Sprouts... hey, is this the fridge that Smithsonian dude got croaked in?

"How'd you know about that?"

"Dude, everybody knows about that mess. Is this it?"

"Yes."

"That's so bad."

"Terrible. His skull was over there." I point my cue at the cabinet where Mr. Simpson's gray matter hung on its door.

"Really? Can I buy it from you?"

"I break. No." I sink two stripes and a solid.

"How about just the one door?"

"Shut up. Your turn. I got solids."

"But you sank two stripes."

"So don't whine when I beat you." Hey it's my table. I'm home a lot. I play alone when I work out ideas. Right now I'm thinking that this is actually my third serious offer for the fridge, proving that this city is truly a sick weird place. Without the fear of some kind of higher being we'd probably be eating each other. Why not? Cannibalism is proven not to be below human meal standards. It's probably why the aliens feel no remorse over eating us. Perhaps we're a galaxy-wide delicacy and we just don't know it yet.

Honestly though, if I were an alien, the Mook-maestro of mystical madness, or one of his clones, I personally would've just stopped here on Earth for a quick kidnap and eat brunch. I might just pack a few frozen dinners consisting of some organic backwoods human tribe. Or maybe I'd go down dirty and take a whole cell block or two of pumped up criminals. I'd hit the open space ways, put the Earth's Sun at my back, and wave goodbye to Pluto while it was still called a planet.

Stop this, Picasso! But they could very well be bottling and black marketing our seeds back to where they're from like some kind of galaxy import/export human fruit stand of the Universe. In the meantime, they're cloning us, living amongst us, as us, and passing their life form from one clone to the other at will between us. Who knows what else they're doing right in this building that I don't even know about yet? Christ, I'm light headed. I hate knowing all this, thinking these things. I can't breathe. "We are not alone!"

"What's the matter with you?"

"What?"I'm gripping the pool table.

"That's the second time I heard you yell that."

"What?"

"We are not alone. Is someone else here?"

"Never mind, I was just thinking."

"You look like you're about to pass out. Try breathing."

"It wasn't good thoughts."

"Spare me the director's cut paranoia. My rich young life is messed up enough as it is."

"You have no idea."

"You really need to see someone, dude."

26

I line up my cue stick to finish the game when a nimble knocking comes from outside my door. It's almost a scratching, like a very large bat is fluttering its nails against the numbers of my room, wanting in.

"Let them in if they have pizza."

I move to the door with the flashlight as the eight ball sinks and the game ends. Junior no longer cares, richly avoiding the taste of defeat. Who's at the door? Do I really want to know? I don't think so. It's not Erin and Janet from 104. Any other tenant would've pounded loud and rude to let me know the lights are still out.

"Who is it?"

"It's us."

I turn to find Junior standing nearly on top of me again. I push him away. What's with this kid? He's so happy.

"It's them. His 'IT' girls." Junior points down to the floor, indicating downstairs.

I put my finger to my lips to keep him quiet while I think it over. This both intrigues me and scares me.

"Can I help you?"

"I smell pizza." Junior goes for the door. I grab his hand.

"Open it and I stick your head in that crisper."

"They've got pizza, man!"

"Where did they get it?"

"Who cares?"

Through the door comes Brenda's heavy Russian accent. "Can't we come in? We brought brewskies and pizzas."

"Where did you get them?" I can't believe I'm asking this.

"Ameci's, that cute little place just around the next corner. They delivered."

"What in hell does it matter? It's friggin' pizza and beers."

"You wish for pizza and beer and magically it's at my door. You don't find that a little weird or peculiar after what just happened to us, happy boy?"

"Happy? Not as weird or peculiar as you making them wait in the dark hall, Sad Sap. Have you seen what they wear? Now honestly, if I had mentioned two gorgeous, nearly naked nymphos, with pizza and beers, that would be weird. Because that doesn't usually happen to me until Saturday. So chill, caveman. You're about to experience some of the other "way out there" world I told you about, that only we sick rich kids enjoy. This isn't just coincidentally cool, man. It's probably him saying thanks to us."

"Right. Thanks to us for cleaning up a young kid's blood. Remember? Did you smoke some more, or what?"

"It's dark and cold out here."

"Lonely, too," Amanda says.

I open the door a crack, filling it with the flashlight. Brenda and Amanda stand there covering their eyes with twelve packs of beer and a pizza each. "Just a minute." I close the door and put the light back on Junior. "What kind of beer do you drink?"

"Are you nuts?"

"Yes. What kind of beer?"

"You... I... okay, I admit, I drink Budweiser. Okay? It's good inexpensive American beer, and I like it. But not in the can only bottle. Sue me."

"I like Rolling Rock, a better American beer."

"You're arguing this point now?"

"They have both."

"Bud and Rock?"

"Twelve pack each. I'm just guessing on the cheese pizza."

"Damn. What kind of pizza do you like?"

"Tomato, garlic, and parmesan cheese." He gives me a 'How gay is that?' look. "What, you're cool because you still eat bar mitzvah pizza? I like garlic. And normally make my own. How coincidental would that be?"

Junior opens his mouth as if he has an answer to that, but nothing comes out, so he shuts his trap.

"Is one of those pizzas with garlic?"

"Garlic? Yuck."

"No stinky garlic."

Junior looks at me."See?"He reaches for the door.

I squeeze his wrist. "He's controlling this. Get a hold of yourself." He just smiles. I look down and he's groping himself.

"Gray sent us up," Amanda says with her English accent. "It's scary out here."

More than they think. "Where's Gray now?"

"He had to go to the studio."

"In this rain?"

"The show must go on," Brenda says.

"Can we come in?" Amanda asks.

I look at Junior. He's almost pleading. He's got the munchies so bad. I open the door. Both girls come into the candlelight. Amanda enters first, nearly matching my six-foot even, not counting my genius bump. She towers over Junior like a big sister. She slides past me in black track, camel-toe-riding shorts, rubbing each delicate cheek against my manhood. Her curls, bouquet perfect, are still cropped and jet-black, pinned down beside her ears emulating a matador's sideburns. She looks over her shoulder into the candlelight with a little girl smile, her teeth perfect. She holds out her long lean hand with the dark reddish panted nails and presents shinny head Junior with a twelve pack of Bud... in bottles. Now there's a Bud commercial. "This, Skinhead, is for you."

Brenda makes her entrance. She's not quite as tall, but is somehow even prettier. Her flowing white blonde hair, brushed no less than a thousand times into a cascading waterfall, hangs nearly down to the back of her bare kneecaps. She slides around the front of me and plants her lips to mine, almost, the little tease. Her handful of breast, with pointy eraser nipples, dart against my t-shirt through her nearly see-through mango cotton tank top. There's something surely illegal here but I'm not pressing charges... yet. She's got heavy Russian vodka breath, her voice nearly a snarl from smoking. "Dinner's served, my lonely lovelies." The girls come together and touch as they pass, making an elegant right into the candle lit kitchen.

"Oh, look a pool table," Brenda says.

"You mind taking off your shorts?" Hey, I also talk gibberish in my sleep.

"Excuse me?" Amanda pops her curly head back around the kitchen door, confused joyful, hopeful illicit smile.

"Shoes, I meant shoes. I have a carpet fetish. And a socially induced lisp."

Amanda sticks her foot out, wiggling her dainty little dirty toes."No shoes." She pops back around the corner leaving Junior and I starving for attention in the foyer.

"Sorry, I...."

"Vivid, dude."

27

I didn't need to ask how they knew what we wanted. I couldn't tell Junior, but I get the feeling the other two are in on the home delivery gag. Gray is playing with us. He must know what Junior's up to, or what he wants, or even that he's been following him. Why else would I be standing at my sliding terrace door watching the rain while two unbelievable young things are sexually abusing a nineteen-year-old millionaire kid in my guest bedroom?

The only thing that is missing from my pizza was the garlic. I got green unions instead. A matter I did not take lightly in the light of the unlit moment. Fortunately, I have plenty in my almost famous headless crisper. So I chopped some up, and reheated my pizza while the girls and Junior smoked dope on my terrace, overlooking Mystery. Yes, I'm listening to myself. But I can't have my tenants coming to me for help and smelling pot at my door. Considering the fact the sun set over three hours ago, and we still have no electricity, I'm finding it utterly amazing that no one has come angrily caroling at my stoop.

I mean, I could roll the gate back manually. But Junior doesn't know that. He's my alibi at this point, so I'm keeping him around. My tenants must be all parking out on the street when arriving home. Or perhaps they are still just too afraid to be wandering around Mystery Towers in the spooky dark. I don't blame them following what I've seen today. The phones still work. The only person to call is my friend and neighbor, Erin, down in 104 to ask if she and Janet could come up with a bottle of wine to ride out the dark. I had to tell her I had houseguests and that it wasn't a good time.

In the din of my situation I can't allow myself to drag her into this sick world I've fallen into. She knows more than she ought to know already. Filling her head with all this ridiculous alien bullshit would only act as a catalyst to screw her head up just as much, if not more, than it has mine. Therefore, without being too huffy about the declining of the wine and spine on the springtime evening, she hung up on me once again. What she sees in me I haven't a clue. But she's the closest and most trusted female friend I've ever had, and she knows this, because I tell her. So she puts up with my weirdness.

I haven't heard from J.J. yet, my dungeon garden studio houseguest, which isn't all that unusual. Sometimes he's acting on location, working construction on low budget sets or house sitting. Most of the time, he is hanging out with some starry eyed fellow classmate and I don't hear from him for days. It's amazing what the suspicion of mass killing will do for your privacy when the lights blowout.

In the meantime, I'm not sure these two young girls aren't killing Junior. Once the girls got a load of my garlic breath they shunned me like daylight. I didn't have the heart to tell them I rubbed a clove down around the insides of my shorts. Some things vampire groupies just don't want to know. Hey, my sweat pants have no pockets for garlic cloves. But garlic is spicy to sensitive flesh and if I could, I'd rethink doing it.

I'm standing here with cold Rolling Rock number four, wondering what Gray will think of all this, when Brenda starts screaming in Russian. It sounds dirty just the way she's saying it. It must be her turn to ride the prophylactic pony. I decide to go outside and listen to the rain. I keep an old pair of slip-ons at the terrace door. I slide my left foot in and I'm attempting to put my right foot in the other. But no go. I look down at my foot, thinking maybe it's swollen from being reattached, but no, it doesn't appear to be.

So I go to my desk chair, sit down with the flashlight, and bring both feet together to take my first real good look at them since this morning when I strapped on my boots.

"What the hell?!"

My right foot is a good inch longer and half inch wider than my left. And it's not nearly as pretty. I pull up my sweat pants. My right leg has definitely twice as much hair as my left leg. And it's darker. I did, sort of notice this in the shower but it hadn't alarmed me." Jesus H. Christ! Mooky, you dirty rotten alien. You ball sucking, bastard!"

The sliding door from by guestroom bangs open. "You okay?"

"What?"

"You were yelling again, dude. You got some kind of psychological syndrome?"

"Bite me." My head is reeling. I don't want to talk to this kid. I have someone else's leg attached to my body! "I'm fine, go back in and do your thing."

"I'm done. I go again, my johnny's gonna fall off."

"Just give me a minute."

But the girls spring out, completely naked, prancing by me to my fully stocked wet bar. They mix cocktails with my shaker, taking them out to the terrace. They shun me, staying clear away from my two garlic smelling oddball feet. Outside, they reveal yet another joint from where I don't know, and have at it. "You want some of this one?"

"What?"

"You okay, Picasso, you're looking at your feet like you just lost a leg or something?"

I can't imagine why.

"These girls rocked my world, man. You should go brush your teeth and give them a go-go."

"Aren't you a little inquisitive, go-go boy?"

"Sure I am. Like right now, I'm curious about why you got two sizes of feet. But as far as outrageous sexy girls go at my height, I don't fret the whys." He goes outside and rejoins the girls. I can hear them giggling about my feet. Vampires.

I, on the other foot, just sit here smoldering. I don't know what to do first. I want to strangle someone, but I can't. So I strangle my new foot. It hurts just like the old one. So I let it live.

The six-legged, naked giggling bubbles back into my apartment and into my oversexed workout room. It's round four. This kid may be a rich little shithead, but he's a better stud than me.

I get up, go outside, without slip-ons, and stand in the rain. It doesn't make me feel any better, but at least I get to watch a car drop Gray McGuiness off out front. He looks up at me as if not seeing me. More like letting me see him, the poser, as he heads to the steps. I wave to him. He's already looking away. This should be good. I'll need more than beer to get me through this one. He must know what's going on. He sent the girls up here. Right?

Brenda's new drink is in a red plastic beer cup on my stone table. My beer is stale anyway, and I don't feel like chugging from the Jack Daniels bottle, so I pick up Brenda's cup and take a sip. Not bad, Cosmo, vodka/cran, and a dash of Triple Sec with real lime juice, shaken not stirred and drank straight up. Wow! Just what the bad doctor ordered. If I stay out here I won't be able to hear Gray's knock at my door. Therefore I won't have to let him in and experience any of the next twenty-four hours of bullshit that's surely bound to come my way out of all this social bloodletting and sharing of body fluids.

The second sip is even better. Man, I need this. Just when I thought my day couldn't get any weirder, it turns out that Mooky had them attach someone else's leg to my body. Whose leg is this? Where's my leg? Who has it? Can I get my boot back? My head is getting light again. Breathe, Picasso, breathe. Something's not right. Something's the matter with me. "We are not alone!"

"Shut up over there! No one cares you're getting laid!" Someone yells this through my pines from a condo building across and down the street. Screw 'em.

What was I thinking? I attempt to chug from Brenda's drink again, moving the red plastic cup toward my mouth. This time a long red trail follows my hand up to my face. I don't get close to my mouth this time. I try again. But it's no good. My mouth keeps moving. I watch my face morph into a Picasso painting, reflecting off the terrace glass door. "What's in this...?" Shit, the terrace starts rocking. I'm experiencing an inner earthquake! I'm weaving back and forth. This is so freaky-scary but feels incredibly funny at the same time. My balls tingle. My nostrils flare. I'm fascinated as much as I am terrified. My heart has slowed down to barely a pump a thump. The candlelight in my living room and poolroom is bouncing, leaving silvery streaks in their wake. What's happening to me? Am I hyperventilating, am I having a stroke, am I on... Brenda's....

I stop. Or try to. My two sized feet seem to. Yet I topple forward against the glass door. My forehead smacks so hard I'm amazed I'm not inundated by shards of nasty sharp glass. I bounce back onto the flooring. The stones are cold and nasty wet. But that's not my biggest problem.

My living room is lit like an Eighteenth Century romance novel. Moving across it, in front of my new flat screen, is Gray in a streak of uninvited by me human flesh tones. Only, he doesn't look the docile Adonis I just saw. His fanged teeth glisten in the yellow candlelight. His long hair is shimmering dark auburn in the flickering shadows. His eyes glow a trailing afternoon blue. He's completely without clothing. His pecker is a night train in route to a head on wreck. If he truly is a vampire, one of the girls must have invited him in. Or she left the door open for him. Or maybe accepting the girls was his invitation to join in. Junior did say that's how it starts. I want to forewarn Junior that it's his turn on the prophylactic pony or worse. So I reach up to the door.

Gray raises his left hand, palm down to me.

I find myself merely leaning forward in a fetus position. I'm completely unable to move beyond rocking back and forth. I don't know how long I stay like this. My mind is falling into a whirlpool of silent dark watercolors. I'm completely somewhere else inside my head. All of everything, including dreams, disappears from my mind, falling who knows how deep inside my mental cave.

What did I drink?

28

When my eyes open again it doesn't really matter what I drank, because the Pacific Ocean is attacking me through the smashed picture window of a Malibu beachfront pad. It's bound and determined to have my sorry drugged body dragged out to Neptune's Grave. But even worse - much-much worse - in my left hand, held by his hair, is the undeniably, yet unimaginable, severed head of the Magical Man, Gray McGuiness.

What the hell am I doing with Gray McGuiness' head? And why haven't I let it go? Did I have anything to do with this? Or am I once again a pawn in some wild Alien board game? Did that little shithead, Junior Burnstein, set me up to once again be the fall guy of the century?

But first things first. I let go of the head. After that I grab for the rapidly approaching windowsill with my newfound foot. These waves aren't kidding. They want me. Luckily, almost all the glass is out of the picture window before I slam into the crown molding. Nice woodwork.

I have zero recollections of arriving here. None beyond me crumpling to the wet sandstone of my terrace. Whatever was in Brenda's plastic cup has finally worked its way through my bloodstream and is now flowing out of me as I wet my pants. Hey, I'm petrified at best.

I try to sit up and get trounced face first by the next gigantic white water barrage on my sanity. Flush, I'm sent sliding hard across the buckling parquet floor. "Holy splinter-butt, Dogman!" McGuiness floats up beside me, eyes open, mouth stuck in a silent grin! "Ahhhhhhhh!" I grab for him again and fling him backward over my head as once more I'm sucked out with the wave toward the windowsill. Damn, how long has this been going on? There isn't a stitch of furniture left in the room. Leaving me nothing to hold on to, so bam, I hit the crown molding again. I realize this time that this is easy because the building has slipped off its moorings and is in a slump towards the Pacific Ocean. If there's one thing we have in common, it's a slump. I'm so far into my slump my past lives look down on me.

Having learned my lesson about sitting up during my last trip down here, I instead rollover toward what's left of the support wall dividing the two immense picture windows, and grab on. I'm now standing on the wall as the wave washes past me and up into what was once a very nice refurbished kitchen. What cabinetry is left is working itself loose with every aquatic blast. It's amazing what goes through a drowning victim's mind moments before disappearing off the face of the earth. I'm actually hoping whose leg I have attached to me knows how to swim better than the rest of me. I'm honestly a natural anchor in a water world. They'll find no gills on this bloated stiff.

My thoughts are saturated by the inevitable retraction of the sea from this tilted room. My backwash of reality has now picked up a large chunk of faux marble top counter and is sailing it right back toward me. I recognize that I'm now struggling within the morning light. The eye of the storm is seemingly right overhead. A gray misty hue tints the room. How fitting since Gray McGuiness' head has managed to roll atop of the counter projectile and is once again surfing his way to the freedom of the open sea.

I don't know what to do about any of this. I have about three seconds before the surge is upon me. I can't just let the head go about bobbing in the swollen surf. So I reach out involuntarily and snatch the head from its perch and pull it back to me by his long flowing red hair. Damn! His head swirls around and around, each time facing me with that insipid knowing smile.

Well, know this, I didn't kill you but if I did I'm sure I had a very good reason. Wash! I'm underwater for longer than I have breath and by the time the wave is past me I'm coughing up half a lung of saltwater silt. Gray is taking all this wannabe a floater much better than I am. There's an advantage to already being dead in downing.

I have no choice on my ensuing move. The next wave is upon us with an almighty force that's twice as strong as the last three. I'm swept away from the windows and deposited inside the kitchen. I hang by my new foot on an open cabinet frame.

The wave washes out and McGuiness and I slop to the floor. POW! OUCH! My brow bounces on the beveled stone tile, blood bursting from the gash. Nice, I have to get me some of this. I don't hesitate though, I've got a split second to crawl to the side door and plant a death grip for dear life. McGuiness is useless in my attempt.

I'm bound and determined to take him with me. I'm alive, and warming from my heroic struggles to save a head. I pull us up with one arm until I'm secure inside the door jam and can look out the side of the house to where Pacific Coast Highway has given away from the coast of Malibu. Then the wind hits me with a deep chill. I start shivering to my bones in what's left of my sweats and t-shirt. I'm shoeless. My feet and hands are turning blue. There's no time to think. The gap between where I am to where I need to be is about thirty-five yards.

Below me is nothing but open air, cold wind, swirling water and the rolling stones. Running along the side of the house is what's left of the sidewalk and steps. Crisscrossing iron bars stick out of the house's foundation, gripping the fragments of cement. Luckily, what's left of the house is giving me a little buffer from the storm. My mind is calculating what I should do next. Giving up keeps creeping to the top. So I push those thoughts down, because there's a major iffy chance of getting out of this mess still lingering along the side of the house. I actually think I can step-stone along the fragmented sidewalk all the way back to the garage, where the sidewalk is still intact. Maybe I can. So, the Magical Man and I are making a run for it before the rest of this house comes a tumbling down.

From the door jam, I sidestep across to the first cement fragment and hope it holds us. Good thing he's not half the man he used to be. So far it's good. I'm using the exposed chicken wire embedded underneath the stucco to keep me from falling. Good old cheap California construction is saving me.

I'm at the fifth chunk when I realize the sixth one is way too far for me to reach. Even with my new larger right foot. Damn! I'm out in the middle of all this with a dead magician's head in hand, vulnerable to all and any prying eyes. All I need is an inch or two more to get me to freedom. Ain't it always like that?

In arm's length is a bathroom window, though shut, and landlocked tight since the wall is completely out of sorts. So am I. I swing Gray McGuiness up at the window and smash his head through the glass. It's nice of him to have such beautiful, long wet hair. There is so much tension on the glass already that it literally explodes sending Gray out of the bathroom and me with him. I'm falling, my right hand fingers frozen on the chicken wire. The rest of us get swung low by Gray's ten pounds of dead head weight. But when it swings back up, I find myself reaching the windowsill by a good safe margin. I have no choice. I'm forced to put Gray's hair in my mouth or drop him. "Yucca tree, Dogman!" Damn, I wish I had that move on tape. Let's see Batman try that one without wires. I'm now hanging by both hands on the bathroom sill and safely able to get my left foot planted on the last cement chunk. With McGuiness staring me blank in the belly.

I'm on semi firm ground again! As firm as knee deep mud will allow. It's then I realize what is making the house slowly slip out to sea. A massive wall of mud from up above has crossed Pacific Coast Highway and has oozed like a colossal blob of taffy against the house. This is only affecting two houses. The unoccupied house to the north is not affected but the house to the south is already gone, even the garage. Things are moving fast, so fast no one has come to watch yet.

Without much effort, I step to the house property to the north with my newfound best friend. We have escaped Davie Jones' Locker. Unfortunately, the silt in my mouth tastes like I still have his jockstrap over my face so I involuntarily heave up what I've swallowed. Gray doesn't seem to mind.

I'm spent, but the cold is no longer shaking me. Sheer adrenalin is pumping my heart. I sit on the bumper of a black Land Cruiser just like the one.... Wait a minute. Could it be? It is. It's Ernie Sr.'s Land Rover. So where are Junior and the girls? Who's got the keys, not to mention the rest of Gray McGuiness? Who wanted him dead? None of the answers come to me. None of the tricky scenarios racing through my head reflect good tidings for me. Who did this to us? What does it all mean? And why did they leave me alive? Oh yeah, it hits me, why kill a perfectly good experienced fall guy when you need to get away with murder?

Inside the unlocked truck there is no apparent set of keys. Why would there be keys? If not, why is it unlocked? If I were setup to have supposedly driven out here, I'd have the keys. Maybe they're still in the house? Or out to sea, and whoever did this to Gray and I didn't expect the house to get washed away. How could they know what Mother Nature had in store? Was it just my dumb luck or something sinister concocted by those who are controlling this?

I put Gray McGuiness in the passenger seat and pop the glove box open. Damn, nice try. "Where's the key, Magical Man?" He just looks at me with those big dead blue eyes, and slumps against the passenger door facing down between the seat and the armrest. I reach over to straighten him back up and something shiny with a black edge and push buttons catches my mud brown eyes.

"What the...." Someone tossed the remote key back into the truck and it had wedged down between the door's map pocket and the seat's power controls. I look at Gray, his grin somehow seeming even wider.

"Let's go home, Cappy."

The mother is still telling me what to do. But, I grab up the key and give them a go. The truck fires up.

I put it in four-wheel drive, and plow us out of there.

Gray just chickens out and rolls onto the floor mat, ending face up, watching me like I'm driving too fast.

"Keep it up, Gray, and I'll turn you into one hideous looking hood ornament!"

29

I make the left off Pacific Coast to drive away from the storm winds, onto Sunset and trek up the twisting hill. I steer clear of the runoff trying to give me the bum's rush back to the sea. Through the wipe swipe of the windshield wipers and the pounding rain, I hear a faint, "Blip." This should be good.

"We can't let everyone know we're here, can we, white boy."

I look in the rearview mirror and Mooky is the Prince Charles of Ernie Sr.'s back seat. I hit the brakes and come to a complete dead stop in the middle of Sunset Boulevard. We're at the very pinnacle of the first real hairpin climbing off the coast. This makes the two in-the-rain-asinine-tailgaters slide into oncoming traffic. They barely escape between oncoming SUVs, fingers flailing my way.

I turn on Mook. "You are one dead alien!"

"What'd'ya gonna do, white boy, poke my eyes again?"

I jam my first two favorite right fingers at his face and my hand passes right through his head. He's a hologram! "You bastard, where in hell are you, Mooky?"

"Calm, Picasso. I got safer things to do than precariously hang around with you all day."

"Whose leg am I wearing?"

"What do you care?"

"Screw you. Where's my leg, Mooky?"

"We haven't found it. You can't have it back when we do."

"Alien bastards!" More people drive around us, honking their horns.

"You better start driving. We don't have a lot of time."

"Time for what?"

"Time to cover one great big universal disaster. Now drive, fool."

"I need some answers first."

"You needed a leg, we had an extra one. It's a done deal. You got lucky. So get over it."

I take my lucky foot off the break, and step on the gas while reaching down to pick up Gray McGuiness' head. It does a spin around-and-around, grinning 3D at the World."

"Good, you still have him."

"No, bad I still have him."

"Look, Picasso, there's things goin' down that you don't need to know all the details about. Just keep his head and the body separated until we contact you."

"You used me to kill this bastard didn't you?"

"If you did, I didn't, they did."

"They? Don't give me 'They' garbage, Mooky aka William Payne Washington. You are 'They'!"

"Watch it, my dimwit human friend, that name could turn you missing these days. 'They' are The Space Travelers Advisory Board and The Alien Council. I ain't on either. I just do sensitive things for both. It's a go-between job."

"There's really a Space Travelers Advisory Board and Alien Council? You have jobs and even vote?"

"You won't find me in the Yellow Pages, but it's a livin'.

"Like Earth is some lost in space vacation destination and we humans are walking talking smörgåsbord of dumbest things to eat?"

"If you want to put it that way. You're also our overpriced companions and pets. You're slaves to our better way of life. In so many ways I can't even begin to explain. Because you don't really want to see the whole picture, believe me. You wouldn't last a day knowing everything anyway. Your simple mind would implode. But know this, everything major that happens here on Earth beyond everyday human whining and tedious drivel is because we either allow it or will it. You are exactly how we need you to be. For now. Yes, you Picasso, are alive today and working for us because we need you alive and working for us. You don't believe me, count your toes, they are the only blessing you'll get from us."

"But...."

"We don't have time for that right now. How you feel about it doesn't matter one iota.

"I got your iota...."

"Look, Gray was becoming too visible. He's human as far as you need to know. Remember those stones?"

"How could I forget, asteroid? They messed up my life."

"You said you wanted a life. So now you got one."

"Screw off. I'm branded. People hate me. My life is ruined!"

"Ruined? Are you listening to yourself? 'People hate me.' WAAAH! What happened to the person ranting and raving about all the misdeeds in this world, huh? What about the two billion people or so who don't have enough energy sources to meet their basic needs? While rich bastards like you, Picasso, can drive gas guzzling toys like this on credit? And take it off your taxes. Shit, you're barely thirty and own your own apartment building. Where's the guy who cried for the have-nots and the end to human stupidity? Huh? Because if he's gone, we ain't friends no more. And you just best shut the hell up around me."

"I'm being lectured about human integrity by a cannibalistic alien."

"Listen, we aliens care more about this planet than you indigenous ever will. You should see where I'm from, because my mother nature's a three-nippled-bitch! Most of them are. The places we come from. These rappers don't sing squat about real ghetto life. The Universe, man, nasty, mean, uncivilized in ways you couldn't even begin to imagine. But, you tree swinging, cave dwelling morons, you're all just a bunch of self-centered twits. Why do you think we're here?"

"To eat us, so shut up."

"We don't eat you, we drink you... this enables us to breathe your air. We don't want to. We have to. Getting rid of you would be much easier in the big picture of things. But we can't, not all of you, not yet, so you all best figure out how to get along with us when the time comes. Consider it a weird alien form of your planet's photosynthesis and you get the picture."

"I don't want to get the picture! Just tell me why Gray's dead? Or leave."

"Let's just say this McGuiness clone possessed stones some years ago, while occupied by a very powerful alien. Much larger stones than the three chips you found. Whole stones with powers beyond anything even we've seen since we divided them amongst us. Powerful alien with large healing stones enters beautifully charismatic human clone equals the greatest personal magnetism shape shifting force that mankind or alienkind has ever or will ever encounter."

"Shape shifting?"

"Oh yeah, taking on other forms, shapes. Only this cat ain't no Disney shaggy dog. It can possess anything at any time. It's got us all freaked out, movin' about as heliograms to keep him from enterin' us, and becoming us."

"Who is this guy? This other alien?"

"That's an ongoin' thing. Remember the It I mentioned the last time we talked up at your place?"

"Unfortunately."

"We don't know It well. It keeps things that way. It doesn't participate within the Alien Advisory Board or Council as we would like. In fact shuns both in retaliation to what they've done to It and It's human clones in the past. They're trying to make It conform to their rules. Some are even trying to harness It's powers. Or end it."

"You mean It could be... anyone?"

"Yeah, or thing. I got too close once in the past and it toasted my best clone. Said to be the only one of its kind. Came from an imploding galaxy, many, many years ago and had a lot to do with who you are today. Powerful. A Being of sheer energy force from what I'm told. That's why this particular alien clones and possesses humans. Shape shifts, so It can walk amongst you. Even amongst us, It comes as It chooses. We never know what to expect. Sometimes it comes as a male and sometimes as a female and often both. In the big picture, not all Beings are as naturally good lookin' as me. Not even you, white boy."

"Isn't that refreshing? Go America! Land of the free to eat me state. The melting flesh pot of the Universe." I drive for a minute. "Why does It call me Cappy? My father called me Cappy my whole life."

"Well, we guess It likes you. It's highly sexual. He may have known you for some time. You into funky freaky stuff, maybe? It might have participated. You wouldn't have even known."

"Don't even.... He...It was in that little man possessing him that night, the one in my nightmare, wasn't It. He called me Cappy, too. What does this have to do with that night? Why was that little guy killed?"

30

We drive for a while, I sense Mook not wanting to answer me. He just sits there. So I stop the SUV again.

"Look, don't hold on to that, Picasso. I don't know what that dude was about to do. I can only tell you that he needed to die if It had him killed. He's very much against the killing of humans otherwise. Sometimes there's got to be witnesses to mindless acts of violence or else it's just some dumb mystery killing. Or a disappearance that won't go away by human standards and gets blamed on mysterious monsters and aliens. There are humans who believe we are here, even if they have no proof. All I can suggest is that you watch your back from here on out. Like Chess, It makes moves that we can't figure out why until many moves later. With It involved, those kinds of events have a way of festering before they work themselves out."

I pull back onto Sunset again."Yeah, but why me? Why choose me to experience this guy's death? Was it a test?"

"That is between you and It."

"Great, can't wait to ask It."

Do you understand the difference this time? We need you to keep Gray between us. You can't tell anyone."

"So it's us now."

"Picasso, you are so far into this thing you can see out the other side. Nobody wanted this to happen this way. But it did. You've got to make sure McGuiness stays dead till he's too decomposed to graciously want to come back as himself or you are no use to us. It's very egotistically sick about Its looks."

"You mean… if I don't…?"

"Can't have you involved if you ain't involved to the end? Know what I mean, bro?"

"We can't just simply explain this one with things happens. Someone's got to take the fall if he shows up dead or missing, eaten by wolves or whatever. People know who he is, that he's staying in my building. He's even shooting a live show. There's completion bonds and network money involved. I'm not that fall guy this time."

"Then just listen. I really gotta go. Because of the stones, McGuiness became a powerful human vampire clone."

"Vampire? So he was a real vampire?"

"The kid only thought he figured it all out. There were many others starting to see through his murderous allusions for a long time. It was getting sticky. The Magical Man's rein was coming to an end one way or the other. So the alien It, using McGuiness, came to the US knowing It had to kill off his precious clone once and for eternity. He just didn't want to. He couldn't make himself do it. He's addicted to being him, the blood, the sex, the living forever as an Adonis. You saw him."

"More than you know."

"Don't kid yourself. It was convinced that to remain living as McGuiness forever he had to get World Wide Media attention. This led us to believe that the show It came here to shoot was a ruse to have The Magical Man, Gray McGuiness, actually die gruesomely live on camera at the Kodak Theater, in the heart of Hollywood. Then It'd bring McGuiness back to life while everyone is standing riveted to their seats with their mouths open. It even had it set so the power system couldn't turn itself off. It was planning to confess everything. Hold the shocked world as a captive audience. Tell the whole truth about us being here. Think of all the talk show bookings as he rats us all out with his life story. He could answer a lot of historical questions."

"Think of the ratings."

"This isn't a joke, Picasso. Some of us have high profile positions. Some prominent families would lose everything if he had gone public. Nations would tumble. History would have to be rewritten. No one would go unaffected by this, to say the least. Not even you or your precious little dog."

"Wait a minute. It's still dead. Wouldn't It, I ... okay give me the punch line. Because I'm sitting here with Its head."

"You see how messed up this is gettin'? We have no idea what It plans on doing now. We didn't expect this to happen."

"Why isn't the Hollywood Paparazzi all over this guy? Most Stars in this town can't wipe their bottoms without the general public knowing which hand stinks."

"They would if It allowed them access to him. They will when It is ready, believe me. He's a real vampire in a very alien form. But nothing that you think you know about them, the things written in human books about vampires holds true to McGuiness. There are no rules to follow here. Putting a stake in his heart won't cure this one. Even the garlic you put in your pants last night won't save you from McGuiness with It inside of him. And you don't have to invite McGuiness in."

"Get me out of this, Mooky. Don't tell me how this ends."

"You have to know. You must do this, Picasso. If It brings McGuiness back to life claiming he can save humans from us in front of...."

"... nearly the whole planet as an all powerful alien. There'd be no killing him again after that."

"Checkmate. Paradise will change. There's no telling how humans will react. With today's media coverage It could be McGuiness forever running the planet. And everyone will know we are here. No Alien Travelers Advisory Board or Alien Council controlling him or us, and definitely no multiple me playin' go between to keep things from falling apart. You see what I'm saying, white boy? I'd be one of the first ones It takes out."

Unfortunately, I do. "Are you kidding me? This is absurd. Something this important and you pick me? A hack Hollywood filmmaker slash mass murderer to do your bagman work?"

"You're involved for a reason."

"What is that supposed to mean?"

"I don't know. We didn't pick you for this. It did."

"I don't even know what this alien It calls himself."

"Lately he's been calling himself Jerry."

"Kiss off, Mooky."

"You get the idea. It's an only need to know process from this point on. Life would change, man. There'd be mass carnage on a scale where either It or we'd be forced to fix the situation. Believe me, we don't want that."

"We again. Then, who cut McGuiness' head off?"

"We don't know for sure. We got ideas. That building. It can hide things that happen from us in there."

"But you're the Mook, Mr. 7*911, you know everything. Mister find-you-a-leg. Garlic in my pants guy."

"You gotta lot to learn. The more we learn about Jerry, the more we learn we don't know jack. We are not able to track him like he tracks us. His power jams even our equipment. But he knows he's got to go, and if we let him do it his way and avoid exposing it to the public, it's a win-win. He calms down and maybe comes back into the fold. We can smooth things out. Maybe. You understand? You may be his out. He's chosen you."

"Wait! I don't want to be chosen! Get me out of this, Mooky. Right now or I'll go national!"

"Try showing up in a newsroom with that head. I dare you. Who the hell would listen to you? They'd shoot you on the spot or we would."

"I don't care."

"I'm about to poke you, if you don't shut up."

"Give it a shot, Hologram Man. Ouch!"

I swerve. Horns honk!

"I'm driving in a storm on a winding road, here, you prick!"

"Then listen. I can tell you this much. The alien using McGuiness' body, is the first one of us here. You might say Jerry discovered Earth way back when and is still here because of the stones It created. Yes, the same stones the Space Travelers Advisory Board and The Alien Council voted to take away because of what Jerry was doing with them. They divided them amongst themselves. The same stones It now wants access to or It'll finish what It plans to do on air. Expose us all."

Great, this will never end well for me. I just know it. My knuckles are about to pop out of their skin around the steering wheel. I should stop this truck and get out right now, but I can't. I tried. "Unlock this door, Mooky."

"Not yet. It is very freaky, from what I've heard, which makes him even more attached to being McGuiness. Very much in the beginning of crossbreeding you people out of your trees and caves. Jerry spent thousands of years genetically breeding humanoids to give birth to as perfect a human being as It could. An Adonis. Every inch of man's history, Picasso, Jerry and we were part of it. We're the cause of most, the Ying and Yang of what you know to be real. Remember Neanderthal? "

"Yes, I think their ancestors are paying my dog to act."

"Well, It got rid of them by breeding them out of existence before the rest of us even got involved."

"It? Why It?"

"Fine, He, It, Jerry, whatever. Just be careful of whom you sleep with until this all blows over. He likes to be pretty."

"This isn't going to all blow over! This Jerry wants to be Gray McGuiness. The Magical Man. If I have McGuiness' head. And there's still a remote chance that Gray could be brought back to life. Jerry will come looking for me."

"It's just a mere side effect of his clone carrying the stones."

"Alien clone termination and sucking human body fluids are not mere side effects. It's a horror film, Mooky. A whole new sick genre. And it's happening inside my building!"

"Yeah. We have to be careful, Picasso. But it gets worse."

"How can it possibly...?"

"Very quickly. We fear that Jerry's whole goal isn't just about exposing his privates in public. He's led us to believe he plans to expose the rest of our asses here on Earth to get rid of us if we attempt to take Gray away from It. He believes he is the Supreme Being on Earth, and wants the Space Travelers' Advisory Board and The Alien Council to give him back his precious healing stones and work under him as McGuiness, leave Earth or dissipate. We don't want that. The only other alternative is to sink life back into another Dark Ages to keep McGuiness from being able to go global. And most of us don't want to do that again."

"Again? What do you mean by most?"

"You don't need to know this right now. But yeah, some of us dig the idea of sending you back to a Dark Ages again and killing off all the smart ones. Your ignorance is our bliss."

"Kill me right now, will ya. Don't do it slowly like this."

"You ain't on the too smart to live list."

"Thanks. There's a list already?"

"You know what I'm talking about. Evolution."

"Look who's a drama queen now. Ouch! Will you stop?"

"At first, we started wars and spread diseases to keep man in turmoil. Remember the gladiators? That was sick stuff."

"Yeah, they're called Hollywood secretaries now."

"Good one. Now war and disease helps you develop new medicines to prolong life and better technologies to kill each other. Those better technologies are bleeding over into public use. It's getting harder to hide how many of you we take a year just to survive. Once man's body evolves to the point where your minds come to the realization of what you are, you'll know we are here, too. Because what you are and why we are here are one and the same thing. Man is here because we are here, and it all started with your good buddy, Jerry."

31

I can't help myself. I suddenly turn the wheel and head for the nearest tree. I'm committing suicide, without even trying. But the SUV sloshes through the runoff, jumps the curb and skids to a complete stop in the mud just inches from going over a hundred foot bluff. I can't breathe. My head is spinning. I can smell my life dissipating before my very eyes. I stink of salty brine from the Dead Sea. "We are not alone!"

"Nice try, Picasso."

"Let me end it now, Mooky! Don't put this weight on my heart. I'm too crazy as it stands. Please! I beg of you, don't do this to me. I'm not strong enough. I'm not the go to guy. My heart is gonna explode any second." Tears well up in my eyes, I'm crying again. Not for me, not for anyone, but for what I know to be true. Even though I refuse to believe it in my head, my heart pains to stop pounding, to end knowing it's true right now. How can this be happening? Why is it happening?

The SUV shifts into reverse and backs out onto the Sunset and into oncoming traffic. I get more of those familiar fingers I've grown accustomed to of late. They have no idea what real road rage means on the interglacial level, so screw them.

"Gray had Junior and I clean up his last mess."

"Of course he did, that's how it works. Gray McGuiness willed you to do his dirty work, like all the others have. So, don't blame me. Regardless of what goes down next, Picasso, Jerry can't blame The Advisory Board, The Council or I again.

We want to smooth things with Jerry. He's controlling this and we've got to continue letting him think that. Are you listening?"

"Yes."

"Jerry knew we were about to sink the world back to the Dark Ages if he went forward with his live show. So now you have his head. It's a game changer. This is what we think Jerry's new plan is. It's simple, Cops will be around your place today. Remember those two?"

"Mike and MacAroy, the Hansel and Gretel of the LAPD?"

"Them's the ones. You've got a big mouth so I ain't telling you everything yet."

"There's more?"

"Just keep in mind these two Police Dogs are involved with Ernie Senior."

"And he's in bed with Jetty DiGarbo."

"Right, who's in bed with your dog, and who's in bed right now with your girl, Claire. You're getting how complicated this is for you, aren't you. How it all works together we don't know."

"What do they want?"

"The two cops? They don't know. They're just being sent to have a word with you about Junior being missing. But they're unwittingly tied tight to all this, so watch out."

"You mean…! Even back then... the little guy's killing in the street outside where I bartended, the stroke of death cover up? They were the two cops that night that shot him?"

"Now you know why they fear you so much."

"Fear? Try hate. They pinned four murders on me."

"I've got your back."

"Why doesn't that make me feel better?"

"Relax, we think Jerry wants those two cops to find McGuiness' body in your place and make that gruesome discovery a national spectacle. You see how this changes things? We have no control over what happens next inside your building. Somehow you ended outside the building with that head, and we made a move to Blip you into the beach house.

Your job is to keep that head and body from getting reattached. So Jerry can't become McGuiness again until we've cut a deal with It.

"Why did it have to be at my place?"

"I told you, your place is a little peculiar."

"Peculiar? The place is a fortified murder magnet. What don't I know about Mystery Towers? What kind of magical mystery tour am I on?"

"Ask Jerry if you see him. But hope you don't."

"Come on, Mook."

"Forget the building and all that magical mystery stuff for now. It won't matter if this all goes down right. Pay attention to what's happening right before you. I mean it, look out!"

I look up and a red Ford F150 is coming right for me. I'm on the wrong side of the road. I slam on the brakes and turn the wheel, skidding to a stop again. I get the usual fingers and serenaded with resounding horns. It's still raining hard enough so they can't get a good look at crazy old me.

"I actually forgot I was driving."

"You ain't getting rid of me that simply, Picasso. Let's finish this. I'm already late for where I'm supposed to be.

"Don't let me stop you from leaving me out of this."

"The two cops only know they did Jetty's people a favor way back when. They think they're being called on again by Jett's people to look for the missing kid. They were only told you are holding him captive up at your place. They won't know about the Magical Man or any other bodies unless they find them."

"Jerry is sending them, and you can't be seen stopping what's about to happen."

"Exactly why I can't be here right now, and ain't. Suddenly it's another big news day… and a national hunt for McGuiness' head when it turns up missing. When found with you, it'll be brought together in the county morgue and reattached.

"Does Jerry know I have it?"

"Probably. We can't track the body or the head but we're sure Jerry can. We're doing our best to keep him from seeing us now. He could be you, and I wouldn't even know.

"Me? What?"

"Forget I said that. Be aware that this is a potential public relations' nightmare for Junior, his daddy, their production company, the studio, and all involved when Junior's prints show up all over your place. Jetty and those cops will have to cover the kid's butt by quickly pinning it on someone else."

"With glee, I'm sure on me."

"You the prime suspect of the millennium. But they will be big heroes publicly and privately."

"Give me a minute to think this...."

"Your sole value to us right now is to keep Gray McGuiness' body and head separated."

"Whose leg do I have?"

"I told you."

"Who were those people in the studio parking lot?"

"Apparently you have a knack of ticking people off, Picasso."

"So they were people? Real people?"

"Really, real people."

"So, do I...?"

"Yes. Lonnie was there and still lukewarm, so we took him. For reasons you don't need to worry about right now. I know you don't see it, but it gets funnier later. I promise."

"Great. So now I'm part Italian?"

"And there's the blood type thing."

"Wait! Do I want to know all this?"

"It might help to know. Like if you want children."

I don't want to hear this part. I turn the radio on.

"Turn it off." So I do. "It ain't that bad. Remember, I got your back. We just had to change your blood type a little. You're universally positive now, and able to accept all types of blood and body parts. In case anyone should ask, or we need to add anything else down the road."

"What?"

"Blip!" I look in the rearview mirror and Mooky's gone. Blipping bastard. So I head home, not wanting to find what I know I will. According to Mooky Man, I'm still lucky to be alive on this planet right now, at this given time, in this age of the Universe. I look at myself in the mirror. Who is he kidding? If I had the nerve I'd end being here right, right now.

32

Coming over the 405 Freeway in a blaze of thunderstorm sets my mind into a stew of wonderment. Not just that we might very well be here in Heaven already. But worse things, too. Like, I wonder if they'll let me have a laptop on Death Row. I wonder if dying is anything like living the life I'm living. I wonder if this is it if there are no tomorrows when I run out of todays? I wonder if this is my one shot. If this is as good as it gets?

The sun is shining down through marching thunderclouds to the north. A rainbow is stretching the entire length of the valley, pot to golden pot. I'm ascending the 405 Pass right now. There is almost no traffic at this very magical moment of time in our Universe. I'm witnessing it in all its natural color and magnificent glory. An unforgettable painting etched on my brain. Seeing this, how could Earth not be Heaven?

I drive like this... in wonderment... "Mother...!" Until a 1992 lost white vanload of fools cuts drastically in front of me! I'm dashed in a frantic wash of road spray! "You Bastards!" They're driving way too fast. They just make the upturn onto 101North.

I'm slapped back into my reality!

What mess am I about to step into when I get home?

I roll down the window for fresh air. Instead I get dirty rain water. Screw this, it's not my leather. I take it. It feels good, too. I'm a Frankenstiened human bagman for an Alien Mob. With all do respects to decent fluid sucking aliens everywhere, both the Alien Travelers Advisory Board and The Alien Council, not found in your local Yellow Pages, can kiss my very anxious human butt!

Damn me. I'm faced with removing from Mystery Towers the body of possibly the most charismatic man ever to walk on earth. Or at least his clone's dismembered body. I look down at Gray's head, tittering slowly on the passenger floor mat. His luscious thick lips curled ever so slightly in a stunning somewhat mocking grin. It's the head of Adonis himself. Elvis would look like me compared to him. Even dead he's playing with me. The alien cloned vampire bastard!

"Well, Magical Man, how do I get out of this biz? Why has your buddy Jerry, the first alien here on Earth, chosen to include me? Why am I having these nightmares? What is he trying to teach me? Is there one answer? Or is it one of those random, multiple acts of coincidences I keep hearing about? SHUUT UUUPP, PICASSO!" I pound on the steering wheel and drive for a while trying not to think.

I look down at my speed. I'm tooling forty-five, heading down hill. I check the traffic in the rearview and pullover to the far right lane. I make a sane progression onto the 101 Freeway, heading south. Two exits and I'm on Woodman heading south again to Graystone. I need sugar. The light is green. I was hoping a hole would open up, swallow and spit me out somewhere deep in the bowels of anywhere but home. Instead, I make a left onto Mystery Avenue and stop in front of my Hell on Earth, Mystery Towers, where rumor has it an extra deposit is required in case of an autopsy when one moves out.

I pass slowly. The lights had been off when I left. But they're on now. I'm not so sure how long I'd been gone. It was dark, about nine when I inadvertently drugged myself unconscious. It's now around noonish. Hey, the rain stopped. Finally. But which day is it? How long have I been out? Did I miss my ball games? Considering the lack of smell from Gray over there, I'm betting it's the next day. This may explain why there are no cops swarming around my place looking for Gray's body, yet. No

Fric or Frac. Nobody I can see. The tenants' cars are all there. Of course, it's Saturday. Everybody's home.

I don't think I want to be caught driving this truck. If they are looking for Junior then it wouldn't look good for me to show up in Daddy's truck without him. It starts pouring down rain again. Give the soil a break, huh. But no. At the end of the block I take the alley west two blocks to where a fast food burger's parking lot meets Stern, a side street. There's lots of free parking available behind a convenience store so I use a spot halfway up. Problem is, I'm packing an extra head. I search the truck for something to carry McGuiness in, but no, there's nothing large enough.

Come to think of it, do I want to bring this head home? I'm supposed to keep the body separate from it. I can't believe this conversation is actually taking place in my head! I'm hiding severed body parts to keep aliens from warring against themselves and ending life as we humans know it. Well, screw them. I dig up a handful of change from the cup holder. I leave the head right there and drive over to the burger joint and order a burger and soda at the drive through window.

33

Back in reality, all I need is one of them oversized burger bags. When I ask for it with my Happy Meal, the tubby Spanish kid at the window checks out the truck and how I look driving it.

"Dude, you stink like Aquaman died."

"He did. I got his head right here. It's all I could save. Wanna see?"

"Not funny, Dude." He gives me the bag and closes his window.

I drive the oversized bag back to my parking spot, making sure security isn't following me over. How could I not look crazy? I do look homeless. I'm still, shoeless in my shredded gray sweats and stained t-shirt. I'm damp, but I'm surprisingly not freezing. I'm in a new SUV. It's probably not such an uncommon scene in LA.

Back in my parking spot, I take out my burger, replace it with Gray's head, and fold the bag closed. What a surprise this would be if handed out the drive through window. I chuckle on that vision as I devour my burger. Until I start to choke on the dry bun! I gulp my soda to clear my pipes. I'm not so happy anymore. The bag has unrolled. He's looking up at me from within. I'm still kind of surprised there aren't all kinds of blood and flies. Maybe it's because he's a clone. Or that he's a vampire. Or that he's being used by a gazillion-year-old pure energy alien to mate his way through humanity. Or maybe he's just a bloodless bastard sent here simply to screw up my life.

And that's why there's no maggot infestation. Look at him. He's so charming. What am I gonna do with this guy?

On the other side of the wall from where I'm parked is a condemned home or small duplex apartment. I'm not sure. It's still boarded up after the earthquake years ago. I guess nobody wants to build this close to a burger joint. I get out, making sure no one is watching crazy me walk around the wall. I get into the side yard of the building by prying open the bent iron gate. Up close, it turns out to be a two unit bungalow knocked off its foundation with big droopy magnolia trees overhead giving me shelter from the storm. The doors and windows are boarded shut. Do I want in? Or do I want to dig a grave big enough for both of us and hit myself with a shovel?

Trying not to look like I'm looking to dig a grave, I walk barefoot all the way around the building. The weeds and dusty, prickly bushes are ridiculously overgrown. There's no way I'm climbing through them to get into a boarded up window without protection on my feet. There's quite a few accessible foundation vents along the back of the building, but it just ain't me. If I force open a door, who knows what noise it'll make. I don't have any tools anyway. Damn. What to do, what to do? I've got to hurry. Think, Picasso, think! The place stinks of mildew, mold and rodents. My head starts to swim. Breathe, Picasso, breathe!

Under the house makes the most sense. No, rats would eat his face. Fitting, but when I come back for it I can't think how hard I'd throw up before Jerry zaps me into epidermis dust. Damn. Think, Picasso! The weedy ground beneath my feet is saturated. It wouldn't be hard to dig a hole. So I move to the overgrown garden of weeds and look for an out of the way spot to dig. Nothing strikes my fancy.

I'm the epitome of a madman. I'm tattered, wet, dirty, stinky tired, panicked, confused, and now bloated by a burger and soda. I'm lost for real answers, wanting nothing more than to bury the head of an alien cloned vampire inside a burger body bag. So that I can save at least part of life on Earth as we know it. Damning us all if I do and damning us all if I don't. I'm a dust speck away from taking my own life. Worse, regretting I've ever lived. I look around again to make sure no one is watching. This place is not the place. But the building across the street is under construction and.... "Duh!"

I get off my knees and head across the street into the dry empty, windswept parking lot below. Now I'm cold. No workers are here today. Or they've gone home already. Good. There's a Jacuzzi about to get poured, which is miraculously not filled with rainwater. My teeth are chattering. I have to hurry. I go into convulsions in the cold.

The whole front of the building is set with pea gravel and rebar for cementing. Once I hide this head, will I need it back? I hope the hell not, but who knows what's about to happen. Mooky said wait until I had both body and head. But I can't carry this around with me. What would happen if I accidentally put them both together in the same room or car while on the run? I can't take the chance that it would be the end of me and my dog, in many painful alien ways.

At garage level, I go through and unfinished entryway to find iron gated arched windows hiding the spa area. Nice. But it'll never get used. Wind, lack of sunlight and LA road grit will see to that. A car comes by. If they look, they can see me. So I duck and step onto a hidden plastic PVC pipe and role down over the Jacuzzi's rebar grid supports into the pea gravel. I hide there for a moment, letting the pain in my ankles subside. I still don't have shoes on either sized foot. I should make Mooky man fetch me two different sizes.

Soon as this rain gives up, they'll be pouring the new cement here. It could happen within a day or two, maybe more. That would give me time if I needed him back. Like my reoccurring headaches, I'm not planning on it, but I won't be surprised when it happens. I use the PVC pipe that nearly killed me to dig a hole past the pea gravel and into the dirt below the rebar grid. I make it wide and deep enough to put the head in. Only the bag rips because this head won't go calmly between the bars. I force them apart with my bare feet, pushing his ears down hard between my legs, and plop, I'm done. Letting go of the bars they lock back down like Jaws. I'm winded. I couldn't pull him back out without a day's rest if I wanted. So I tuck all his red hair into the hole down around his face. I cover him up with the remnants of the bag and pile first dirt and then pea gravel, tossing the remaining gravel across the Jacuzzi area. And smooth things out between us.

Once out of the Jacuzzi I look back at my handy work. Jimmy Hoffa's bagman would be proud. I buried McGuiness good. Even I can't tell where, except I buried him, so I don't count. Unless they decide to redo this Jacuzzi someday, there's no reason why they just won't cover it up with cement forever. If I decide I need it back after that, I'll deal with it then. But just in case, I step off the burial spot on the opposing walls. Three steps to the west wall, and four steps to the north wall. Like some pirate's treasure. I'm Captain Blight lost in a sea of my own insanity. Considering my newfound leg and that I own a bird that rides on my shoulder, I peg leg it out of there.

34

Walking back home barefoot in the rain, sipping my soda, I start wondering again. If this is heaven, then making us die in the end is a hell of a thing. I don't blame Gray for wanting to live here forever. The guy had the whole package. Everyone loved him, respected him, and wanted to be him, even me. So I don't blame Jerry the alien for wanting to be Gray. I don't even blame Jerry for me ending up with Gray's head. What I do blame Jerry for is one of the two meatheads now waiting outside my front glass doors by the name of Sergeant MacAroy.

This only means that the revenge of the meathead twins, stocky Detective Mike Tucker, is waiting to torture me back by the pool door, or worse down in my dank dungeon. Were they here when I drove by? If so, were they both already in my apartment? Is the jig up and I'm the only one left dancing? I don't have keys anyway so I'm not entering by means of a door. So, screw them with a stick. If I get in it's by a neighbor's window.

From across Graystone, and behind a tree, I can see Erin's plum Ford Explorer down in her parking spot. She has a key to my place. There are baby pine trees growing wild outside her roommate Janet's stain glass bedroom door. Her bedroom is right above the studio in the garage. When I sneak across the street and through the busted gate, I can hear someone going at it hot and heavy inside the room. Janet's a noisy lover. The howling only adds to the haunted roomers and helps keep the kids at bay. I often hear her on her lunch hour when I'm walking Bubba. This time is nothing. Usually, two or three people stand there waiting for ghosts to appear out of the loose stones. So I tap first with my foot on J.J.'s window. It's set back into the wall and just above ground level. He pushes back an armful of curtain, taking in my washed out to sea demeanor as if I'm just another extra on the set of one of his mega disaster films. I hold my fingers to my lips. So he slides the window open.

"You lost, little boy?"

"Just my sheep."

"Good, it's you."

"Go up stairs and knock on Erin's door and come let me in Janet's bedroom."

"You can't hear that?"

"I can hear it."

"He's a horny lawyer."

"Good, I'm gonna need one. Go now."

I wait. We agreed after the last time that we needed a code. He wasn't sure what had happened and I didn't tell him the whole story about Mooky and the stones. I can't tell anyone, especially not now, not with what I've learned today. He didn't want to know anyway. I just made him promise if I ever disappear he'd say 'you lost, little boy?' when he saw me again. I guess he figured this was the time.

Within a minute the haunting stops with a loud pounding and "What do you want?"Followed by Erin, J.J., Janet and Stevey hoisting me in through the open stain glass window.

Once inside I can see that Stevey wants nothing more than to get back to cheating on his wife, so I lead Erin and J.J. to the double hall doors. I signal to keep our voices down because Mike may be just outside in the pool deck stairwell.

"Erin, let me use your cell phone, and I need my backup-backup keys. To my Jeep, too."

"Jozeph...?"

"I can't tell you guys yet. Okay? Look, I...."

"The cops have the place serenaded," J.J. points at both doors. "Those same two, guys."

"Surrounded?"

"No, they're both out there singing in the rain. Both of them. In and out. It's been like this all day. So happy to be standing out there in the cold. It's spooky."

"I'm sure they're just glad to stomp on me again." The prods. "When did the lights come back on?"

"Not sure"

"Those cops talked to everyone who's come home. Showed us a picture," he adds.

"Of whom?" Like I didn't know.

"Some dumb kid," Erin says.

"They're looking for Ernie Burnstein's kid," J.J. adds.

Great, he knows him. "I'll explain once I get upstairs, okay. I'm doing you both a big favor."

"Don't do us any, Picasso. I have but one nose to give."

Stevey and Janet start going for it again. I don't know what he's doing to her, but she's getting it good.

"Jozeph. Are those people back?"

"What people?" I feign innocent. Apparently, I'm not good at it. They just look at me. It's my move. "Yeah. Worse."

"Maybe you should see someone. You know, talk this out."

"J.J., these people are for real."

"I know, I was meaning someone from our Government."

"The only people I can trust right now are you two."

"What do they want with you now?" Erin asks."

"A favor."

35

I make my way alone past apartments 105 and 106 and hang a left at the end of 103 into the same staircase where Junior and I found all the blood. I don't go outside this time. Instead, I head up the stairs to the third floor. There's no roof access just like the sign says. I retrace my steps, but on the third floor this time. And hang a left again past 302 and 307. I go through the fire door, past the garbage chute and elevator to my slightly left open apartment door, 308. Not sure what to expect, I push the door the rest of the way open anyway. "Hello?"

"Where's the kid?" Jumping Jell-O beans, Dogman! It's dark but I know to whom I'm speaking. It's Cyber Thug and Scare Face. Ernie Senior's two office goons.

"How'd you tenderloins get in?"

"Door was left open."

"What's with the two dicks downstairs?" I don't really care. I'm looking for footprints on my clean gray carpeting and at the mess my kitchen was left in.

"Where's the kid?"

"We talking about Junior?"

"You were last seen leaving the CBS Studio Center together, yesterday in the rain."

"He gave me a ride home."

"And then what?"

"Maybe we should call the cops up."

"Just tell us where he's at."

"Last I saw him he was pulling away from dropping me off."

"He called home from here."

"He did? When?"

"Last night, about 7 p.m. We had his cell traced. There's no record of it leaving here."Cyber Thug moves over to the empty pizza boxes left on my pool table. Then picks up a half eaten cheese slice out of the kitchen sink under the Bud beer bottles piled on top. I figure he's probably had to go fetch the kid a few times, so he knows the kid's lack of taste in pizza and beer.

"Oh, yeah, he came back with pizza and beer. I'm a little cloudy, okay? Designer drugs. You wouldn't... listen, this is kind of private. Hollywood stuff you don't care about. We're dating, okay? Autumn-Spring lovers. It's special, though. He bought me pizza and I let him suckle me. We didn't want Daddy to know until after the honeymoon."

"Shut up. Where is he now?" Scare Face seems jealous.

"Buying me flowers?"

"Let's go, grab some clothes."

"I got news for you, Cyber Thug. You too, Scare Face. I'm a wreck and I'm not 'let's going' anywhere but into that shower. You want to join me, bring your own towels and soap. If you plan on staying out here, take off your shoes."

I go into the master bathroom. Slam the door and lock it! What can they do? Beat me? They're rental cops. In the bathroom, I turn on the shower. What the hell, I get in. I don't feel brave enough to take off my tattered clothes yet, but in lieu of falling into a convulsion from being cold, I wash my hair. If Ernie's goons hadn't found headless bodies lying about, then I probably won't either.

When I get brave enough to get out of the shower, I get undressed and dry off while moving down my long bedroom hall to my closets and change clothes, half expecting them to be waiting for me. But no, I'm alone in my bedroom. Black jeans and a white A-shirt, blue T-shirt, then a gray sweatshirt later, I reenter the living room to find the two meatheads.

"Well, well, well, well, well. Look-e-here."

"Glad to hear you've worked on that vocabulary, Milky."

"He's getting' wise already," MacAroy tells him.

"You ain't got nothin' to be glib about, Picasso."

"Glib, Mike? That's a good one. You read that word on a bubblegum comic?"

"We got orders to bring you downtown. We know you like that trip."

"What for?"

"Possible missing persons."

"I don't think so. Try again."

"We still owe you one, Picasso, for those sodas in my car, so don't make us own up to it on purpose," Tucker says.

"I don't know what you're talking about."

"We do," MacAroy says.

I take out Erin's cell phone. Dial. Erin picks up. "It's me. I thought you were coming up. There's two meatheads up here I want you to get pictures of. Yeah, those cops that harassed me last time. Bring Stevey with you. I plan to sue this time. Right now. Have him bring one of his cards."I hang up, watching the two lugs make their way to the door, past my pool table and through my walkthrough kitchen.

I thought so. Here unofficially.

"We just want to know where the kid is."

"Tell Ernie that Junior and I are in love and I'll send him home once we've spent all of Grandma's inheritance money on me and my dog."

"Either we get the kid or we hurt you, Picasso."

"Go ahead. Mooky wants to talk to you guys anyway."

"Him? He's involved in this?"

"It's a threesome. Mook likes us both. It's that Frenchy numbers thing Hollywood keeps writing about."

They look at each other. They know I'm bullshiting. But they got pensions to worry about. Then their eyes change. Way too big for me just having said Mooky's name. I turn around and Mooky is standing beside my new sixty-inch TV.

"You rang?'

"Yeah. Clone these guys as lab rats for me, please."

Mooky raises his hand and Mork and Mindy are out the door so fast, they actually leave a stinking cop vapor wake. Man that was.... I hi-five Mook. Right on through. "Hologram."

"Still. Where's the head?"

"Use that one." I point to my spare bathroom. I can't help it.

"We don't pee, Picasso."He walks over to my pool table and stands in front of my new watercolor I've been coveting for a long time, and nearly blackmailed the artist for."That's the biggest difference between Earthlings and most of us Space Travelers. Byproduct. Without it, your world wouldn't be what it is. And we wouldn't be here to share it with you."

"You're here because we poop?"

"We're all here because everything on this planet poops one way or another. You decay. We dissipate. We're not sure what Jerry does, beyond the creation of those healing stones."

"Jerry created them? As part of eliminating waste?"

"No. But like I said, Jerry's way beyond even us at this point, but the stones have something to do with the basic principles of human souls."

"So we do have souls."

"I guess." He studies an old watercolor painting on my wall. "Very nice. Do you know who he is?"

"Carlos, a bass player. He lived near us in Hollywood back when I lived with a friend of mine, Roger O from Detroit at the corner of Santa Monica and Vine."

"Above the Army Surplus Store."

"My first apartment in LA."

"I remember. He'd check in on you once in a while? "

"He's one of you? How long have you been aware of me?"

"You spent the money I gave you on a painting of an alien?"

"No, the artist brings me work when I let her stay in my place. She comes every June or July from up north, usually with a new boyfriend or husband. I help her throw a little networking party here. She pays me with a painting."

"I thought you didn't have any friends, mister everybody hates me."

"People who don't know me."

"Big difference. Have you found the body yet?"

"I just got here and found company. I thought you weren't supposed to be involved."

"I'm not."

"Where's the kid? Junior."

"We think Jerry's got him. And the girls."

"How long have you known of me, Mook?"

"Ask Jerry that question when...."

We're not alone. Erin and J.J. stagger into my open double doors. I turn quickly to Mook and... Blip... good, he's gone. Looking closer at my two friends I find that J.J. is actually holding Erin up. She's in shock. What now?

36

With very little effort, J.J. and I pilot Erin over to the couch and get her down on her back. She's mumbling something, I don't know what yet, but it's not good. I look at J.J., he just shakes his head.

"What?"

"You better go have a look see of your own, Picasso."

"Just tell me what happened."I pull my rain boots out of the closet.

"She stopped to put a bag in the trash chute. And a thing this long jump out at her."

"A thing? A rat?!" I sit at the door and pull on the boots. Ugly, but they both fit.

"No. The thing of things. A foot at least. The big one eye."

"The.... Stay here. Don't answer the phone." I run out and down the stairs to the first floor. I look first outside to the front stoop. Good, both the cops and thugs are gone. I back track to the garbage chute door right next to the elevator and push it open. There's a small rectangle room there. At the back is a metal door with a handle just about large enough to stuff a body.

"You better not be in here McGuiness."

"You talkin' to me?"

I spin around. Timothy Sparks, a young director slash editor, from apartment 108 is standing behind me in galoshes and a great big on location yellow raincoat. He's shuffling through his junk mail. His large brainy head, under a matching rain hat, bobs on his broad shoulders as he reads.

"Timothy! I didn't... I'm just, you know, I was... the garbage chute, it's clogged again. Dead full.... ah...."

His childish big blue eyes flash me some knowing pity. Damn, he knows. "I didn't do it," he says.

"Of course not."

"I never put boxes in there."

"What?!" I start laughing... I thought, shut up Picasso.

"Serious."

"I know, Timothy, look... how's things on your projects?"

"I was just on my way up to talk to you. Do you have a low budget thriller scripts lying around, and not pitching?"

"Something I might be using as a door stop, you mean? Or perhaps my real life?"

"I got a pitch meeting tomorrow, and well, I was hoping to have back up."

"Ah, sure... I ah... let me go through my stuff and I'll bring something down later. I may have something in synopsis. All my doors slide but the front, so I'm blanking."

"Great."

"I thought you had that other project all lined up." What are you doing, Picasso? Get rid of him.

"What? Oh yeah, you know... still in the works. They like the changes, thanks."

"That's good, you're welcome. Well, hang in there. I gotta...."

"Hey look, I don't know how to put this. But... um... well under the crummy circumstances. And I love your work. You know that. It's just that...."

"I know, Timothy. No one's gonna let you shoot my work."

"Yeah, remember that last meeting I had, though?"

"I remember."

"Well, those people didn't click with me over pitching a script with your name on it. Someone, a grip I think, even keyed my truck in their parking lot."

"Really? What parking lot was that?

"CBS in Studio City."

"You kill a few tenants and you're creatively dead in this town. What can I say?"

"I didn't hear that. But you know, I hear O.J. still got laid. So, would you mind if I...? You know, just in case."

"You want to put another name on my work, Timothy?"

"Jesus, I'm sorry, never mind... it's shitty, I hate what this town is doing to you."

"Look, I need cash right now. I'll look and see what I have. It'll cost you more if you sell it. And I pick the name. I better get this...."

"Thanks, sorry, it's just a backup anyway, I...."

"I'm used to it by now. I'll talk to you...."

"It'll blow over, someday, Jozeph. Even some of those old McCarthy guys found work eventually."

"Yeah, those Commies... got to love them."

"Seen J.J.?"

"J.J.? Ah, no, no I haven't. Why?"

"He wanted a jump on his truck. If you do...." He comes at me with his junk mail like he's thinking about putting it into the chute.

"Here, I'll take that."

"It's okay, I'll...."

"The chutes cockfull, ah... chockfull. Sorry, Freudian I'm sure. Use the... ah, here, I'll just take it."

"Well, all right. Some messed up couple of days, huh?"

"You have no idea, Timothy. And it's not nearly over, so...."

"Jozeph, is there anything... I was... I'm sure you're...."

"What?"

"There were cops around earlier."

"Oh, those guys. You know, once you're a suspect you're always a suspect."

"Yeah. Ernie Burnstein Junior. Have you seen him?"

"Yesterday, he gave me a ride home. Have you seen him?"

"Well, actually, last night. With two girls about midnight."

"Really? Where?"

"Getting into a Town Car. In our garage."

"So, you saw them leave?"

"Yeah, I told the cops too, Mike and MacAroy. That's why I brought it up. What I didn't tell them is about how freaked out they were. Because they were asking about you."

"Really? The cops? Or Ernie?"

"The cops were asking. Ernie was freaking. The girls were just helping him walk."

"You know young rich kids. Drugs and all that. Trauma Queens."

"Yeah. And just so you know, he was in a lot of pain."

"Really?"

"They stopped talking when they saw me. But he was holding himself funny."

"You're kidding."

"No, not that. Back here, walking funny, but like it wasn't humorous to him." He holds his hand out over his backside.

"And you didn't mention any of that."

"It never came up. So, how's Bubba doin'?"

"Dog's life, in the arms of sexy, beautiful, famous women."

"Lucky dog."

"Yeah." Timothy is watching me.

"Gotta run."

"Yeah, I'll bring some ideas down. Thanks, Timothy."

"Hey, you scratch, I scratch." He goes into his apartment leaving me behind with what I know I'm about to find. McGuiness' body. I open the metal chute door and there's a set of manly hips and naked legs jammed tight with bags of loose garbage. But worse, his St. Petersburg slumps out. "Damn!" I'll have to touch it to close the door. No wonder Erin was in shock. Even dead he's hung a lot better than me. He nearly made it all the way down to the bottom of the shaft where it curls out towards the garbage dumpster below. Who else could've seen this? Actually, it's almost a good thing that I emptied the chute yesterday because who knows what would've happened if he ended up somewhere between floors and I couldn't find him until he started to stink.

What the hell am I to do? Maybe I should change the signs on the door to read: 'No boxes or dead bodies, small bags and animals only.' Maybe I'll add it to the lease terms. I use my new booted foot to push it out of the way and close the door. One half step later and I'm at the elevator, finger on button. I can't leave him like this... as much as I'd rather just burn the building down around him.

In the dungeon, the coast is clear, so I move to the garbage dumpster slash elevator motor room, and turn on the bare bulb. A sizeable blood sucking bug circulates, casting eerie vampire like shadows overhead. I open the heavy, sticky right side door to get a better look up the grime coated metal chute. I have to hold the door to keep it open. I look. Ah, geez. A hand. Palm up, clean nails, and half a juicy garbage stained arm sticking from a pile of newspapers that pour out of oily stained grocery bags.

Let's see, this would be the... right hand. I can't even describe how both poetic and heinous this is. Hey, you never know when you're gonna need an extra hand in this building. What can I do? I don't want to touch him. But I've been swimming with and transporting his head around all day and night, so what's the problem? The problem is that I'm showered now and I just don't want to reach up into all this stinking garbage to pull a headless naked vampire out of my garbage chute, cloned or otherwise. I'm sure it's hardly noticeable over the dumpster reek but my life sure does stink like rotting flesh right about now.

Any other normal human being on this planet could just call the equivalent of 911 and someone would bust out and take this away. But no, not me. I'm on an alien mission from the Space Travelers Advisory Board to save the Universe as we know it. Dark and far-far away is how I knew it, and that was good enough for me. Instead, I look into the dumpster and under a few plastic bags there's a pile of perfectly good clothing. I reach in, staining my sweatshirt on yuck knows what, and grab up a pair of jeans. They're the baggy jeans Junior cleaned the blood up in and rinsed off in my shower.

I push the dumpster a foot further into the room so I can get a better stance. Holding the heavy metal sticky door open with my right boot, I wrap the wet jeans into a makeshift glove and reach up to shake hands with Mr. Gray McGuiness. I give him a yank. Nothing. Not even the newspapers move. Damn it's today's paper and I haven't read it yet. Stubborn bastard. I reach up and brush away coffee grounds from a headline. Hey, I didn't have coffee or read the paper. No wonder I'm having a bad day.

Okay, I'm gonna have to bone up and give this guy a joint popping yank. Putting my foot up against the doorframe, one-potato, two-potato, yank-potato-four - I really yaaaannnnkkkk! SNAP, CRACKLE, and POP! I fall back, losing my footing until my left elbow pounds hard against the dumpster sides. Ouchy mamma! The sticky door swings shut on me, thud, pinning me between sticky heavy door and filthy stinky dumpster.

"Goddamn it!"

37

I'm insane, but it doesn't take me long to not believe my luck. I'm actually standing here pinned between the sticky door and the filthy dumpster with Gray McGuiness' entire arm in my hand! "Will someone just shoot me?"

"Jozeph?"

I turn around, hiding the arm behind me! Banging my hand and cutting my finger good on the stinky rusty garbage can. "Timothy?"

"I left my jumpers in J.J.'s truck bed. I gotta go."

"Right, jumpers, no problem, I'll..." I push the door half open. Putting my cut hand into my black jean pocket.

"I'll be home in a couple of hours. I got a meeting."

"Great, Timothy, I'll ah... this stinking door... be careful out there."

"Yeah, this rain's a killer."

"You can't trust anything these days." I smack the door out away from me, meaning to move out of its way.

"Did Gray McGuiness move into the building?"

"Who?" The door swings back closed on me. Thud. It nearly pushing me back in. Just to be safe I move away from it.

"The Magical Man. Come on, you can trust me. I know he's in town to do a live show. I can't wait to meet him."

"Oh yeah, if I get the chance I'll let you guys shake hands."

"That's so cool."

"Yeah, room temperature almost."

"How's the computer?"

"It's good, Timothy. Thanks for taking the time. I owe you."

"I've got some software I'll bring up later."

"Great, stay alive. Ah, dry."

Timothy goes, glancing back at me more than once. Hey, how do you look normal when you've just dismembered a naked, headless vampire stuffed into your garbage chute?

Three of the things I like about Timothy best is that he's a Star Wars fanatic, a whiz at computers, and has saved my neck more than a bunch of times. With some of the money Mooky gave me, I bought a high-speed laptop computer. Timothy used his zip drive to transfer all my hard drive files, and saved me a lot of work. He installed all my Microsoft and writing programs and my Internet. It might come in handy in prison if I'm caught standing here with Gray McGuiness' arm.

So I put the arm into the half full dumpster and look back up into the chute. Damn, what do I grab a hold of now? The guy was naked when he entered my apartment, and he's dressed that way now. Still not a drop of blood from this guy. I'm gonna need some help. I wonder what day laborers charge for dismembered body disposals. Hey, all is well if it pays well.

Maybe if I tell Timothy, smiling and waving from his keyed Black Ford Explorer Sport, that this guy is a vampire human clone, inhabited by the first alien on Earth, he'd help me get rid of the head and body in separate graves. How many times did he pay to see Star Wars plus the Laser Disks, and now on HD DVDs and probably Blu-ray Disks? I won't even charge him for a live interactive alien experience once Jerry finds out what we've done to McGuiness. I kid myself, because I know I have to go upstairs and offer J.J. and Erin that very same experience without telling them the truth. Or I'm really screwed.

38

If I never had to ask my two good friends and neighbors to help remove a headless body from my garbage chute I'd be missing something. Like the dumbfounded expressions on their faces that I'm looking at right now.

"Who are these people?"Erin comes out of my master bathroom with Peroxide and Band-Aides.

I'm in the kitchen trying to get my finger to stop bleeding. My right arm is sticky from that garbage door. Washing it off isn't easy when you've got an open wound attached.

Propped on a barstool under my pool table light, J.J. raises his hand as if he has to go to the bathroom. Smartass. "Your building is messed up, Picasso."

"Having you in it, J.J., makes it all that much better."

"Hey."

"You were here, though, when all this happened?" Erin asks.

"Yes, but drugged unconscious."

"No one will believe that."

"I'm fully aware of this. Under the pomp and circumstance of my last adventure I'll be the first guy they tar and feather."

"We'll get back to that. You were drugged unconscious by whom?"

"I just drank from the wrong drink on that table out there."

"And now you've got to dispose of this body so that factions of these underworld mob guys don't start warring against each other, messing up the World? Are you sure you didn't fall asleep watching The Twilight Zone?" Erin asks.

"I wish, but that's about it in an Andy Gump. Except... well, there's a head I didn't tell you about."

"A head!? Who's head?"

"The body's head, McGuiness'. I... look you don't need to know any of this stuff. Come on you guys, please, I need you to trust me."

"We do trust you. If we didn't we wouldn't be here," Erin says. "It's just, well...."

"You left out the part about why you," J.J. says.

"I don't know why me. It just is. I'm in the middle of all this somehow. Partly because of what happened last time. Or my punishment for being alive. I don't know. It might have something to do with a shooting outside a restaurant where I bartended, that somehow led to me buying this building."

"The nightmare?"

"Yes, the little guy. McGuiness may have known him."

"And this Jetty guy is involved with the mob?"

"Yes, he caused what happened in the restaurant that night."

"We never really bought your explanation last time, and this one seems even lamer," J.J. says.

Erin has my hand in hers, putting on the Peroxide. "Jozeph, did you kill this man?"

"How can you ask me? Ouch!" She tugs the bandage around my finger.

"You deliberately hurt me."

"I did not. It was just a knee jerk reaction to all the bullshit flying around this room. If you can't tell us the truth, then why even involve us?"

"Because I need help and I don't want to hurt you guys."

"Lying to us doesn't hurt? We're your friends," Erin says.

"Erin, I'm involved in things I don't even want to know about. Things that are driving me nuts. Do I look happy? Have I not been acting strange? If I tell you, you'll hate me."

"How do you know?"

"Because I hate the people who told me!"

"Oh... well, okay then."

"I gotta smoke." J.J. gets up and moves to the terrace doors, stopping short of opening them while he pats himself down for his lighter.

"Call the police."Erin says."I'll call them if you want."She puts gauze around the Band-Aid to keep it clean.

"The police will want to pin it on me."

"Ah, hello, is anybody seeing what I'm seeing?"

Erin and I move out of the kitchen to look out at the terrace. Oh, man! Caw is sitting on the baker's rack, picking at McGuiness' bare arm between his claws!

"Oh my…!"Erin passes out on the carpet between the pool table and the kitchen floor. I try to catch her but she's a fast fainter. I take a pillow off the couch, put it under her head, and pull her white sweater back over her exposed bra.

"Tell me you guys see this."

"Apparently, we do."

"That's a real human arm, isn't it?"

"Yeah, McGuiness' arm, I'm guessing. I'll take care of this." I go to the hallway outside my spare room, open my linen cabinets and pull out a faded beach towel. I move over to open the terrace door and hold it out. Caw drops the arm into the towel and does one of his weird wanting to say something human cackles."Oh, shut up."He just lets loose on the stones below. "I'm helping you."

"This is getting way too weird, Picasso."

"J.J., this is Caw."Caw flutters a wing as to wave hello, and looks J.J. in the eyes, connecting with him.

"Intense. You know this bird?"

"They gave it to me."

"Damn. How many pieces is this guy in?"

"Well, three at the moment."

"I'm not hacking this guy up for you."

"We only have to hide him as is."

"Whew, that's a relief," eyes still locked on Caw.

I'm not sure what I'm seeing, "We have to move fast before anyone else sees him," I say over my back as arm in arm in arm I march to the door and grab my smelly slicker."You coming?"

"Are you kidding, I wouldn't miss this for an Academy Award." He moves to the theater chair and puts on his dirty tennis shoes. "What about Erin and the bird?"

"We'll come and get her on the way out. Caw is on his own."

"She'll be mad if we don't let her help hide a body."

"Come on."

We go out, me carrying the arm in the towel, taking the stairs to make it quick. We pile out onto the first floor and look around to make sure no one is watching. We couldn't look more suspicious if we tried.

"What are we putting him in?"

"Huh? Oh yeah, stay here, no one gets in there."

"Sure thing, Cappy."

"What did you say?" This isn't happening!

"What?"

"What did you just say?"Please not J.J.

"I don't know, I said yes. What's with you?"

"You said 'Sure thing, Cappy.'"

"Is that a crime?"

"It is around me."

"Picasso, isn't this moment eerie enough for you, without dragging in your pappy nickname phobias?"

"It's... never mind... I'm just.... Right, I'll be back."

I go down the elevator and move over to my storage shed where I keep extra paint and lighting supplies. Cappy. He called me Cappy. I've got a large blue plastic tarp. I grab it up and take it back up stairs. It's very noisy. Note to self, cloth tarps to remove headless bodies from now on.

J.J. is smoking out under the overhang at the front door when I get back. Smokers, an unreliable, suicidal bunch. Could it be possible that it's now Jerry inside J.J.? He sees me and comes back in, after flicking away the evidence into the downpour. Sure seems like the real J.J. to me. I open the chute, transfixed at what I find.

"How we gettin' him out?"

"We won't have to."

"You're losing me."

"The chute is empty."

"What?"

I stick my head in. Nothing. Not even garbage. "He's not in here." I pull my head out. The dream just keeps getting better.

J.J. looks. "Well, he didn't get up and walk away. Did he?"

"The dumpster." You can't see it by looking down because of the bend at the bottom that makes it clog up. We go down. I'm stuck between two wishes. One is that he's fallen into the nasty dumpster. The other is that someone has come and taken him away. When we get to the dumpster it's evident that some wishes do come true and others still just suck. "He's got him."

"Who does?"

"This is bad. There's this... person... a powerful person who... I can't do this to you, J.J., sorry. Just leave it at 'it's bad'. Trust me on this."

"And stinky. What now, Mystery Man?"

"We've got to hide this arm. I hate to say it but the fate of the World depends on it. And even this may be too little."

"The rain brings out the drama queen in you, Picasso."

"I'm not exaggerating any of this. This is a major faux pas on a scale this World has never known!"

"He's a lonely dead guy, not even a whole one. What's the big French Potato?"

"The big French Potato is that the body isn't here now. And who has him will be back for the rest of it very soon. Unless we hide it."

J.J. moves away from me and lights up another cigarette. He's thinking this over.

"You know I spent three years in prison?"

"No, I didn't."

"Drug bust up in Berkeley."

"This has nothing to do with drugs."

"No, this is a lot worse. This is mutilation and murder of a famous person. This is a modern day Black Dehlia. You know what those cops will do with us if they find us with that? This guy is huge, man. People with cameras, pencils, and guns will be swarming all over this place."

"J.J., if we get away with only jail time on this, we're lucky."

"I'm not going back to prison."

"Give me a minute to think this out."

"While you think of something clever, I'll get Erin's keys. My truck's dead. I'll dismember it later," he says.

J.J. goes back up in the elevator. What am I to do?

Outside my building, a truck sloshes out of the rain behind the pines and splashes to a stop at the top of the driveway. A nice big government blue one. A truck I'm sure I've seen before. I duck around the elevator's always-open fire door. I can't see faces from this angle but I know it's the Mustachio Twins coming to have a nice unfriendly chat with me again. I'm sure Tucker and MacAroy checked in with Jetty as did Cyber Thug and Scare Face. Considering I'm wearing one of their clan's legs I'm getting the notion to put it into motion.

The elevator starts back down. It could be J.J. coming back. It stops at the first floor. I can't wait for him. So I take off through the parking dungeon, through the laundry room, then out and up the back steps. I hit the Graystone gate at a sprint. I don't even bother to wait and see if anyone is looking. I'm not sure, but my right leg seems to be faster than the rest of me. Then again, I'm still a paranoid mass murdering slash sometimes filmmaker running for his life. So who am I to judge? I just head west on Graystone with every intention of just dissipating into the rain. That doesn't happen so I keep running. With any luck I'll make it back to Ernie Senior's Land Rover. By the way, having three arms doesn't help in the game of sprinting for your life.

39

I'm on the run again. I've got two right arms and another man's hairy right leg. I'm the perfect fall guy, driving east on Ventura. Where to? I don't know. Okay, someone beat me to the body. Jetty or Jerry? How did someone all of a sudden know where to look? My guess is Ernie Jr. panicked and put the body down the chute with his bloody clothes. I can only imagine the story Ernie Junior is weaving.

But wait, didn't Mooky say that Jerry had Junior and the girls. Oh-oh. If Junior cut McGuiness' head off then he would've released whatever Jerry is into whatever realm he exists when not inhabiting one of us. How long does it take alien Jerry to recoup a body? Why do I ask myself these sick questions? I don't know the healthy answers. Will somebody stop this insipid rain! The rain just stops. I should've thought of this earlier. Hey, I'm connected.

At Coldwater I start wondering what I'm doing. Where do I go from here? I can't think of anyone who'd be glad to hear from me under these conditions that wouldn't want to turn me in or kill me. What the hell, I make a right up Coldwater heading south into the hills.

The storm clouds are dark and incredible. Maybe they'll engulf this truck and finally make me disappear. They don't, so at Mulholland I make a right heading west. It's a winding adventurous road that snakes along the top of the hills dividing the have ocean breeze homes from the have auto vapor homes. The clouds extend in both directions forever. This rain is here to stay... for now. People are sandbagging their homes against the mud streaming down the canyons. I'm letting my instincts take me where they may. At Beverly Glen, my instincts may have bottomed out and I'm forced to manually take over. So I phone home on Ernie Burnstein's car phone.

"Erin, pick up."

"Jozeph?"

"Are you alone?"

"For the moment."

"What do they want?"

"You."

"Are you in danger?"

"No, but J.J. took an awful beating in the elevator."

"Where are they now?"

"Searching the building. J.J.'s with them. He's got a master key. They have FBI badges. What are they looking for?"

Don't even. "They're not FBI. They're MOB."

"MOB...? The Mob?"

"Yes."

"Jozeph, there's another BODY."

"What? Where?"

"In 102. A kid. In one of the tubs."

"Oh, the kid. Who else knows about this?"

"The five of us so far. You knew this?"

"Call the police."

"Are you sure? There's blood everywhere, from the kitchen to the bathroom, all the way across the carpet. It's horrible."

"Yes. No. What do you think?"

"You didn't do it, right."

"Erin. I'm not a killer."

"What about the other body... the one with the... my god, did you see that thing?"

"Unfortunately."

"I may not have sex again."

"So we'll both die born-again virgins."

"This isn't funny, Jozeph."

"Who's laughing?"

"These two men say you have McGuiness' head and arm."

"Well, not exactly. Technically, I have his arm. His head I buried."

"Jozeph!"

"I had to. Please don't make me explain all this. Just call the police. Do it now. Call Mac and Mike. Keep them busy for me."

"Okay. Where are you?"

"Call those cops, Erin."

40

I hang up. Damn. Would Junior do this then tell Daddy? Why are the Mustachio Twins at Mystery Towers and what do they want with the rest of Gray McGuiness? How do they know I have the head and arm if they don't have the body? I'm getting good at asking dumb questions. I suck at smart answers. I call Claire. I'm not sure how she will react to hearing from me.

"Yes, Ernie."

Caller I.D. "It's me."

"Jozeph? Where are you?"

"Not far. How's Bubba?"

"Just fine, he's right here. Say hello to Daddy, Bubba."

Bubba barks. He's so good. "Kiss him for me."

"Tell me what's going on and I'll think about it."

"First tell me what you've heard and I'll fill in the details."

"They're saying you killed Gray McGuiness."

"Prevaricating bastards."

"Then who did?"

"Who's saying this?"

"Burn. Police are looking for you. A MacAroy and Tucker."

"I bet they are."

"And there's more. Jetty's brother Leonie is missing and there's eyewitnesses who claim you shot him in the head."

"He shot himself!"

"Jozeph, what's going on?"

"I can't tell you, Claire. I wish I could, but there's a lot going on. Much more than you'll ever know... hopefully."

"Please, Jozeph, this is maddening not knowing."

"You should see it from my end. But this thing with Jetty and Leonie goes back to a shooting where I bartended."

"Jetty and Leonie killed someone?"

"No. But Jetty caused it. Those two cops, MacAroy and Tucker, were involved and kept Jetty's name out. They're on Jetty's payroll."

"Oh, come on."

"We shouldn't talk about this on the phone. Are you alone?"

"Just Bubba and I. Are you coming here?"

"Yes."

"Alone?"

"Almost."

"Jozeph, don't push my buttons, please!"

How do you tell a beautiful woman you have an arm in the back seat of a stolen truck when you're suspected of killing him? That you're heading to her place to convince her of your innocence shortly after burying his head at a construction site? No good answers formulate. "Maybe I shouldn't come."

"No, come. We need to talk this out."

"Okay, but you should know they found another body."

"Where?"

"In my building. McGuiness' room. A kid who got in."

"Who killed him?"

"I think McGuiness. But I'm not sure what happened."

"Gray!?"

"Yes. Claire, this is complicated. I should stay away."

"No, you're in trouble. You need a good lawyer. I know one."

"How about a headshrinker?"

"How about a kick in the butt? Get over here. Call me from the street and I'll let you in the garage. Okay? Jozeph?"

"Thanks, Claire."

Claire now lives along Wilshire Boulevard in one of the high security buildings. Condo Lane. It's just a jump over Beverly Glen from us alienated folks in Sherman Oaks.

41

When I get out front of Claire's place, I call her again. Her machine picks up this time. Damn. So, I hang up. They've gotten to her. Who, I'm not sure, but my guess is Jetty or someone in the production crew. Maybe it's the snotty production assistant who loves me long time. So I continue driving west on Wilshire. Where to now? Just before I make Westwood Boulevard, Ernie's car phone rings. Do I pick it up? Is it Claire, or is it Jetty? Maybe it's Mooky.

Blip! "Pick up the phone, Picasso."

I nearly jump out of my skin!"Mooky, will you stop this?"

"The game is starting to change. Pick up the phone. See what he wants."

"What he wants is to frame me for murder."

"He wants his brother."

"Well I don't have him."

"Yeah you do, white boy."

"No I... wait... I have his brother Leonie's leg."

"Funny, huh?"

"No! Not really... kinda... come on, Mooky. I've got Leonie's leg attached to me. They'll kill me when they find out."

"Don't worry, no one's finding the rest of him."

"Where is he?"

"Gone, Picasso, gone. Now answer the phone. If you want to mess with his head, just tell him the truth." Blip! The bastard's gone.

I pick up the phone."Mom?"

"Shut up, Picasso. Where are you?"

"Where are you?"

"Waiting to kill you."

"Why?"

"I want my brother."

"The aliens have him...."

"Ah.... what?"

"Don't tell anyone. They'll think you're nuts. Trust me. And I'll deny ever telling you. But it's the truth. An alien trained crow grabbed his gun hand and made him shoot himself in the head before he could kill me in the CBS Studio parking structure. Ask his two Mustachio Brother friends claiming to be FBI. They saw it happen."

"I'm not buying any of this garbage, Picasso."

"You don't have to, Jetty. It's free. McGuiness was a human clone that became a vampire because of alien healing stones. He's thousands of years old. An alien named Jerry bred him and cloned him into the Gray McGuiness we all know today and used him to walk amongst us. Only Jerry's been breeding us like dogs since the beginning of mankind and is very sexual from what I was told. Not a He or a She, an It mostly. Pure energy and shift shapes into however it wants to be seen. You, me your latest squeeze, you'll never know for sure that you're not really sleeping with Alien Jerry from now on. You getting this all down, Jetty?"

"You crazy bastard. Shut up, and listen!"

"No. Ask yourself why McGuiness didn't have any blood? You've got his body now right?"

"Stay away from Claire. This is your last warning."

"Jetty, before you go. Remember that smiling little guy you punched out in Charlie's Restaurant on Third Street, way back when? That little happy wafer that got shot down in the street by two rookie cops named Leonard MacAroy and Mike Tucker because of you. Remember him?"

A long pause. "No."

"Ask MacAroy and Tucker who he was. Who I am. Ask them about the aliens. Ask them who Mooky is while you're at it."

"Shut up! There are no aliens."

"Yeah, I bet the knuckle beating nuns failed to mention that in bible school, huh, Jetty. Makes you wonder who we really are, though."

"All it's doing is making me want to kill you even more."

"And religious freaks want to know why I avoid them."

"We have ways to make you come to us, Picasso."

"Jetty, you don't kill the fall guy. You set him up for a rainy day. Like this one. However, I got a riddle for you. What has one leg and is feeding aliens' through his testes?"

"What the hell...?"

"Leonie. Get it? Your big brother, Jetty. The same knucklehead hood brother you sent to kill me. What a way to go. In some eternal alien's test tube, a human caviar machine. It's a nutty world they live in."

"I'm gonna hurt you real bad, Picasso. You and your whole family, your friends... and your dog."

"I'm not the only one who loves that dog, Jetty. You hurt Bubba and Claire will never speak to you again. Isn't that what this is all about? You, Claire, and I. Well, I got good news for you, you dumb ginney. I didn't get the girl. The dog did. I'm not licking her on her show or anywhere else, Bubba is. Think about that."

"It don't matter, you're finished in this town. You're dead."

"Yeah, well that's no news to me. But listen up. I think the little guy you punched out at Charlie's was occupied at the time by Jerry the super nova alien. For some unfinished reason we're all back together again. It's you, me, Jerry, Tucker, and MacAroy. Just like old times. Only, you can't make this one go away by getting me fired. Or buying off cops, or having your brother threaten to break my legs in the wee-hours of the morning. I have nothing to lose this time. I'm already dead. You listening, Jetty? There's no covering this one up. There's no telling what Jerry's planning to do. He could be playing all of us on this. He could be anyone around you. One or all of us is going down on this one, Jetty. You still there?"

"That one is you. There are three eyewitnesses who say you killed McGuiness and my brother."

"You mean, Junior? And your twin flunkies? I got news for you, Jetty boy. If Junior is back amongst you, he ain't Junior anymore."

"You're talking crazy. Ernie's kid told us everything. You came in with the Israeli army knife that you keep in your desk drawer, and cut McGuiness' head off and ran away with it. We even have the knife. What we ain't got is his arm and his head. You still do, you sick bastard."

"Sure I'm the sick one. I also shoved his body in the garbage chute."

"Right. Now where's my brother? And you can have the rest of Gray."

So that's why they grabbed him up, a stiff ransom? Only in this sick town does that make sense. "I told you, your brother is feeding the aliens through his hairy balls." Click. Let him chew on that vision for a while.

42

Overall, I thought that dialogue went fairly well. I'm not worried that Jetty will hurt Bubba. Claire would go Jane Q. Public on him. Pedestrians would urinate on his Hollywood Star. Killing famous French poodles like Bubba over jealous fits of stupidity doesn't go over well in tinkletown. Thou, killing unemployable writers nearly goes unnoticed, and directors get murdered by the press daily with no one caring, so I have to be careful. I don't see them reaching out to the center of Lake Michigan to drown Pop. Plus Pop carries rifles and handguns. But there's always Erin and J.J. to be concerned about. So, I dial home.

"Where are you, Picasso?"

"This you, Mork?"

"Don't play around. Come home," Tucker says.

"I didn't kill that kid, Milky, McGuiness did."

"We know that. His fingerprints are all over the place. What the hell is going on?"

"Remember that last thing? The thing with Mooky Man?"

"We don't know what you're talking about."

"In case you remember later. This is more of the same. But mind bogglingly worse."

"We've got an eyewitness who claims you killed McGuiness up here in your room. Two others who claim you killed Leonie DiGarbo at CBS Studio Center."

"That wouldn't be the same witness who watched you and MacAroy gun down that little guy outside of Charlie's many moons ago would it?"

"Don't go there, Picasso. I mean it."

"We're already there, Tucker."

"Where's Leonie and don't...."

"He shot himself. I had to jump in the LA River to get away from those other two New Jersey clowns. Jetty sent them in that parking lot to whack me. You and I both know which Walk of Fame why?"

"I don't know nothin' about that, either."

"Of course you don't."

"Bring yourself in, Picasso."

"There's not much chance of that. Jetty is out of his mind."

"Think of your dog."

"Leave my dog out of this. There's someone you don't want to know putting this all together. You're on the wrong side of staying alive.

"I'm on the side of saving my pension. Now come home."

"Gee, you almost had me there. Let me talk to Erin."

"She's not here."

"Who is?"

"A neighbor, Timothy. Said you had a doorstop for him."

"Where's J.J.?"

"Ambulance took him to UCLA. Someone beat him bad."

"Those were Jetty's boys, the Mustachio Twins. The two guys who were trying to whack me when Leonie shot himself."

"You're wanted for murder. I suggest you bring yourself in soon before someone else gets their hands on you. From the looks of your friend, they ain't gonna be as understanding as me and Mac."

What to do, what to do? I'm stuck in the flunky files again.

"By the way, the CBS Studio Center has taken a restraining order out against you. They want you to stay away from their Lot and their cast. That means Claire. You got me?"

"Burnstein?"

"Yeah, Burnstein signed it himself. Apparently his kid was sodomized last night and Mr. Burnstein plans to press charges against you."

"Me?"

"For raping his kid."

"What? Why me?"

"Because we knew you was a fruit, sleepin' with that fur ball. Apparently, the kid had some internal bleeding last night, and two women took him into Cedars-Sinai. We should've expected this from a guy like you, Picasso."

"Eat me, Mike. If that kid was assaulted it was by those two girls and McGuiness."

"Not according to him."

"He's saying I came in and gave him the Howdy-Doody-handshake before or after I killed McGuiness?"

"He didn't say. I'll ask."

"Yeah, why don't you do that, Mike? And I'd bet your mother that you have no idea who or where McGuiness' two girls are. That just happens to be my two alibis out of this mess.

"Let's leave our mothers out of this, Picasso. The two girls were gone when we got there. They didn't leave numbers. Nothing showed up on security cameras for visual IDs."

"A glitch in the hospital camera system?"

"Something like that, yeah. It looked like the kid was alone. But there was a report of two young girls with him. We got no leads at this time."

"They're vampires. That's why they're not on camera."

"Don't start this mental stuff with us on this one."

"So, in the meantime, kiss off, okay."

"We ain't interested in your sexual preferences. Just bring your faggy butt in before anyone else ends up heartbroken."

"Like me."

"Especially you."

"This is all bullshit. But you know that, don't you."

"I told you not to mess with us again. You comin' in?"

"Hold your breath. When you turn LAPD blue and pass out, I'll be there to catch you."

"The next time you start smartin' off about being some mogul's kid's lover, you better make sure it don't turn up true." He hangs up on me.

The hump hangs up on me. Cops don't get prissy and hang up on suspected murdering sex offenders. I can't believe this. This is getting way out of hand. Now I'm a mass murdering gay rapist. Why is it so easy for me to become all these disgustingly bad things and so hard to become a successfully good filmmaker in this town? I'm not even sure, because I was unconscious at the time, but I think we just established a motive. The kid got raped and went crazy. Did Junior really kill McGuiness and stuff him down my garbage chute?

He should've had some of my garlic pizza. I never even got a kiss goodnight. There's a moral to this sordid story hidden somewhere, but I'm not seeing it right now. I'm sure when it comes my way it'll bottle rocket over my head unnoticed. This must be part of that 'way out there world' Junior told me about. The world that is way too wacked to be part of any story an almost dead filmmaker would know how to write. If it is, I was better off not living it. If it's not, I still don't want to. In either case, I'm in it deep, looking for a way to swim back home to my dog and laptop.

A large glob of bird drippings hits my windshield. I duck and almost put the SUV into a tailspin. I look up and Caw is up ahead looking down on me. What the hell? He circles back and levels out just in front of the truck, flapping just hard enough to keep off the grill. At the light he circles again and heads south on Westward. I've had subtler hints in my life, so I hang a left and follow. At Santa Monica, he does the same thing. So do I.

Eventually, I'm heading back through Beverly Hills, driving east on Third Street. Ironically passing the very corner where the little guy was shot down. Charlie's has been closed and it's changed hands a couple of times now. Cedars-Sinai Hospital is up half a block on the left at the next light. I didn't know that back then. Thump. Caw is on top of the truck. He's pecking. I guess I'm here. I smack the roof and he flies away. I get the feeling someone wants me here. I get the feeling it's Jerry leading this expedition all along.

It's still not raining much. I'm driving Ernie's stolen SUV. Therefore, I don't want to circle the building more than once, so I drive it over to the Beverly Center and park. It occurs to me that I have no wallet or change in my pockets after I'm already parked. Outside the SUV I double check to make sure there isn't a neon sign blinking that a mass murdering fag rapist resides, waiting to get his butt kicked by some neo-nutty gangbangers. One can't be too careful in my position.

The only sign I find is one saying free theater parking. I'll figure it out later. I use the car phone to call the reception desk and ask for Burnstein's room. Room 625B. If Junior is bleeding, that might mean Jerry doesn't have healing stones on him, if he is indeed occupying Junior's body. Or if he had been. Or maybe he wants Junior to feel the pain. Or maybe, just maybe it's all Spartan to me, and I have no idea what in hell is happening. I'm not even sure what I'm doing here.

I am sure I'm the last person anyone from that side of the family is expecting to see and or wants to see. Yet, here I am counting the floor buttons in the elevator. Seems like no matter what I do I'm pushing somebody's button these days. If I had money, I would have brought flowers. Considering I'm accused of being this kid's gay rapist, maybe flowers would push the issue into a blooming confrontation.

Exiting the elevator, I step out with three other people who shield me from Cyber Thug and Scare Face sitting on either side of the door of room 625B. Great. Not that I didn't expect them to be here. It's just that I was hoping for more leeway in entering this floor to observe things. But no. There they are. I turn the other way and scamper away from them. No gunshots or yells of dirty fagot come my way. I'm assuming that I'm unnoticed. This is ridiculous. I don't know what I plan on proving by coming here. I'm suspected of murder on top of sodomy. Who wants to see me besides the police and selected prison guards?

On the opposite side to where I want to be is another reception area just like this one. I position myself in a chair against the glass so I can watch room 625B from afar. I'm still wet, my slicker smelly and now I'm cold against this glass. If I don't look like some shunned gay lover lurking in the shadows of my boyfriend's recovery room, dog-eared down from sadistic love, then what do I look like?

Just inside 678A there's a TV on loud enough to wake the dead. I'm not listening to it but suddenly out of nowhere a female voice starts talking about me."Gary," she says, "I'm standing outside of Spooky Mystery Towers in Sherman Oaks. Just moments ago, a body was removed in a body bag from apartment 102, rented by currently missing Gray McGuiness, The Magical Man. You might remember that this same haunted building, owned by the infamous Jozeph Picasso, the landlord slash sometimes filmmaker, was the scene of a gruesome murder just months ago. According to the lead investigator, Detective Tucker, Mr. Picasso, is once again, wanted for questioning involving a murder in his apartment complex that took place sometime last night. Police are withholding the name of the victim, who appears to be a minor, until next of kin are notified. According to a neighbor living just next door to Mystery Towers, who declined to speak on camera, 'We can only hope if Mr. Picasso is involved in this in anyway, he'll be apprehended shortly so those of us good folks of Sherman Oaks can go back to feeling safe on our community streets again.' I think we all feel that way, don't we. Back to you, Gary."

I'm up on my feet by this time. I may not be well liked, but now I'm well known in this town. I go into the bathroom. I can see the new rental application forms with an added space for

'What planet are you from?' In case they plan on screwing up my life any further?

What am I doing here? Somehow, I know that I must visit Junior. Why? I have nothing to say to the little punk. But if... I know how this sounds... try thinking it... but if he is being... what? Taken over, possessed, shift shaped, or whatever. Then I need to talk to this alien Jerry It energy thingy. To see if we can come to some kind of common ground understanding so that I just don't totally set him off. And make him turn me into a bowl of white boy pudding. I know how this must seem but I get the feeling that Jerry is using Jetty and his clan of marauding buffoons to gather up McGuiness into one location. Could I not be controlling my own destiny and I'm here to talk things over with Jerry? I look in the mirror. I don't look like I want to be here. "Am I?"

"Is you what?"

"I thought you aliens don't pee."

"We don't."He comes out of the stall."People tend to get nervous when I Blip in and out of public view.

"What am I doing here, Mooky?"

"Jerry wants to talk."

"Why?"

"It wants McGuiness' arm and head."

"When you said It has Junior, you meant possesses Junior."

"Right."

"With his butt bleeding in a hospital?"

"We took his stones away. It's why we all don't get along."

"Right. The stones belonged to him."

"Yes. The Alien Advisory Board controls them now. As you know, It was turning his clones and friends into vampires with them so that they wouldn't die on him."

"Why am I involved in all this?"

"Ask Jerry."

"How?"

"It is waiting for you."

"Burnstein's got his goons at the door. My name and picture are on the tube. Do you realize what is happening to me? What people are calling me? I'm now a gay murdering rapist."

"Yes, you better work something out with It or we're toast."

"The guy is lying in bed because in some form of weird alien reality he did himself in the backside, and he's blaming me?"

"Funny how life turns out, huh?"

"No it's not!" Blip! "Mooky?" I turn and this dried-up frog in hospital slippers and gown stands at the door looking at me as if I might stop him from using the urinal. "Sorry, come on in."

"Don't stop talking to yourself on my account."

"I wasn't talking...."

"It's okay. This place is full of dead people. It's hard to get them to talk back though."

"Yeah, isn't that the truth. Enjoy."

"At my age, you bet I will. Hey, ain't you that wanted Picasso guy on the tube?"

"I used to be wanted. I'm just dead to this town now."

"Ain't we all? I used to be someone wanted, too. Now I'm talkin' to the dead. Waitin' to hear back from 'em. Good luck."

"Thanks." I go out, back into the hall. Jerry's waiting for me. How do I get in the room without getting beat to smithereens? What the heck. I walk over to the B-Side of the sixth floor and prance right into the room."Hi, boys, see any good men lately?"

Cyber Thug and Scare Face look at each other for an instant, not believing that I'm simply waltzing into the room to see my boyfriend. I'm standing at the foot of the bed before they can get back to me. In a second, they have me on the floor, beating me. I just cover up with my slicker making it almost impossible to get at my face. Eight or nine punches into their "Hello, how are ya?" they stop and leave the room, and the door closes behind them. I uncover my face and look around. I'm in a private room. Junior is looking down at me from the bed. That stupid skinhead grin of his.

"Hey, Cappy, what took so long?"

43

"Don't be mad."

"Mad isn't the word for it, Jerry."

"It's not easy being me, Jozeph. I'm lonely."

"Going around killing people, raping them and screwing up my life won't change that."

"All I want is to be like you."

"Well, you're not like me, get over it."

"Show me some compassion."

"What I'd like to show you is my new extra large right foot."

"If you knew what I really looked like you'd understand."

"What I understand is that you've accused me of sodomizing this kid you're possessing and now the mob wants me dead."

"The Mob wanting you dead is your own fault. And it was this kid's father who pointed fingers, not him nor me. To cover up killing McGuiness."

"So Junior did kill you... or McGuiness."

"He thinks he did."

"Then who did?"

"I can't tell you. You'll get in my way if you call the police."

"I might call them anyway."

"Then I'd have to turn you into white boy pudding."

"Stay out of my head."

"Daddy decided to make you the fall guy. Jetty is just seeing it through. He thinks you killed his brother. He's afraid of what you know and who'll you'll tell. Claire in particular."

"Leonie shot himself. Mooky's friends gave me his leg."

"I know. Jetty's a jealous, weak minded man. All Dickey Trout thought he wanted to do was express his amazement over the statue to someone, anyone. Violence is never the answer to man's insecurities. Jetty will get his one day soon. I'll see to it, if you help me."

"Help you? You nearly let Dickey take my head off with a shotgun. Why did I have to watch you get that little guy gunned down by those two lug heads, MacAroy and Tucker? Why have you been haunting my sleep?"

"Okay, you got me, Cappy. You had a choice to make that night. You chose to cover your backside. You were broke. You were scared of losing a good job. You let Jetty get away with what he did. Now I've come back to haunt you to condition your mind so that you could stand before me today without freaking out.

"Who says I'm not freaking out?"

"Keep it down. There's more to that night than you know."

"Do tell. It would be refreshing to know all my nightmares weren't a waste of sleep and that the Mob has a virtuous reason to want me missing."

"That little guy was on his way home to kill his family."

"Damn, he had kids?"

"No, he didn't. He had a caring mother and loving father who worked with the elderly, singing and dancing in a studio just down the street from where you worked. I had my eye on him because I would often occupy one of the little old women who'd dance there. Sweet Patrice my dance partner Arthur called her."

"You dance?"

"I rocked his world. But Dickey had been let out from where they had him held. He came looking for his parents that night for putting him there. I took him over and had him wander into your place hoping he'd just forget about it and go to sleep."

"You were saving other people?"

"The guy was out there. He was sick. He didn't know it."

"Big talk coming from an Alien rapist."

"Jozeph, I'm sorry you got involved. You were nice to Dickey. I only meant to detour him until his family had packed up and left on vacation. That thing with Jetty punching and kicking him was out of my control. And not the first run-in I've had with Jetty and his friends."

"That asshole."

"Please."

"Sorry."

"I left him slumped over his wheel. You would've been dead if I hadn't gotten back into him in time. When the cops showed up, I had to end it, take him out for the good of all."

"What does any of that have to do with McGuiness?"

"I deserve this pain. McGuiness was a long time project. An Adonis. Humans are so fallible. It was so hard to breed him into existence. I couldn't let him go. And humans were dying, my friends fading away. It's painful to lose so many loved ones. So I had him carry the stones knowing what it would do to him eventually. He helped so many people. Many more humans would've died if he hadn't carried those stones for that long. You know The Dark Ages, The Black Plague?"

"Not personally."

"Don't even make me chuckle. I have fifty stitches up this kid's bottom. It was killing aliens and humans alike. My stones are very powerful. When those body fluid sucking others realized I could heal them by using the stones, they took them away from me by threatening to destroy all of mankind, everything I had built. Then they cut the stones up into many pieces to share the power amongst The Alien Council and Alien Travelers Advisory Board. So that they could live here forever, leaving McGuiness one small piece."

"But the bodies, the one in apartment 102?"

"They eventually tricked us and took the stone away from McGuiness to take control of him. Their goal was to keep him from revealing his inner self, or myself as being the Supreme

Being. That's why these bodies started to appear throughout Europe. He could no longer bring them back to life afterwards. The last stones to be accounted for where those you helped retrieve."

"Healing stones, I've held some in my hands. It made me feel strong and manly. Am I in danger?"

"No. You showed great wisdom in giving them back and not let that Ziniken get to them."

"Mary Devonshire."

"She's evil. Her whole lot is. With her own stones she would've forced a messy war within the Council to take control of Earth. Don't think this ordeal with the Zinikens is finished yet either. These kinds of power struggles take time and can span centuries to reveal their full meaning."

"It wasn't wisdom that made me give them back, it was fear. She shot me five times with a laser gun."

"Keeping these stones to themselves is the principal reason why they won't let me teach you our technologies. It's already getting very difficult to hide being here with the limited technology that you have. Recently, they've been forced to pluck satellites from the skies and replace some with their own to keep you seeing only what they want you to see. You must understand their tenuous situation. They are taking funds away and forcing a slowdown of NASA research because of what they know will happen to us if they don't."

"Yes, if the masses became aware they'd have to kill us off because we'd become uncontrollable?"

"Yes, but, only those humans who couldn't handle the news. And the Advisory Board and The Alien Council, of course, are split on that because not all of them drink you to stay here. I won't even try to tell you how many they're taking daily. Thousands. And hide it by controlling the media."

"Which side does Mooky work on?"

"Neither. He is a missionary. But when you see Mooky again, tell him I said to kiss my alien butts for not giving me

181

back a stone like he promised he would if I didn't get involved and let The Alien Council handle it last time."

"You got butts? I was told aliens didn't leave behind waste."

"Purely metaphorical. And yes, advanced civilizations have evolved to utilize all that they ingest. Trust me, it makes space travel much more pleasant not to soil your space suit."

"On the list of things I don't need to know." I realize I'm starving. "Hey, are you eating this?" Jerry hasn't even touched his hospital food. He pushes the tray towards me without actually using Junior's hands. So I dig in. It's cold, but who cares. This is a lot to think over. After a few mouthfuls, I look up at him and he's smiling at me. How gay is that? "You're scaring the Alien Travelers Advisory Board, Jerry. You obviously know all this, so why am I telling you."

"It was McGuiness. He's a human clone, with human desires and weaknesses to be great and powerful amongst humans. When I'm in him I tend to lose control. Even though I am the most advanced Being here. And deserve to be known as the Supreme Being on Earth and worshiped like the Sun, whether the others accept me or not. But I don't want to be known as It. No one wants to see what It really looks like. Even if they could without going blind and turning to ash. But McGuiness, by being him... he was so much fun, he was more than the Sun, he was a star."Jerry waves Junior's hand dramatically as though he's on the stage of life. "He wanted to live forever. I, as him. The magical shows we put one together. There was only one way he could, that I could, that we could."

"And that's by coming out of the alien closet?"

"Ha, yes... you funny human bastard."

"But you were him. I was told these were your plans, to expose yourself in front of the whole World."

"Surely, you understand sexual addiction. McGuiness was otherworldly charming. I gave birth to him in so many ways. He was my son, my father, my love, my soul mate if we had one. Gods were created in his vision. He was beyond me, much more than I even dreamed he could be. The power he possessed was a force felt tenfold by me while inside of him. He consumed me. I was he, but he was much more than I could ever be on my own. My pure power ran unbridled through his human clone veins. I am the glow that leapt from his smile. I was the twinkle in his eyes. That was I shining through, don't you see. That was who I am if you could only see the real me in my hearts.

"He was loved. So I was loved. He felt love. So I felt love. He climaxed in ways that were unimaginable. A pure ripple in time to the bone, head to toe, and I felt those heights ten times over. But as him, I could never get enough, hence the sucking of the blood. That was my only way out of him. It would spring me out of him. Leaving me, not him, racked with quilt, hating myself, punishing myself. The only way to relieve the pain was to become him again and heal them. Inside him, peace grew in my hearts. His human heart and mine there was no remorse, no guilt for what I'd do as him, just madding lust for human life. Human life! It created a powerful vicious cycle of self loathing and animal lust. Why? Why did I as McGuiness have to hurt anyone? Why did he have to become one of them, sucking fluids out of those I only wanted to love? Why? Do you understand? Of course you can't. You couldn't."

I can only nod, my mouth being full of his food. Thoughts are too consuming. I know I should leave but I can't.

"You okay? You look like you're about to start singing."

"This is all so.... It's been driving me crazy, though I must admit I'm feeling groovy now that I've eaten. Even my stomach stopped hurting."

"You're welcome. I can still ease minor pain and illnesses without the stones. Think healing hands. It all has to do with why the sky is blue."

"The light we process?"

"By developing bone behind your eyes to keep your eyes better focused. It allowed your early ancestors to eventually see what you think is the full spectrum of light. To see that food had color. Helping you eat better. And climb out of the trees, and eventually to walk. That was some of the hardest parts of your evolution for me. It hurts me to see the unnatural processed ingredients they are force feeding you now. If you could see the truth about what they spray on your foods, most of you still wouldn't believe it. For many, it's too late to turn back."

"We don't see the whole truth because we can't process unknown colors?"

"Yes, the fourth primary color. You're that close. With all that's here, setting the clock back would nearly be impossible. We'd be forced to move forward and so many of you will parish. That's why there are those factions of the Alien Council and Advisory Board who are manipulating Mother Nature to make these drastic climate changes seem to happen naturally by man's stupidity and greed. You see, it's why McGuiness wanted to take control, to save all of you from them. Even though I as me knew it would only make things worse. He was taking over, and I was losing control. So he had to go. You're still aware that you can't tell anyone."

"Who would believe me? I'm doing my best not to believe it myself. I'm hoping to wake up with my dog at any moment."

44

"There are those who do believe. They will eventually find you. You must not tell them, even if they already believe it. Proving the truth would not set them free as they believe. The Council would take every last one of them. And have and will continue. Think lost civilizations and you get the picture of what the Council is capable of doing to you humans. You must not trust these people to ease your mind."

"I don't want to be the instigator to the end of every sense of man's order. The poor would riot against the rich. People would stop trying to be good. We'd have a very dark age for a very long time. Hell knows what atrocities would occur if we found out we're not the top of the food chain. I mean, man is cruel enough to each other without knowing you guys are here."

"Don't clump me in with those cannibalistic Space Travelers. I don't drink your people. I live off inner energy like a sun or star, emitting solar energy. You might say I'm a giver."

"Just tell me how to get out of this situation before I give jumping out that window a go."

"Okay. Sit down. I realize it's over now. McGuiness left a bloody mess again. A young boy's body in a bathtub this time. He's out of control without stones to repair what he does. I'm nearly powerless of his desires while in him. I still can't let it end this way. You understand? I owe him a fitting magical death. Even if he is but a human vampire clone suspected of murdering someone in your building."

"Yeah, thanks a lot. But he's gone. I have his head hidden and his arm out in the truck. Isn't that how the trick ends?"

"His brain is still intact. Right?"

"Yes, but...."

"Don't think too hard, Jozeph. Me hoping I had created this perfect immortal human. The folly of it all. There are so many other kinds walking amongst you now. Vampires, children of the night, horrible blood thirsty things. Even man eating alien werewolves hidden away in the mountains."

"Alien werewolves? Please, I just swallowed food."

"You must know all this, Jozeph. Otherwise the limited knowledge you have now will continue to drive you crazy. And they'll end up putting you away."

"They still might."

"I'm such a romantic dolt. I've destroyed him."

"Who wouldn't want to be hung like that and live forever?"

"Both male and female of all species on this planet are so fascinating. You humans actually enjoy intercourse. Many species here do... the romance, the courting, and the fight to be the Alfa male. You really have no idea how lucky you are. How unusually lucky this whole planet is to have that drive, those desires and heavy passions. Those dark inbred animalistic basic needs to explode into orgasmic bliss."

"Don't get yourself all worked up. You ain't doing me."

"Shut up. Many of them envy you enough to want to destroy you. All because of just those basic physical needs they lack."

"They don't court one another on other planets?"

"Most advanced Beings don't enjoy intercourse outside a dish. If they do, it's more of a pleasureless pollination giving birth to tissue to be used for creating more of themselves in the form of spare parts and clones. To go on living as they travel across space for sometimes thousands of years. Here on Earth you evolved through generations like the changing of seasons, birthing, growing, and dying. It's very beautiful and yet poetically sad. Like watching beloved leaves evolve through their enchanting changes. Only to be destined to decay back into the soil over the winter. They gracefully help feed and give birth to the next generation in spring. Humans are no different in their growth and decaying than anything else sprouting or dying on this planet. It's slow, yet so amazing to watch the seasons of your lives. We are all in awe of the uniqueness of your Mother Nature. Some fear her even greater."

"So we are evolving?"

"Of course, evolving into the light of knowing what is really happening here to you. What we are doing to you. What you have done to yourselves. It'll take a generation or two more before the environmental adaptable differences are noticeable beyond simple abnormalities. Like extra spinal vertebras to accommodate newly developed nerve passages from increased brain usage. It will eventually adequately connect the right-brain to the left-brain and enabling the use of this new understanding of Sun's light spectrum. And well, things will change. Like the activation of that portal lump on the top of your head. Your apophyseal."

"My genius pump?" I finger my bump. "Is a portal lump? An apophyseal? What is that?"

"A prominence, an outgrowth, to you a projecting part of a bone or calcium deposit buildup. It's actually being caused by the bombardment of media waves in the atmosphere. Your brain is finally doing it independently from your body in its attempt to control mind over matter. All outer species that come here already have this ability to travel from place to place within a gravitational field. None more than me. It's a matter of catching a wave and traveling with it. Surfing the waves means more than humans know. But to your great-great grand kids, it will at first mean the capability of riding in the back seats of SUV's without actually being there. Like The Mook does."

"Holograms? Astro travel?"

"Teleporting your image is good. Moving from place to place entirely is possible. Not by you on your own yet. By those with the powers to control you, manipulated you to be where they want you to be. When and in whatever capacity they need you. Be aware of that from now on. You will not be able to stop them from doing so. It's not a rare occurrence. It's being done with many chosen humans and even some animals, and has been for three generations now. None within your family tree has this power other than you. You are the first of your bloodline. What you call a mutation, a genius bump, we call the ability to take full control of where you are and why at all times."

"They can control me, are they controlling me now?"

"Yes, more and more as this all unfolds. I got you here didn't I? There's nothing you can do about it. In this case, I didn't want to freak you out, so I didn't transport you. I just pulled you here, gently with suggestions."

"By sending that bird, Caw."

"Yes, the bird is for you to use. He means you no harm and is programmed to protect what is Jozeph Picasso.

"Birdman of Hollywood."

"So be it. Unfortunately, if man survives long enough these gifts will practically go unnoticed for many generations until it's accidentally stumbled upon like fire was. Monumental evolutionary changes are often hidden within mutational stigmatization. As things stand, man as you are hasn't enough time left for me to create another natural Adonis. If I clone this one, at best he'd just be the same trouble or worse if the unthinkable arises. Such as the evil gene."

"The evil gene? Get real."

"Oh yes, it's real. A series of dominant gene factors actually. In McGuiness' case it would be disastrous. An evil power that humankind would never recover from. Space would never be safe to travel in again for any of us but me. Perhaps you are beginning to see the importance of why you are involved. The consequences that could occur if any portion of McGuiness were to fall into the hands of those of us capable of cloning him for their own evil plans are unthinkable."

"Like Mooky's bad clone."

"Mere child's play in comparison. Perhaps you noticed McGuiness had no blood."

"Stop right there. Please, Jerry, I'm hanging on by a thread of sanity. I don't want to know any more. Please, I beg of you."

"Okay. I think this kid's cute, and he's rich, and my girls say he was mighty randy. Maybe I'll just stay inside him and make movies with you for awhile."

"He's a pothead, and walks around with his cheeks hanging out of his pants. Abduct someone else. Someone far-away."

"You'll hurt my feeling if you keep this up. What can I do to help? You're not going to cry, are you?"

"What? No, I just... it's... how will I sleep knowing this?"

"I'm sorry. Problems won't arise until Man begins to clone himself. It's not for some time. I'll be here to help. Mistakes will still be made and it will lead to your downfall. It has a lot to do with what they are spraying on your food and homes."

"Chemicals. Great, in the meantime, you need to get me and Junior off the hook. If you don't I'll go to jail for sodomy-lobotomy and murdering McGuiness. Or Burnstein will have Jetty joyfully take me out."

"I've got an idea that could serve us both."

"I was hoping you brought me here for a reason other than to push me over the edge."

"I'll need McGuiness' head and arm back."

"Jerry, the guy is wanted for murder. There were finger prints all over apartment 102."

"I know. Why do you think I sent for you? He's done. No games. I just can't let him go out like this. You met him."

"Yeah, he was really cool."

"I couldn't forgive myself. And I'll need five of my stones."

"Now wait a minute."

"They owe you this, Jozeph. You have no idea how bad this could've turned out for you if I didn't like you. Not everyone on The Advisory Board is fully against me ruling this planet.

There are those who would benefit greatly with a shift in power. Something I rightly deserve. You're all here, alien and human alike because I'm here. Remember, I am the most advanced Being on Earth. Unfortunately, I'm also the ugliest."

"I see. Look, don't you cry."

"Oh, shut up, you handsome bastard. Get Mooky to bring you the stones. Have him go before The Alien Council and The Advisory Board if he has to. Just bring them to me. You'll know where by just being there. Keep them away from your skin unless you like the taste of blood."

"Thank you, no."

"Keep them in their protective case."

"There's one thing I gotta know before I go bananas."

"Why you?"

"Yes, surely there are more worthy humans. So, why me?"

"Because you are who you are."

"That's it, because I'm me?"

"You touched me when you reached out to that crazy little guy. Even if he didn't die that night, you might've saved his family without even knowing it. Just by keeping him there, showing him a moment of compassion. I chose you because you are the right person to help me. I knew this day would come. I knew the moment you were conceived."

"Conceived?"

"Yes, all life, yours and mine is but one long mathematical equation. Mine much longer than yours naturally. With the proper perspective, the results, the variations of one's life are plain to see. Sadly, I can see yours but not my own. I can see all the others, but no one here can see mine. There's no one thing, no being with a greater perspective than I to see beyond me. It's so lonely at the top. But I could see that you would and will help me give Gray his proper out. This little man was a test to see your heart and now the time has come."

"But he was already happy. Did you have to kill him?"

"Yes, because he was insane and pushed to the edge by unkind hearts. Jetty set that path in motion. The others on the Board and Council now know they can manipulate you to do their work because of who you are. Because of your bump, because of your gene, your extra vertebra, your ability to withstand what they are about to put you through and survive. Alive, you are valuable to us. So I led them to you. For what you are about to do."

"I'm a bagman to an Alien Mob because of you."

"You are a chosen one by a power beyond your imagination. Smile. Your life as mundane as it may have seemed to you just months ago was always predestined by aliens to turn you into what you are today if and when we needed to call upon you to help us again. You proved once before that you would do the right thing. So I had you buy Mystery Towers."

"Mystery Towers? So this does involve my building?"

"Is that so hard to believe? Now go, I can't tell you anymore. Just don't try to sell it until you're instructed to or else."

"You don't scare me, Jerry."

Junior laughs in my face, and tears as quickly roll up in his eyes as I can see the sudden change of emotion is tearing at his bottom. "Get me my stones. I'll stay here in Junior and keep his mouth shut. Go with your instincts and we'll see each other soon." He holds out his hand and I take it. All my troubles wash away like footprints in the morning tide. I look out the window and the Sun is breaking through the clouds. There's a crow high up in the sky. It could be Caw. None of this matters but the view. "Earth is a paradise, isn't it, Cappy?"

"Yes."

"I wish I weren't here alone. Don't spend your life alone, Jozeph. Find that someone to love. Find that someone special to share this gift from the cosmos. Procreate, pass life on to another. And don't try to live forever."

"Okay."

"Now go, before I kiss you."

45

Outside the door, sit Cyber Thug and Scare Face. They look up at me from their chairs. I don't know what Jerry did to them. They're as docile as a hernia patient in a rehab room. I stop in front of them, trying to conjure up something witty. Their puppy eyes just give me the glassed over grin. I no longer hurt from their beating. Frankly, I'm really feeling groovy. Revenge on these two is the farthest thing from my mind. But they're sitting there, shoulder to shoulder, and they beat up J.J. So I reach over with both hands and clunk their heads together. I mean cluuunk! I put a little backspin into it. They bounce off each other like human marbles and plop off their chairs onto the floor. I turn to the reception area to witness every hospital worker in the ward reach for a hotline to security. So I refrain from adding any odd sized foot to these guys and high step it to the nearest staircase.

Outside the hospital, I'm still feeling groovy but winded. I'm really out of shape. I probably would've keeled over going uphill. But I'm out in the fresh air without a care in the world. Until security shows up! I'm groovy but I'm wanted. So I take off down the street, my new right leg leading the way. I make it back to La Cienega, apply translated from Spanish meaning the swamp, or marshes considering the muck I'm stuck in. I'm facing the Beverly Center with the world on my tail.

Maybe clunking those two clowns wasn't such a bright idea. I just can't help feeling good about it. Given my situation, I have nothing to smile about. But this world is a beautiful place after a refreshing torrential rain and meeting his Jerryness.

Enough feel good moments, Jerry. Get me out of here. I have to make it back to the truck and get the arm. Do I need to do it right now? Is the truck good where it's parked? Do I have time for this asinine indecision? These thoughts and less are raging through my mind as I wait for the run don't walk light to wave me a sign of freedom. I don't have time for this. I've got an alien enhanced body to put back together and an unsuspecting crazy world to save. So I jaywalk.

Halfway up the ramp I find a Black Lincoln Eldorado coming my way. Guess who's driving? Half a step of getting out of his way later, Blip, I'm sitting in its back seat heading down the ramp. Damn, it's true. They can move me at will using my apophyseal. I feel no worse for passing through the car. Mooky is grinning at me in the rearview mirror. Cop cars are screaming up the ramp past us!

"Holograms drive?"

"Got a little present for you, Apophyseal Man."

"You projected me back into my boring life?"

"No. I'm here to give you a hand."

"Let me guess. McGuiness'?"

"Right arm, my man. At your fetish."

I look down and my towel is on the floor. Inside I'm sure is McGuiness' hand and arm.

"Your little conjugal visit go satisfactory?"

"Jerry's a very nice... whatever."

"Whatever is right. Nice he ain't. Sometime I'll tell you his real deal of how he got here."

"It told me to tell you to kiss Its butts. Metaphorically."

"I bet It did. Where's the head?"

"You in on this now?"

"I ain't out or in. That's not my game. Where's the head?"

"I don't trust the undecided. If you want a second head, grow your own."

"Don't start this game of chicken and peas of yours with me again, Picasso. I ain't taken a bullet for you this time."

"Too bad. In the meantime, I'll let you know when we're at my stop for getting out of this."

"If you want out, we have to do it Jerry's way. For now."

"Which is?"

"Give McGuiness his respectable goodbye."

"He wants his stones back."

"We know."

"What's the chances of that?"

"When you need them, we'll let you know."

"Get me the stones, Mook."

"Just get his head together with that arm and call Jetty when you do."

"These guys will try to kill me."

"We're depending on it."

"What?"

46

I go for the back of his head and jam my hands into the windshield of my Grand Cherokee Jeep. Bastard! Awe! All my fingers really hurt. But I'm back at CBS sitting in my own truck. The keys are in the ignition. Unfortunately, McGuiness' arm is on the seat. I look in the center council and my hotline to alien protection, my cell phone, is there, but no wallet.

Outside the parking lot, I look up to watch a news helicopter hovering over the Tujunga Wash. Oh, oh. My thoughts are collating the good from the bad chances that my real right leg has turned up stuck in that shopping cart. Okay, how would they know it's mine? Damn it! I've got my name written in the tongue of all my shoes and boots. Even my slippers. Don't even ask. A habit my mother taught me. Ice skating, bowling and fishing trips.

Okay, let me think this through. They find my leg. The boot on it has my name and current phone number. A possible coincidence? Not likely. What does that tell them? They don't know it's me driving towards the studio lot's main gate. They know my truck, they know me, but if they have my leg, how could I be alive? If I'm dead, then I'm free to roam around. I'm a ghost in their eyes. I need many things, but I'll settle for a wily diversion to slip by this guard gate. I stop within a stone throw of it to watch Caw land on the roof of a car stopped by the guard. From there Caw takes a short hop and he's on top of the poor defenseless guard, pecking him to the ground.

By the time I'm out in the street and the broken guard arm is resting on the exit drive, Caw is back in the air leading this cape-less crusader into stupidity and beyond. In my rearview mirror, I can see the guard standing over the broken gate arm scratching his head. Others are running up to him. He must've been screaming bloody murder. Everyone on that lot probably knows that Caw is mine by now. Great. I can't wait to hear my welcome back. Even dead I'm a winged ratlike pest.

In about ten minutes, if they are indeed dredging for the rest of me, a celebration will erupt around this town signifying the fitting death of the big, bad murdering slash sometimes filmmaker. Drowned like a rat in the flooded sewer. My phone rings, bringing me out of my pending funeral plans. "Hello?"

"Congratulations, you're officially dead."

"You let them find it?"

"We had to. It's your perfect cover."

"What about my friends, Mook?"

"Don't call them."

"I don't have a will made out. People will ask questions."

"I'll handle everything. Just let them bury you while you work out getting that head and arm to Jetty and his boys."

"All they got to lay to rest is a leg."

"You complaining?"

"What about Jerry?"

"It's his plan."

"What about Ernie Burnstein's people?"

"Trust me, they will be thrilled. The whole town will be."

"Thanks. What happens when I turn up alive?"

"We'll deal with that if and when you do. Go get the head."

Click! Uhhh, I want to poke that alien soooo bad!

Erin will kill me when she finds out I'm not dead. What about Bubba and Claire? Who can I trust on this? Damn, I hate being dead already. I have to talk to someone. Where will I stay? I probably should check in on J.J. but maybe that's not such a good idea in person. After the beating he took because of me he might want to make my death wish come true.

The sun is out and the birds are feasting on the worms. I park in the burger joint's parking lot, across from the building where I buried McGuiness' head. Caw has flown off somewhere and I'm sitting here watching the crew pour cement through the opening in the spa room from a gigantic cement truck blocking my view. Maybe I should walk over there and say boo and scare them off. Maybe I should just go over there, dig McGuiness' head out of the wet cement, and freak them out. Maybe I should just shut up, lie back, and take my eternal nap like a good dead guy. So I do. Fitfully.

47

When I wake up, it's close to dark. The workers have all gone home for the day. The Sun is down behind the burger joint. I'm the only dead person sleeping in this lot. I'm not sure how long it'll take the cement to harden, or my legs to feel like rigor mortis has set in, but in any case I have no way of getting him out.

Blip!

"Use the laser," Mook says.

"What laser?"

"Any closer you'd be sittin' on it."

I look down on the front seat and there is the same kind of laser gun I watched an alien posing as District Attorney Mary Devonshire use to explode my sixty-inch Hitachi four months ago. Then I watched Detective Mike Tucker blast both her and one of Mooky's bad clones in the head, and then... never mind. "I don't know how to use this thing."

"Just point and click the red button."

"We're not talking Microsoft here."

"How do you know?"

"Look, Mooky...."

"Picasso, you ain't sittin' on a lot of leeway here. Just take that thing over there and cut the head out."

"What if I damage him?"

"Cut a wide chunk, and put it in your Jeep."

"You make it sound so simple."

"The only thing simple here is you. Just be careful, don't damage the brain."

"Why can't you help me?"

"I'm not standing in a room with you while either of us is armed, hologram or otherwise."

"Oh, come on, I... we're fixing this...." I look back at him. "I still kill you?"

"Eventually."

"But...?"

"I'm not good or bad, Picasso, you are. Eventually we'll end up on opposite sides again. If it makes you feel better, it will be self preservation."

"Wait a minute, this is it for me. I'm getting my butt out of this sticky mess. I'm walking away from you, your bird, Jerry, the Space Travelers Advisory Board, and The Alien Council... forever."

"Nobody walks away from us. Once you in, you in for life, my dimwitted Philadelphia Cheese boy. Ain't you ever seen Good Fellows? Just be careful. That thing packs a wallop."

Blip!

"You blippin' bastard, Mook!"

48

Across the street I'm standing at where McGuiness should be buried with an alien laser gun in hand. This is so absurd I wouldn't know how to explain it if I had too. So please nobody show up to witness this act of alien espionage.

"What in hell do you think you're doin'?"

Damn. I turn to find a spent man. Melanoma is eating away at his ears and nose. He's standing at the door with a baseball bat and a cigarette dangling from his dried up stubbly face. This guy looks as close to Oklahoma dust as he can get without blowing away.

"How's it going?"Dumb question.

"Depends. You gotta pee, there's an Andy in the garage. You plan to carve anything in that cement I'm gonna have to pulverize you and probably bunch up my spine. Which is it?"

"Can I take door number three?"

"Not likely."

"You believe in aliens?"

"Look, goofball, I got maybe five or six good months left on this planet and I ain't about to spend them wondering what you're talkin' about. So why don't you be a nice little Hollywood whacko, and beat it, before I beat you."

"Now, is that a nice way to treat a super hero bent on saving the world?"

"It is when he's standing in my world over fresh cement on my watch. What'll it be?"

"You recognize this?" I show him the laser gun.

"I ain't playin' twenty questions. Once I start moving I'm gonna beat you to a pulp."

"Okay let me show you something." I point the laser to the left of the spot where I think McGuiness' head is and push what might be the right button, a blue one. ZZZZZZZZZZZZZZZ-ZZZZZZZZZZZING! A beam of blue light erupts from the nozzle. I'm thrust backward against the wall. The beam starts to ZZZZZING all over the place, cutting holes through the walls as it goes. Wrong button.

The spent man dives out the door just in time for me to widen it and clip his bat in two. Chunks of cement ceiling are falling down where I've cut holes into an apartment kitchen above us. Exposed water pipes burst sending water everywhere. Buy the time I get up on my knees I've undone about five weeks of work. I've cut holes through just about everything in the room and beyond. I'm talking practically ruined.

"You still there?" Nothing. "Hello? You have my permission to beat me now."

I walk over to the deformed door to the parking lot expecting an on slot of lasered off baseball bat to my head, but nothing. There's just a burning cigarette smoldering on the cold cement floor, and the top to the Al Kaline bat. The spent guy's gone, but not my craving to pick up the cig and take a toke. At least he's not lying there in pieces like the rest of the room. I back track away from the heavenly smell of lit tobacco to McGuiness and discover I've managed to cut up everything but my intended target.

I get on my knees and make sure I'm ready. I clench my teeth so I don't bite my tongue. I push the red button this time. ZZZZZZZZZZZZZZZZZZING, out shoots a much more controllable red laser beam that I use to quickly cut a square hole. Big enough to fit the head out and more, right to the packed dirt, pea gravel, rebar and beyond. This still won't be easy. We're talking about a hundred pounds of cement, steal and head here. I'm parked across the street. "Give me a hand here, Mooky."

Blip!

"You don't listen well, white boy."

Blip. The laser gun is gone.

"It was an accident."

"We better move fast. People are coming. You managed to put on a flashy laser show."

"Help me."

"You sure you got him?"

"I stepped it out. So, I think so."

"Gonna have to do for now. Put your hands on it." Blip, Mook's gone. Big help. I look over my shoulder at voices rushing my way and Blip. I suddenly find myself looking out my Jeep driver's window at the sun's last leg setting behind trees.

That may have been a weight off my shoulders but about one hundred pounds added to my groin. The cement block is now resting between my belly button and the steering wheel. Somehow, the cement must have seeped down around the head and encased it in rebar, pea gravel and dirt. Maybe the gravel settled, maybe it was the water seeping past my hurried repacking job. Anyway, if I guessed right, all of the head is here in my lap. Alien bastard humor!

Across the street the building is swarming with neighbors. From where I sit, I can take in the full damage to what I've done. Not only did I cut into the first floor but I managed to cut through all the floors to the roof above where a small plume of smoke rises to the sky. I also cut the railing off the building entry steps next door. And cut the balcony above it nearly diagonally in half. The rest lies in the balcony below it. Good job, Jozeph. You make one fine alien sympathizer.

The spent guy is hopping up and down with his lasered off bat, demonstrating what he saw me do. He's making sure he's not taking the fall for this. I don't blame him. I can't hear him. He must be getting into the alien part because everyone is backing away from him. He's almost pleading. But like all alien fearing humans, this spent guy's nuttier than Picasso on a laser binge. I'm seeing firsthand how people would treat me if I started telling the truth. That we are not alone, and aliens are controlling everything about us. If I were a better human, I'd go over there and put his poor mind to rest.

Sirens fill the air, rushing up Graystone.

I'd like to watch what happens next, like any other normal morbid, non alien made person. Instead, I start my Jeep and pull west across the parking lot to Colbath and hang a right. At this point, I have the feeling I haven't many human rights left. So I'm taking all the rights whenever I come to one from now on. So I make another right on Graystone and head past my place to find a small crowd outside my building. Maybe I'll get lucky and they'll burn down Frankenstein's castle.

49

What to do next? It's the eternal question of dead men driving. I have options. The first is to just drive this Jeep off Mulholland and end it all right now. The second is to call Jetty and let him end it all his way. The third is to go in front of the press with this cemented head and severed arm and let the courts decide how it all ends. The forth, and the one I'm favoring, is to just keep driving and forget it all happened. I would if I thought it could all end. Mooky and his friends will find me.

Blip!

"You gonna make that call or talk to yourself all night?"

"The line is busy."

"Try again."

"Get out of my truck."

"Ungrateful human."

"Look who's talking in tongues. I saved your life. Now look what you've gotten me into."

"You're not gonna start that sniveling again are you."

"Whatever happened to eye for an eye?"

"That's right. I still owe you a poke or two."

"Ouch! Damn it, Mooky. That hurts!"

"I found it so refreshing when you did it to me."

"Remind me next time to let you dissipate into thin air."

"I'm saving your life right now. So we even, white boy."

"How?"

"By being your friend. Even if you don't know it."

"Give me just a minute. I'll make these tears of agony look cinematically touching."

"You know, Picasso. I can think of a lot of people who'd want to be in your shoes."

"Oh really. Which size? The old eleven D? Or the new twelve double D?"

"Keep it up. Make that call. Keep telling him the truth."

"Hologram bastard. I want all my shoes and boots replaced." I dial again. It rings through this time. "Jetty, please."

"You got 'em."

"Oh, hey, Jetty. Jozeph Picasso here."

"Who is this?!"

"Of course you think I'm dead because your idiot box says I am. You recall that little guy you sucker punched at Charlie's yet? That night I was bartending and then lied to help keep you out of it? Then your no neck brother called to threaten me anyway? Remember? Well, I've got news for you, Jetty. That little guy's gonna take you downtown. He's finally getting that last punch, postmortem. And all you can do is stand there and take it. Just like he did. As he kicks you in the behind. "

A long pause, as the actor turned producer bobs and weaves on the other end while thinking. I know he's working it over because I can hear him breathing.

"They pulled your body part out of the Tujunga Wash, Picasso. I saw it on TV."

"And TV wouldn't lie, would it. After all, look at the stellar image it made of your life."

"Who is this?"

"I'm not kidding, Jetty. It's me, Jozeph Picasso. My dog peed on your shoes in Claire's dressing room. She laughed about it in front of everyone in that studio. You were the butt of our joke."

"If you ain't dead, whose leg was that?"

"No, no, that was my leg."

"Ahhh... that must 'a hurt."

"It's okay. I don't need it."

"You usin' your pecker for a Pogo Stick, or what?"

"No, you see, I'm using your brother's leg now. Remember?"

"Leonie's leg?"

"Yeah, the right one. He's a hairy bastard. His foot stinks kind of woppish, but it's got nice toenails. Did you know big brother painted them pink?"

"What'd'ya do with my brother?"

"How many times do I have to tell you? He's feeding alien babies through his balls now. It's good work for a dead guy if you can find it."

"Shut up. Where are you?"

"Pick a place. I'll show you my foot first hand when I kick you with it. Oh, I have that head and arm you wanted, too. Only the head is encased in cement. But that shouldn't be anything new to a tough New Jersey thug like you, right."

"Enjoy this, Picasso. It won't last long."

"Is that anyway to talk? We're practically blood brothers. One forth brothers anyway. By the way, this leg likes to dance to that crazy disco beat. I can't stop it. Did your brother moonlight from the mob as a ballroom dance instructor?"

"Keep this line free."

"Jetty? You still there? Hello?"

"Just bring the rest of the body."

"He hung up on you?"

"I wonder why?"

"He'll call back. Give him a minute to think it over."

"What if he doesn't?"

"Then we move to plan B."

"This plan B as dumb as the A plan?"

"In plan B we call your two cop friends."

"Mike and MacAroy? Why?"

"You'll need witnesses. What better than two cops?"

"Witnesses to what? These guys couldn't point their mothers out of a lineup without implementing themselves."

"Witness to murder."

"Wait. Not mine."

"Only if things don't work out."

What do I say to that?

"Hey, come on, Picasso. The unknown happens all the time."

"Is this one of those 'need to know' things you've warned me about? Or is this one of those 'goodbye sucker' times?"

"Just call your two buddies. They've talked to Jetty by now."

I dial Tucker's number. "Is this Milky the Clown?"

"Shut up and listen, Picasso. I don't want to know how you and your friends done this. But write down this address."

"Just a sec. Okay, shoot."

"Roscoe and Owens Mouth."

"That's an address? Sounds like a vacant lot in Sun Valley."

"Just bring what you got for Jetty. Meet us there. And look, keep your mouth shut. Don't call nobody else. And show up alone. If you know what I mean."

"You mean, no aliens."

"I don't know what you're talking about."Click.

"Talk about a cop in denial."

"You're on your own."

"Wait."

"Just keep telling the truth as you see it, Picasso. Sooner or later Jetty's gonna have to make a move based on what he believes his life to be. If it doesn't work out, it was nice knowin' you, almost. Oh, if he doesn't believe you, show him the tattoo on your butt."Blip!

"Tattoo?" What tattoo? I've been tattooed? I've got Leonie's tattoo? A tattoo of what? I'm not standing in a vacant lot, dropping my pants, and mooning a bunch of east coast hoodlums to stay alive. Unless of course, it's a deal breaker.

I'm wanted enough as it is. So I can't just stop the truck and drop my pants to look and make sure my inheriting Leonie's tattoo isn't just more alien humor. But think of the beating I'd take if Jetty called my bluff and Leonie's tattoo wasn't there. There's no need to be wanton and lascivious, too. I'm rationalizing all this after subconsciously driving over to the Sherman Oak's Mall off Riverside Drive to do a little shoplifting. I've made it as far as the dressing room behind the register with a new set of clothes and two sizes of black shoes. I know I have bad people waiting for me. I know this isn't a good time to be goofing around. Well too bad, let them wait. I'm wet and dirty and I want to see my bequeathed tattoo. Frankly, I'm in no hurry to be declared dead twice in one day. So I drop my pants and twist my torso to look in the mirror. "Holy LA Ink!"

50

"Dirty rotten alien bastards!"

The young female checker taps on the dressing room door. "Sorry, is there a problem with the pants, sir?"

"What? No. Never mind. I haven't tried them on yet. I'll be right out." I'm yelling because I'm standing here looking at my one hairy cheek in the mirror. The words 'Debbie Does Dallas' is enshrined in a six inch purple heart with a broken yellow arrow stuck through it. Somewhere Leonie probably got his heart broken by some stripper and had it immortalized. Of course, I'm speculating here and Debbie just may be his ex-wife. Or his high school cheerleader sweetheart. Or maybe his father produced the sex film and made a lot of money. And this is how he celebrated! I may never know.

But that's not my real big concern. In this better light I'm finally able to give the two legs the scrutiny they deserve. I've got to say, this Leonie was one hairy guy. Thank Buddha, I didn't inherit his back. I mean, this guy's a gorilla. Or he was. How do I tell a woman that the leg isn't mine? That I have no idea why Debbie has done all of Dallas on my butt? What woman in her right mind would trust me after that? How far do I carry this lie? If I have premature ejaculation, can I lie and say "Hey, it's not my dick, either."

"Sir, there's women and children in the store."

"What? Oh, sorry, did I say that out loud?"

"Yes, very loud. How are the pants? Would you like to try another color?"

"Maybe we should go with something with more of a relaxed fit. One of my legs is a little bigger from surgery."

"Fine. And the sweatshirt?"

"This is perfect."

Once dressed, I stand at the checkout counter purposely closest to the parking lot exit. Moredetta wants to run my store credit card. She looks up at me funny as I use her pen to write down vital information. Does she know I'm dead? Or did I just freak her out with my Turrets Syndrome babble-on in the dressing room?

"So, you don't have your store card or ID?"

"Just my social security number. Here, I signed an IOU, and added an extra hundred dollars for your trouble."

"I'm sorry, without proper ID or your store card you'll have to take those clothes off." She looks inside the shoeboxes. And you have two sizes of shoes on?"

"This is an honest national emergency."

She looks at my signature on my signed IOU. "I hope you don't find this funny?"

"Look, I wrote down my address. This is my real phone number. You can call me anytime."

"Are you aware that Jozeph Picasso is dead? It was just on the radio while I was on break. It's big news."

"Yes, but don't tell anyone you saw me? Bad people are after me. And the aliens have made them think I've been dead since yesterday so I can save the world for them. Please believe me. I need your help. You're the only one I've ever told. Honest."

She backs away from me. "Yes that seems perfectly logical, Mr. Picasso. These things happen all the time." She picks up the phone. I'm sure she's not buying it though.

"Look, technically I am Jozeph Picasso, most of him. I wish I were totally someone else. Quite often actually."

"Let me call my supervisor. Her house is haunted. She's writing a script. She'll want to meet you."

I force the phone back down. "Relax, I promise, by tomorrow I'll be the undead. I'll come back and pay cash."

"I'm sure you will. Now, let me make one little call to get us someone who can authorize payment arrangements."

Bingo. I start backing away towards the exit. "I know how this must look. Just put everything I'm wearing on my card's number. I swear on my mother's grave I'll stop by tomorrow... if I live and the aliens aren't eating me by then. I promise. Okay? Thanks."

"Security!"

51

This is the karma I have for being such a smartass. I make a run for it. Once again, my newfound hairy leg is leading the way. This guy sure must've been a bagman or something because he really knows how to run away. I'm having a hard time keeping up. Out in the parking lot, I make it to my Jeep's parking spot. Just in time to discover that the spot is empty.

"What the...!"

Someone stole my Jeep. I look back and security is coming my way. Fast. So I make another run for it toward the steps at the far northeast corner leading down to street level. This is all I need. What do I do now? How do I explain this to Jerry, Jetty, Mooky, Hassle, and Grizzle of the LAPD? This is probably why stupid crooks always look in such good shape. The getaway part of crime never seems to work out as planned.

Whose got my Jeep and what will they do with it? If it makes its way to a chop shop, will they get the joke when they find more body parts then they bargained for? What happens to McGuiness if they do? I look back. These guys are gaining on me! Whatever happened to little old retired security people who can scarcely stand up? Oh yeah, they work in banks so that it's safer for the bottom trolling public to rob them.

At the bottom of the parking structure I've got no choice other than to sprint across Riverside Drive and do my best to get lost down an alley behind the office buildings.

"Where are you, Mooky?"

Blip!

"What are you doing, Picasso?"

"What took so long?"

"I can't be popping in and out of public shopping malls every time you need to change your underpants."

"I've got some strippers' name tattooed on me!"

"No, a famous porn character."

"You alien dipstick! How am I to explain that?"

"Believe me, you got a whole lot 'a explainin' to do. Just bunch it all together and let them lock you away when you're done talkin'."

He's right. Who'd believe any of this inane stuff? I can't tell anyone this is autobiographical. Aliens gave me a hairy butt. Well, half and the tattoo. Wanna see? Clang! My life fades into defiant laughing echoes down a dark dank hall to Purgatory.

"Where's the Jeep?"

"It's gone."

"So, fool, you aware you lost it at least."

"Someone stole it, Mooky, from the parking lot."

"You dumb cracker. What were you doing in there?"

"Putting on dry clothes and examining my tattoo. How could you do this to me?"

"Look, I'm not a doctor. I'm not even a wet nurse. So you got a problem with your new leg, take it up with the AMS."

"Alien Medical Society?"

"You catch on real quick."

"Ask those bastards where my Jeep is."

"Just shut up. You ready?"

"For what?"

"When you get there, make sure you keep your hands on both the arm and head."

"Mooky, don't...."

52

Blip.

I'm sitting in the back seat of my Jeep going about eighty-five miles an hour due west on the 118 Freeway. All around us cars are swerving to get out of our way. It's pandemonium in Technicolor, as cop lights flash from everywhere. Up above is a total nights of thunder of searchlights. In the front seat are two scared kids in wool caps. They haven't caught on to me yet. It's a good thing, because they've got guns. Bam! We clip a station wagon and bounce off the cement guardrail, throwing sparks back at about fifteen cop cars. Hey, I've got Alien Car Insurance with zero deductible. But I'm back live on World's Dumbest Criminals again.

"You keep driving like this... we should put on seat belts. We could get a ticket."

They look at each other to see which one was moving his lips. Then look back at me in complete dumbass surprise. This will be more fun than I thought.

"What the double jack?"

"Man, did you two meatheads pick the wrong Jeep."

The darker of the two teenagers puts his gun on me. The lighter one does his best to keep both hands on the wheel while facing me. "Shoot, the motha'!"

"Wait a minute, you don't have to. I'm already dead. The cops will think you're shooting at them. And you know what happens next."

"You got that right."

"Here, take a look at this." I pick up McGuiness' hand and arm, unwrap it, and wave it for them to see. "Nice, huh?"

"Is that for real?"

"Feel, it's not even stiff yet."

"Hell no!"

"You, one crazy mooootha'!"

"No, I'm one dead mooootha'. This is my truck and you're in a dirt load of trouble when these cops catch up with you. They're gonna think you killed me for it. That's why they're after you. You get it now? You're not just car thieves, you're suspected murdering car thieves."

"Shit, what'd we ever do to you?"

"Besides stealing my Jeep?"

"See, I told you this not the truck for us."

"Shut up, an' drive. You a ghost?"

"How do you think I got in here?"

"I'll be a Jiminy Crackhead. He's a real motha' ghost!"

"He ain't no dead dude, Crackhead. He's messin' wit' you."

"Messin' wit' me? You here, too." This shuts them both up a moment. I can only wait them out as options strike home. "Okay, if you so dead, white bread, prove it."

"You ever hear of a Jozeph Picasso?"

"That mass murderin' filmmaker?"

"The one they pulled his body parts out of the river today?"

"That they been talkin' trash about on the radio? Mister, nobody likes you. Everybody glad you're dead. We even glad you're dead. An' we don't even know you from bull spit. They think we done it. We get a medal or parade down Hollywood B or somethin'."

"Yeah, even white folk glad you dead. I ain't heard so much happiness in one city. They were even calls from other states, somethin' Springs Colorado."

"They only found but one leg. And they about to throw a b-q hoedown to dance on your grave."

"That's right. I'm that motha' writer/director that everybody hates. You hear that, Mooky? I'm a national hate holiday!"

"Who you callin' Mooky?"

"He's bullshitin' you. He got both his legs. See there? He got two new shoes on. Even if they ain't the same size."

"I'm dead. What do I care how many pieces my body's in?"

"Yeah, then who's that you got there? Whose arm is that? Your old momma's?"

"This is an arm belonging to a human clone. One that an alien named Jerry used for thousands of years to walk amongst us in. And inside this block of cement is his head. I know this because I saved it from washing out to sea and put it in there. And both of them are hung better than you and maybe slept with your mommas."

"You hear that? Both of them slept...."

"Say what?"

"He one crazy motha'. Even if he be dead."

"You two lifers have no idea."

"Keep your eye on the road, dummy. How do we know you this Picasso dude?"

"Look, there on the floor. See? My registration. Jozeph 'the hated' Picasso. Only your DMV knows for sure."

My cell phone starts ringing. "Could you answer that?"

"Who is it? If you dead?"

"That would be the New Jersey Mob wanting this arm and this cement encased head. Ask them who I am. If you don't believe me. Or I could show you my tattoo."

"Man the mob is into some funky biz. We ain't nothin' just stealin' these toy trucks. Ain't no respect in this child's game. Look at all these cops on our butts. This ain't nothin' but diss time to them."

"Don't worry. Soon you'll be in prison. You'll meet all kinds of mob guys who'll be glad to introduce themselves, personally."

"You think so?"

"I wouldn't be surprised if you spent every night for the rest of your life with one or more. And guess what? They don't pick up the check at the salad bar."

"Say what?"

"Shit, we gotta lose these cops, man!"

The darker one opens my center council and answers the phone. "What you want?"

"Who is this?"Comes over the phone.

"None of your business, is who this is."

"Let me talk to Picasso. Is he there?"

"Yeah, he here. But he dead." He looks back at me. "It's for you, dead guy."

"Told you. By the way, don't bring me up to these cops chasing you. Mums the Picasso word."

"Got that straight."

"Mom?"

"Shut up, Picasso. Where are you?"

"Heading west on the 118 about Topanga Canyon with an organized electric glide posse on my trail."

"We're waiting for you."

"Them the mob?"The lighter one asks.

"Relax guys. It's not the New Jersey Mob. It's some low life LA cop on the take named Milky the Clown. He's got his brains stuck in some hole and doesn't know how to get it out."

"Who?"

"Two schmucks I'm trying to forget. Listen, Milky. I've been carjacked. I'm trying to get the arm and head back. So have fun waiting. I'll be there when I'm there. Unless you want me to lead these guys and their entourage over there right now."

"Get here as soon as you can, Picasso. Alone, or a little friend of yours is taking a ride not so alone."

"You touch any of my friends, Tucker, and I'll have my friends take you for an intergalactic ride. Far-far away, to another galaxy. I'll have them suck air through your balls while they keep you alive by feeding you stinky alien substances."

"You tell him, dead guy."

"Stinkin' pigs. Diss that motha', man. You know, for a dead white dude, you ain't such a bad cracker."

"Who is that?"

"Two gangbangers on their way to sleep with you guys in prison."

"Get over here, Picasso!"

"Say hello to the Mook for me."Click.

"Look out!"

I look up and we're rear ending a slowing flatbed truck deliberately getting in our way! I hug the cement block and arm to me and close my eyes. The glass shards attack my face and the two gangers take the back of the flatbed full frontal in a millisecond gone wild! There's nothing I can do but join them in death.

53

Blip! How many times does a guy gotta die to get out of this mess?

I uncover my eyes. Thank Buddha. I'm out of my Jeep but I'm here. I was right, Roscoe and Owens Mouth is a vacant lot with a six-foot high sandy mound all the way around. Turning it into a secluded artificial reservoir to kill people in. Only, it's not entirely vacant enough for you know whose safety. Standing with their backs toward me are five dark figures with what appears to be a large cargo trunk. Not the kind of trunk my parents stored in the attic full of army memorabilia stuff that they thought I'd want someday. It's a fancier kind of magic prop trunk, a portmanteau. A large trunk that opens into two equal parts. Probably the same one I let two stage hands lug into McGuiness' apartment. My guess is this is the trick they used to make Gray's body disappear from Mystery Towers.

Wait! I don't have Jerry's stones yet!

What I do have is one hundred pounds of cement and an arm wrapped in a towel. If I am bleeding anywhere from my Jeep's windshield coming my way I don't feel it at this time. It's dark and dank where I stand with the festering tang of exposed algae. The figures before me subsist as mysterious shadows against the cloudy industrial lit sky. The distant glimmers of high voltage power towers are silhouetted by Sun Valley Mountains. As far as we humans know, slow moving lights in the sky are incoming airplanes. They dodge left behind cumulous clouds heading out of Burbank Airport. Now would be a good time for the rain to start again and cover my tracks but it doesn't. Tracks? I look down and both sizes of my new shoes are ruined by mud and photosynthetic organisms. Damn it. Oh, how I'd love to be on one of those planes bound anywhere.

If this is Jerry's plan, and I'm to see it through, it would be nice to understand the strategy. I'm unarmed, undermanned, and uninformed. From the movement of these other people, for the moment, still unearthed.

Cement? I never got a chance to check if the head's actually in this block. I mean, it looks like he is, the shape and all. But with the day I've had, I've got my reservations. Damn, this could really turn up bad news for me if McGuiness is planning on some kind of Magical Man reunion and he has no mind to get me out of here alive.

A car is heading this way. It peaks over the mound, a black SUV. Looks like Ernie got his truck back. All the monkeys are here now. So I crouch down to avoid the headlights bouncing about, hiding behind nothing but lonely shadows... and watch. Moments later, Ernie and his son Ernie Jr. get out of Ernie's Range Rover. Remind me not to name my kid Jozeph in case someone is pathetic enough to write about us and want to call him Junior. They cluster around like warts on pirates, sloshing about the muddy foot of the far west bank. No one seems to be happy about standing out here. I feel their pain. And hope their shoes are as ruined as mine. Both Ernies have shovels though. They start digging where another points his finger. My guess from his shortness, it's Jetty the wonder jerk. I turn around to leave....

Blip! "Keep your voice down."

"You see that? They're digging a hole!"It hurts to scream hysterically in sotto voce by the way.

"I can see that."

"I don't have the diamonds."

"You don't, that does."

I look down at the hand and inside its death grip is a small gold box.

"What's about to happen?"

"Ask Jerry. Just think it out logically and those that can, will make it happen. Think smart. Good luck."

"Good luck? I'll need a miracle to slog off this lot!"

"You needed plenty to get here. Cheer up, I'll see you around."

"Get back here, Mooky."

"You're almost home."

"I'm almost dead in their eyes. Tell me what to do."

"Just tell them the truth. Oh, if you find yourself speaking in a weird tongue. It's just us subliminally teaching you." Blip!

"Blip this!" Weird tongue? This isn't weird enough?

I can hear their voices pick up as the two Ernies dig. "He wasn't in the Jeep," Ernie Sr. says. His voice labored from many years of pointing his silver spoon at lousy writers from behind his desk. Maybe writers the world over will get lucky and Ernie Sr. will collapse and fill the grave.

"I called him there. Those two punks picked up the phone and handed it to him," Tucker chimes in. He lights another cigarette, having just flicked away the other. Bastard.

"I don't care. There were just two decapitated dumbshits. No one else." Daddy Ernie almost seems concerned.

Junior, moving deliberately slow, takes a sweat wiping break. Is Jerry still in him? Is that how he's getting here? Is Jerry digging his precious clone's grave himself? Is this self flogging at its lowest?

"Where is he, Mike? That bastard did something with my brother." Jetty must really like me because he's getting upset over me not being here. He's a second rate hoodlum with heart. Front page news. Perhaps a rock to the back of his skull will ease his pain.

"If he ain't in the Jeep then he's on his way. Trust me, he wants out of this as much as we do. So he'll be here. But I'm tellin' ya, there're things about this guy you don't want to know about. And don't want to be messin' around with him over. Just take the head and arm and let him go. So we can end this thing tonight."

"He's a scumbag nobody sittin' in my way of happiness, is all I need to know," Jetty says. So it must be true about me. I'm a scumbag nobody. Who am I to argue?

"All I'm tryin' to say is...." Tucker looks at MacAroy. Mac shakes his head. How do two cops tell anyone that we aren't alone without ending up in the hole that drops before them? "He's got friends, is all I'm sayin'."

"Shit, I got friends. You got friends. We all got friends. All that creep's got is some dumb dog that cozied his snout onto my show. I'm gettin' it or you two off my dole, one way or another." Jetty is looking right at me. Yet he's not seeing me. Odd, huh?

"He's got a thing for that dog."

"Don't we know." MacAroy looks at Ernie Sr.

Ernie nods yes. Oh-oh, what's going on between them?

"What are we doing here? This is useless if we don't have all of McGuiness."

"Maybe Junior will think twice before gettin' so wasted he takes it from some horny freak next time," Jetty answers him. "Now dig."

54

Blip!

"Digging for treasure, Captain Blight?" I'm suddenly about fifteen feet due east of them. Don't ask. It's just where it made sense for me to be. Just out of arms reach, and here I am. So that's how it works. I'm picturing every blade of grass in Idaho, but that one's not working.

They all turn to me, mouth a jar, looking as though they'd been caught smoking crack in the school's shithouse. Ernie and Ernie are both knee deep in mud and counting.

"Where did you come from?"Jetty asks. He's looking at me like I'm a monster. Why not, ain't I the Frankenstein of my generation?

"From listening in, over there."

"You bring what we told you to bring?"Tucker isn't as happy to see me as Jetty. Probably because he knows they're in an alien load of trouble if this gets out beyond this mud pit.

"The head and arm. Sure. Here, they're under warranty, right?" I look and Gray's massive fingers have all but made the gold box with the diamonds disappear.

Jetty motions over one of the Mustachio Twins and he sloshes near and gives me the east coast smarmy smirk 'I know you are gonna die' look. Ha, the jokes on him, I'm already dead in the eyes of the creative world. He takes the head and lugs it over to the magical portmanteau, where the rest of McGuiness waits in a makeshift body bag. The other twin props up the magical trunk lid and dumps the cement incrusted head inside.

"How do we know the head's in there?"

"Break it open if you want. I didn't have time. I'll lend you a hand."I hold out Gray's arm.

Jetty looks over to Ernie Senior. "You wanna give it a whack with the shovel a few times? See if we can break it open?"

"Why don't we just whack him until he tells us the truth?" Good old Ernie, he's always looking out for me. What a man. What a producer. What a gigantic prick.

Ernie Junior isn't looking my way. He has his head down and is still digging. He must sense me looking at him, because he glances up with nothing but sorrow for me in his eyes. My good buddy. I still can't tell if Jerry is in there or not. But my guess is yes. I've been known to be wrong, though.

Tucker and MacAroy are looking at me sadly for other reasons. You see, Tucker and MacAroy know there are aliens. And if Junior is himself, he suspects there are real vampires. All three know if they keep playing with me things could get real ugly for everyone involved. Problem is, they are forced to be here by Jetty. Jetty holds all the cards because he also holds a silenced gun. The only thing he's sure of is that there's gonna be hell to pay if the others don't dig faster. Judging by the look on everyone's face, yep, they're whacking me. Damn.

I look Junior over as close as I can in the dark. From the cautious way he's moving around I'm now thinking he's not Junior with Jerry inside after all. He's just Ernie the dumb lucky rich kid, wannabe director again, with a very sore disposition. Too bad, I liked him better as Jerry.

"So what's the game plan? The Magical Man just disappears and we call it an unsolved magical murder night?"I ask.

"That's close," Tucker says.

"Tucker, Mac, what would your fellow officers think? You know how they get about whacking innocent civilians when it comes time to decide who makes Captain of Detectives."

"What they don't know won't hurt our promotions or retirements. But so you know, we ain't for this. Just in case."

"In case what? Mooky finds out? Or I make it out of here?"

Tucker and Mac look at each other, then over to clueless Jetty. "Somethin' like that."

"And you, Jetty, don't you think Claire Davis would be disappointed? She was looking forward to working with Gray McGuiness in *Crazy Kind Of Love*."

"Get the arm."He motions to one of the twin flunkies. "Picasso, get in the trunk and shut up."The flunky comes over and takes the arm, dropping it into the trunk on his way back.

My job is finished here in case anyone is listening or watching. Hello? Damn. It's time to stall. I can't carry a tune or dance, so my options aren't overflowing. So I do the one thing I know will get their attention."I'm not getting in that trunk until I show you this." I turn around, drop my new pants, sans undies, and Moon them good and plenty.

"Jesus Christ! Pull up your pants, Picasso, this ain't no peep show," Tucker says, not in the least surprised by my rebuttal to Jetty's request.

"Show some self-respect," Mac adds. Look who's talking. Mr. Revlon cover-up himself.

"You recognize that tattoo, Jetty? Here, take a better look at the hair. Part of your big brother still lives in me. Consider this a message from behind. You bury me. You bury what's left living of Leonie out here, too."

"What's the matter with you, Picasso?"

"Take a healthy look, you guys. Because me and it are about to button up and walk out of this mud pit."

"Christ. You got one hairy cheek with a tattoo. So what?"

"It's Leonie's cheek. His right leg and his tattoo, that's what's so what. The aliens gave them to me to replace what I lost jumping into the Tujunga Wash while running from those two twits. Go ahead smooch it. Give it the big hug. Kiss your big brother goodbye, Jetty. I know you want to."

"I'm out of here." Tucker makes a move to leave and Jetty puts his gun on him. So Mac pulls his gun, leaving the mustachio twins the last to pull theirs. This is getting beautiful. So I pull up my pants. The trick to any good moon is in knowing when to turn off your love light. Wouldn't it be neat though if they started killing each other? Like a Mexican standoff Hollywood buys in almost every Quentin Tarantino flick? Leaving me to kick them all into the mud hole and drive home by myself. Please? Any one, if you're tuning in? Where are all the good alien action film fans when you need them?

"No one's leaving until I know what's going on here."

"Look, Jetty, you don't want to know," Mac actually seems to feel sorry for the little prick. But Jetty isn't settling for that lame excuse.

So I give it another try. Why not? Mook said just tell them the truth. "We're not alone on this planet, Jetty. Wise up. Having your brother's butt and leg attached to me is living proof to that. Remember, they found my leg in the river, with my boot still on it. I'm dead to the world, aside from you cruds, and a few million Aliens. Who've decided to make me the messenger from beyond God Particles. I'm here to save the world by keeping the Alien Advisory Board from warring against each other over this dead vampire clone. Ask Junior, he knows. DNA on his sore butt is also proof they probe us in many ways. Right, Junior.

Junior looks up, wanting to answer.

"Shut up, Ernie," Jetty tells him.

"Then ask your boys about the bird that made Leonie kill himself before he could kill me. Caw is an alien trained bird. He's smarter than all of you. And he doesn't garble his dialogue nearly as much as you do, Jetty."

Jetty looks at the twin studs.

"We just saw something dark and heard screeching and screaming. It came at Leonie from out of nowhere and grabbed his gun hand. They struggled. It went off. He ran off. We couldn't see who actually pulled the trigger."

"And what happened to his body when you got back from chasing me into the river?"

"He was gone."

"And who took him?"

"We don't know."

"But Tucker and MacAroy know. Don't you boys? Space Travelers. They're breeding us all like dogs and cloning us so they can live as us. From the very beginning of man, and they're eating us, too. We're a smörgåsbord of stupidity to them. A must stop vacation destination for the rich, powerful and cannibalistic aliens from out there. Way beyond our solar system. Right, Tucker?"

"We don't know nothin'. Only, Jetty this isn't such a good plan. He was bringin' both the body and head. Now we got him here. That's it. Let him go. We don't advise that you whack him out here like this. Your brother already tried that. Just let him go. Who's he gonna tell? He's part of this, as much as we are."

"Tucker, Mac, I'm touched. I'd think you two lugs would be the first to want me deadened. I think I'm getting all misty-eyed here. Does anyone have a tissue? Come on, let's hold hands and give a prayer to say goodbye to McGuiness. Kumbaya my Lord, Kumbayaaaa ...."

"Shut uuuuup! Get in the box, Picasso!"Jetty points his gun.

"I'm not getting in the box. And if you make me, my alien friends will only Blip me out of here."I hope.

"Picasso, just get in the box. He don't believe you. And we ain't claimin' nothin' other than you got a messed-up filmmaker's imagination. So get in the box. We ain't drawing fire over this."

"I'm not getting in that box unless you get in there with me, Tucker. And I don't care what you draw. You know what will happen to all of you if you continue with this. You want McGuiness gone. The aliens want McGuiness gone. And I'm okay with it. As long as I'm not gone with him. Okay, now put the guns away. Get out of the hole, and let's get this event over with."

"Get in the box."

"No."

"Get in the box or else."

"I'm not getting in the box. If you want to shoot me, fine. Leave a bullet they can trace. But otherwise, forget it, Jetty, I'm not getting in."

Jetty looks me in the eyes. He's thinking his options over. He's got cops who don't want me dead watching him. But he doesn't seem to think that's a problem. His family owns them. A card here hasn't been played. I get the feeling I'm not the lucky dog holding it.

"Yes you are," Jetty says.

"Not while I'm breathing."Okay, show me your hand.

"It doesn't matter to us."Jetty points a gun at me.

Mike stops him. "He's right about the bullet. He screwed us once before on that. We got a friend of yours, Picasso."

"I told you to leave my friends out of this. Where does the killing stop?"

"Get the dog."

"It bit me."Ernie Senior says.

"Wait, you got Bubba? Bubba!" I call out to him. My voice trails out into the night. At first all I hear is his toenails on glass. Then his muffled barking. He's so good. It's Bubba from inside Ernie's SUV. I jump on Senior Ernie and start beating him. Right there in the muddy hole. I don't care. He's my dog, and nobody messes with my best friend without getting a punch in the eye. The two Mustachio Twins pull me away and hold me off the ground while I kick at them. I land a good one on a knee and they throw me back into the hole. Junior jumps out of the way. I catch the shovel blade on the side of the head. I pick it up and hold it like an ax. I turn on Jetty. "He's a TV star just like you. Except he's good at it. How can you hurt him?"

"Either you get in the box on your own. Or we put you in it dead, with your little dog."

I swing at him. Glang! Right on the kneecap! "Jetty, you hurt Bubba and you can just forget about being happy with Claire. I'll come back from the dead, I swear. And both I and McGuiness will screw your career up good."

He's hopping up and down. "You messed up my thing with Claire already, you crazy bastard! Take that away from him!"

The rest look at me. I give them the 'who wants it next' look. They back off. Jetty points his gun at me. He means it this time. Mike doesn't look like he plans on stopping him. So I hand Junior back his shovel. He doesn't want it, but takes it anyway. "Look, it's not me she wants, Jetty. It's the dog. It's working with Gray McGuiness. It's not my script she wants. I'm not the one in your way. It's this guy, and he's already dead. So let's just bury him and call it a fright night. You and Claire don't have to do my script and Ernie Junior can direct whatever he wants, like he planned. Or not. I don't care. Just don't kill me or hurt Bubba."

"You still know too much. Get the dog. Don't worry, we ain't doin' your lifeless script, Picasso. Never were. Now get him out of there. You two, get back to digging. Faster and deeper! Put a little back bone into it, Burnsteins. If either of you two can find one."

I get pulled out of the hole and both Ernies get pushed back in and they start digging faster. I guess they're digging here because somebody knew the sand like soil beneath the muddy silt would be soft to the shovel blade. I'm not catching the full logic of us being this close to civilization. I guess I don't have to know everything. How many other lost bodies are out here is crossing my mind though. Maybe the deserts are filling up with them and it's standing room only for the mob these days.

Maybe I should test how fast my newfound leg can run. And how accurate their aims are in shooting unemployed hacks in the back.

229

Jetty turns to Mike. "Get the dog."

"No wait. Bubba stays in the truck. I get in the trunk. You take him back to Claire. That's the deal."

Junior finally speaks up. "I'll make sure he gets back safely, Jozeph." Everyone turns on him. "No one harms the dog, if he gets in. That's the deal."

I look at all the other faces, Mike, Mac, Jetty, Ernie Senior, and the two Mustachio Twins. A Hollywood lynch mob if there ever was one. For the love of Bubba. Oddly, Junior's the only face I can trust in this crowd. Fine. I walk over to the trunk and step inside with the body and the cement block. The gold box is still firmly in the arm's grip. There's not a lot of room to move left over. "Did you guys think this out? I'm not a short little prick like you, Jetty. There's not enough room."

"Get the chainsaw."

"No wait, I'll fit. Just... here, let me take off my shoes. I get in. Before I let these mugs shut the lid, I start untying my new muddy shoes. I'm just stalling. The body's all there, so get me out of here. No Blip. I try to Blip myself anywhere but here, nothing. Something's wrong. I'm out of stall techniques. So I crouch down around McGuiness' body. Damn he's stiff. I mean lovesick rigid. Is this a sign? Stop it, Jerry. One of the Mustachios Twins pushes the trunk lid down over me. Big smile. At least someone's looking forward to this. Blip me already!

"So long, Picasso. Have a nice long smothering death."

I grab the lid to give it one more go at stopping this. "Mike, you're a cop. MacAroy, you can't let this happen."

"We don't have a clue to what happened to you, Picasso. We were never here. As far as anyone knows, you got washed out to sea like LA trash. If your friends show up, we tried to save you and failed."

"Don't do this."

"Shut up, everybody. Close it," Jetty says.

The two Mustachios push the lid all the way down over me. I'm practically straddling McGuiness, bent in half. I look sideways at my last ray of hope as the lid fully closes down. Mike and MacAroy just look away. I'm dead. Click. Latch. A chain is wrapped around the trunk. A padlock snaps shut. Of course, I'm inside the Magical Man's Mystery Chest. And McGuiness is here with me.

This has got to be Jerry's plan. "Jerry, if this is what you had in mind, then my part is finished. Have fun."The trunk starts sliding along the wet silt. "Jerry?" Then without much fanfare, it topples sideways, and we roll until I'm on my back. With the sole weight of McGuiness' on my belly. Worse, the cement block comes crashing down on the side of my head at the end of our last roll. Putting me mercifully out like a crushed light bulb.

Thankfully, that's all I recall.

55

If you haven't been licked awake by your best friend while lying on the bed of a SUV then I guess you've never really lived in West Hollywood. My eyes open and Bubba is so in my face he's nothing but a slurpin'-lovin'-puff ball and boy do I need it. "Get up, Dogman! They're coming now!" The doors open and the two Ernies get in front. They don't say a thing. They're breathing tells the whole story. They just dug a hole and buried an unemployable filmmaker alive in a trunk with a famous dismembered Magical Man, who sodomized one of them and then got his head cut off in return. If I have to tell them what they really did, wouldn't that be an archeological moment?

From where I recline, the difference between a heroic archeologist and a dirt bag grave robber is one thousand years of avoiding decay by misunderstood local victims. My two favorite gravediggers put their truck in gear and bluntly drive back over the sandy rim. Neither of them is making sure Bubba has his seat belt on so I hold him in my arms and he just keeps licking my salty face.

"What's that?" Junior turns back at us. It's dark.

"It's the dog."

"Lit'le bugger's always licking himself."

"You're just jealous." Hey, Bubba can't really talk, so I help.

It must be the thing to do in these situations because they look at each other to see whose lips were moving. Just like the two dark kids did in my Jeep.

"Would you drop me off at the Van Nuys Police Division? My Jeep got stolen and crushed on the 118 before I got blipped to this stink hole."

"What the...?"

"Fine, stop if you don't want to help. I'll take a cab."

Senior Ernie stomps on the breaks. He still doesn't believe it. His head may have rotated a one-eighty on his pencil neck. But like I said it's dark, so maybe not.

"Come on, Bubba we're leaving. These guys stink like B-movie producers." I climb over the seat to get out the door.

"Now hold on. Are you seeing this, Son?"

"He's there. What's happening, Picasso?"

"Hey, he's the Magical Man, Jun. Ask him."

Junior looks from me to his daddy. He's not even surprised. "Drive, Dad. We're really in a shitload now. Burying them? Dumb stunts like this are why both my grandmas hated you, and left a messed up stoner like me everything."

"Shut up. Jozeph?"

"You may call me partner, Ern. Jun, you can produce, but I'm directing Crazy Kind Of Love. And Jett touches my dialogue over my dead body." I open the truck door. Bubba looks at me as if I'm on catnip. I don't care. I'm not staying put without a green-lit movie deal.

"Wait!" The two Ernies look themselves over. I hope they like what they see. I kind of dig it. Dirty, sweaty, and scared. "Okay.... If you make it alive to my office in the morning, it's a done deal."

"Tenish, then?"

"Tenish. You want that lift?"

"Bubba does, so yes please."

"I don't want to know what happens next, Picasso." Ern puts his foot on the gas.

"Neither do I." I just want some more kisses. "Take me to Claire's old place in Studio City, her little bungalow hideaway. Call her and let her know we're coming. She doesn't need to know what has happened. Any of it. That's between you, Jetty and me or who's left breathing when this is all over. Agreed?" I guess it was a rhetorical question. "In the meantime I'm dead to the world... and remember Claire thinks I'm dead too, so make sure she's alone. I don't know what's about to happen. But I get the feeling it's gonna be theatrical."

Junior picks up the phone. Daddy gives him a look. "What, you want to tell her about Aliens and Vampires?"

"Naw, it's your picture."

The phones ringing. "Claire Davis, please. Ernie Burnstein Junior. Thank you." He puts his hand over the phone. "There are other people who don't sound happy. I think I heard crying."

"It's probably laughter because they think he's dead."

"Tell her you found Bubba and you want to meet her."

"You hear how guilty that... Claire!? Whaddup, girl. Ernie... Junior. Yes. No, everything's fine. I just wanted to call to let you know I have Bubba. Yeah. I'm on my way to Studio City. Could you meet me... my Dad and me at your old place? Sure." Junior hands the phone to Daddy.

"Claire. Yes. He was walking in the parking lot. How should I know? He's a smart dog. Maybe he needs a shrink. Believe me, I'm just glad we have him back. Who's all there? They are? The whole cast but Jetty? Damn. Could you come get him? Come alone, I don't want to see any of those people until morning." He looks at me.

"Way to go, Ern."

He puts his hand over the phone. "She was bringing people."

"Tell her you have inside information you need to discuss with her leading to my death. Information you don't want to share with others right now."

"No, she'll think I'm nuts. Would you come after hearing those words?" I can hear Claire's suspicious voice. Good for her. Never trust a producer. "No, Claire. Claire, come on, it's okay. Just come get your dog. I just don't feel like driving over the hill or putting up with this little butt licker all night. I've been drinking. Now come get your dog. Be there in twenty minutes. We'll wait. Connard Street. Got it." He hangs up and looks back at me in the mirror. "I don't think she'll come alone. What do you think?"

"Ern, I think you're always lying. Especially when you're telling the truth."

"Shut up, you dead writer."

"Murdered filmmaker. At least get my end credits right."

"Where's McGuiness?"

"He'll be around."

"He mad at me?"

"He loves you long time, Jun. And Ern, don't be surprised if he grabs you next."

"Shut up. I don't know how you got out of that box, Picasso. But that freak rapist is dead in there. I should know."

"So you killed him?"

"Hell no. Jetty made me help dig him out of that garbage chute. Disgusting. I'd rather produce daytime game shows."

"You then, Jun?"

"Believe me, I was being held down."

"That only leaves one other guess. Was it Jetty or his boys?"

"You didn't hear that from us."

"So, Jetty thought Junior was casting his film behind his back and the tragic end came unexpectedly."

"Saved my life."

"He's a hero. It really shows. Only I'm having a hard time believing you guys."

"And what about your leg, Jozeph? She'll know you're not dead. How do we explain that? How do we explain any of this? What about those two young girls? What happened to them?"

"They won't be a problem."

"Stop the truck, Dad."

"Why?"

"I'm gonna throw up."

Daddy pulls the truck over and Junior sticks his head out the window and heaves. At least he ate."

"Relax. They found my boot on someone else's leg. I give clothes away all the time. It's called Goodwill."

"The leg was your blood type. They're running a second DNA on it just to make sure." Daddy almost sounds like he's still hoping I'm dead. "Have you seen the news?"

"I'm sorry my friends suffered over nothing."

"Who's suffering? Everyone's glad you're dead."

"Surely someone."

"Some Erin chick on talk radio. She digs you, spaceman."

"Oh, and they interviewed your dad."

"Pop? Really."

"Said he hadn't heard from you all year. Been on the lake fishing for months. Said you were always getting into trouble with your Hollywood dreams. You came off as a lousy son."

"And yours is sitting pretty to one side."

"Not funny."

We pull onto Connard and stop up the block.

"Is that her?"

"Where's she going?"

"She's too smart just to drive in and park."

"She's casing the joint," I tell them. Lucky girl.

"I think you're right."

"She owns a gun?'

"I don't know."

"What do you know about her, Ernie?"

"I know what I pay her. I know you better not hurt her."

"I can guarantee you if she's got a gun, she didn't bring it because she's worried about me."

Ernie Senior flashes the truck lights. But Claire isn't about to come running. So Daddy and Dumbshit get out. I let go of Bubba and I'm forgotten like yesterday's bad breath. He's out the door and into Claire's arms so fast you'd think she drove up with him. I stay down in the seat. I'm not sure what to do next.

I can see Claire kissing Bubba, the little bugger. The two Ernies must be telling her about me because they keep pointing at the truck. Claire seems to be trying to see through the tinted glass. What do I do? Do I let her in on this? Or do I leave the two schmucks holding the dog trick? How do I explain all this? I know I don't want to even try.

"Jozeph?" Shit, that voice, she's calling for me, her presence illuminating the night air. I can smell her sweet killer essences from here. "Jozeph? If you're in the truck, come out. Please?"

I almost float and come forth. I fight the animal urge to show myself, and don't make a move. Something's not right. If Jetty thinks I'm dead, and finds out I'm not, anyone who sides with me will be in danger. Including Claire and the two Erns. Them I don't care about. Claire I do. So I don't answer. Ernie Junior shakes his head. He's figured I'm not gonna show.

"He ain't there," Junior tells them.

"What do you mean? I swear, Clair, he's alive. He was right there in the back when we pulled up."

"Well, he ain't there now," Junior says.

Claire pulls a gun. That a girl. "Step back, you two."

"Now hold on, Claire. He was there. Look, I'll show you."

"Dad, he ain't there now."

"Come out, Picasso. It's okay. You're freaking us out." They start to move towards the truck. Let the world think I'm dead.

"He's in the back."

She has them at a gunpoint now. You go, girl. "Open it."

"Put down the gun."

"Just open it, Ernie."

"Come out. Claire, Jesus, is that loaded? Picasso?"

Junior just waits.

Bubba isn't in on this, so he waits, too.

Claire motions with the gun for Ernie to open the backdoor. Bubba starts to wiggle. He's heard guns before. "Run, Dogman!" Senior Ernie double clicks the backdoor button. It swings open! Blip!

56

Wow, that was close. My head is spinning. I look around. Nothing I'm seeing is anything I've ever seen before outside of picture books. It's all of earth origins but no time and space where I've been invited. The walls are of thick cut stone white washed in painted plaster. The whole room is lit only by candle chandeliers and sconces. An ancient wood table spanning about two first downs expands out from my belly. How my elbows got on it, I'm not sure. I'm underdressed for the occasion whatever it is, I'm sure.

A bounty of food sits before me, and smells out of this world. I haven't seen, or sensed anything like this before. Everything in wood or stone bowls and nothing looks as though it belongs in this Century. Not even the burgundy ornate knit cloth napkins. Have I traveled back in time? Or perhaps I'm on some weird movie set? Or worse, maybe there is a Heaven beyond Earth and I'm about to be shown what I'll miss for not believing? I don't make a move though. In the back of my mind I'm thinking wherever this place exists, it might disappear if I even change my avenue of thought. Maybe this is my Idaho and I've finally made it. Playful female voices come trickling in from a far away corridor off in the corner of the room. It must lead to a hallway or something of that echoing nature. But the voices are no strangers to me. It's them, the two with McGuiness that night. My pizza with beer girls.

"Hello?"

"You like, Cappy?"

"Jerry?"

"Please, here in McGuiness Castle, I am known as Gray."

He's standing behind me. I don't want to know what he looks like after what we've done to him. Maybe he's sparing me the details by staying behind me. "So, you made it back."

"Yes, thank you. It will be a short uncelebrated revival. A few handwritten notes of goodbye. But still, you lived up to your end of the bargain. You got in the box and saved your precious little dog's life. You are a brave man, Jozeph Picasso. Even if Gray must still die in the end."

"What happens next?"

"It's best that you know when the time comes, so don't fret."

"Thank you. Are those the girls?"

"Yes. Not to worry. They are fine thanks to the stones. Packing to travel abroad. I want to give you something."

"As long as it's not a kiss."

"You are very funny. You should write comedy. I want to give you a choice."

"You mean I wouldn't have one otherwise?"

"No."

"Because I'm dead to the world?"

"Yes. In Hollywood, the infamous filmmaker, Jozeph Picasso is dead to the world. Quite gleefully actually. You're being cremated tomorrow. No expense will be spared, thanks to the Burnsteins."

"Hailed a saint? I doubt it in that town."

"You might be surprised to what happens to an image of a scoundrel with the right spin to polish it."

"Nothing surprises me, except the level of depravity from my fellow man and Alien invaders. Are you joining me for dinner?"

"Yes, but I must warn you, I'm not my lovely self."

"I can imagine. It's okay, sit down. I've lugged your head and arm around long enough to be practically immune."

Gray comes from my left. I don't look up. From where I sit I was expecting Jerry to be wearing something richly flamboyant.

Due to the dire situation Gray hides under something that appears from the Carthusian orders of medieval monks. They adhered to strict rules. They wore undyed wool for their monk's clothes called habits, to proclaim their poverty, generally a grayish-white. Both of his arms are there. That's a good sign. He has the hood off to allow his thick red hair to flow down his back. From my point of view, his head seems to be firmly attached at the neck. That's a better sign. I'm not sure what I expected to see. I'm open to whatever, as long as this leads to a conclusion to this mess. At the end of the table he turns towards me. Oh, gees, he's a mess. He didn't even try to repair the damage the cement must have caused drying around his face and the ravage of decay. Not far off from a zombie. He just made himself functional as a whole. Makeup!

"Jerry...."

"Gray, please."

"Gray, I'm sorry."

"Don't be, please. Eat, if you still can."

"You're not that bad."

"I'm hideous, zombiish, I know. This is my own doing, so I walk the earth this way while I still can. To remind me that even I, the most sophisticated Being to ever set foot on this Earth, cannot manufacture a perfect human soul. Even though I've tried and failed to conglomerate it. I'm not sure it doesn't still exist in many pieces scattered amongst you across this planet. What's the maxim?"

"No one's perfect."

"Yes, so sadly true. Breeding you with other species that possessed higher qualities only gave rise to false gods, myths and loathing. When you humans start cloning yourselves in Southern California soon, you will find out. It's your souls you can't manufacture in a Petri dish. Only Mother Nature, from the grains of her body, from what makes up all that is on Earth, can evolve a true living soul. Like a snowflake, human souls are all one of a kind. Humans without souls will be a bane on your civilization in ways you couldn't imagine."

"Like 3D digital actors, they don't actually bleed or cry real blood and no actual tears?"

"If you must see it in such a cartoonish way, yes. But don't mock me, Jozeph. It's not too late for us to save the others."

"Us?"

"It's your choice to help me or not. I can't do it alone. I failed you all miserably. I left you all fallible in your souls and warlike in your hearts. Oh to be human, to feel as you do. But I can't. I'm not. I am me, an It. With nothing left to love me for what I am. What I'll always be, until the end of time, just me."

"You tried for a long time, Gray. Don't be so hard on yourself. We're only human. Where would we be without you?"

"In trees screwing your sisters, most likely. Oh, I know. The power of sexual pleasures upon Earth is greatly appealing. It is so addicting that the constant need to take the sense of its joy up a notch is endless without moral stop gates. The foundation of your god fearing notions helps place a cap on mortal pleasures of which even the best of men and women have succumb to over the ages. Including inside the church's who created them. Without it though, humankind can only destroy itself at the pinnacle of depredation.

Unreciprocated love is not just a metaphor for when its power is put into physical action. Rape involves mind, body and soul, violent and/or otherwise. Even in show and tell Hollywood man must have a soul to survive the temptation of evil. The reality of sexual pleasure is seldom greater than what the human mind conjures up for itself in its attempt to insure the survival of your species. It's in part of these natural human qualities. The sexual imagination. Those your species uniquely enjoy. That makes you so appealing to an It like me to inhabit. It drove me to breed you relentlessly into what you are today, beautiful to look, touch, and taste.

You humans are so lovely with an even stronger more deliciously touching inner beauty. Though you're hopelessly flawed with being insanely jealous at heart. That one human quality, that basic flaw, has put an end to Gray McGuiness. The closest humankind will ever come to experiencing a perfect human being. A true Adonis, he was, in both mind and body. Lacking only an infallible soul. Because even I, with all my unearthly powers, could not manufacture one for him. Yet, he was murdered by human hands in a fit of jealousy. By a bad soul of no more true character or talent for real life than a toad has for hopping to catch a bug."

"Jetty?"

Gray just looks at me with his gray eyes, seeing through me from all I can tell. But he doesn't answer, yes or no.

"Our ability to fantasize and desire to masturbate is our one true human gift to the universe? How sad is that?"

"On the contrary, pollination of many Alien Species is no more or less exhilarating than a gentle breeze or seldom as adventurously random as an inquisitive bee. Your ability to masturbate, your desire to fantasize, and choose your mates have made you a target of Alien domination. My fear of this happening is why I kept you to myself for so long. Incinerating the others for centuries as they arrived without them even knowing I was here.

At first they thought it was the level of ozone and proximity of the Sun. That proved to be mathematically improbable and started them suspecting that something was amiss from Mother Earth. That she was protecting her subjects from them in some kind of mystical way. I only revealed myself at last because they started snatching whole human civilizations from above. They tortured you to death in horrific experiments by the thousands, while trying to figure out why being here on Earth wasn't incinerating you like it was them.

It was comical at first, zapping them like flies. I kept them at bay for hundreds of years. They will never forgive me for this. And look at me now, their final revenge. Taking the one thing from me I coveted the most. My one chance at true human physical perfection. Surely, Mooky filled you in about me and what I'm capable of doing."

"He said he would someday. But I understand, I think. You were protecting humans from the others."

"No, I was hording humans for as long as I could to feed my own lust for perfection. In search of the mix of DNA that could give me what I wanted, a spiritual door… an access to your souls. In the big picture I am no better than them. As humans evolved, so did your focus on personal pleasures. Your sense of vanity that I purposely bred into you to fulfill my own vain needs. It weakened your moral fibers and has kept you from developing farther as a race in so many other intellectual ways. It makes me shudder to think that I failed you all so miserably.

In short, my personal lust to prefect human beauty and my desire to use it for my own satisfactions, inside and out, has allowed all of the others who visit here to manipulate and cruelly enslave you for their greater otherworldly pleasure. Their power and greed spreads across the entire Universe and beyond.

There's very little love spread out amongst the stars. Primarily a thirst for supremacy and a gluttonous need to physically occupy all they can get their hands on. They fully plan to take over Earth once humans have built out modern civilization as far as they want it. Someday you will no longer be needed on the scale that man populates Earth now. You'll be replaced by your own clones and their droids."

"They are using us to heat up the Earth, but will need us as janitors and maintenance men for the future growth of their civilization. So that Nature doesn't reclaim what we've taken from her."

"Yes, and to test your DNA for the gene that will help them become you. This is not over. They will continue this search until they find it."

"Isn't that what you are doing?"

"Yes, but in a much more humane and sexy way."

"How does becoming Gray, and shift shaping to physically molest us, make you the same as them? You're not eating us… well, I guess Gray was… and your girls. Okay, I get it."

"So you have spoken to Mooky about this."

"Yes about that and about them feeding on us.

"As I've stated, I'm a vegetarian. The blood thing is a sickness I can't control. Gray can't control. It's an Alien side effect of using those stones in this form that I am truly ashamed of. It both created and caused an end to this. To me, living amongst you as Gray McGuiness. Pass the potatoes, Cappy."

I look at all the food before me. The stone bowl of baked potatoes lifts off the table effortlessly and travels the distance between Gray and myself. This is his last supper, and perhaps even mine. Besides that bowl, you name it, there's some of it on the table. There's beefs, fowls, pig, a cornucopia of fruits and both raw and cooked vegetables. Surprisingly I'm hungry. So I dig in. Everything of vegetarian nature shuttles back and forth effortlessly between us. No tipping necessary. I look at him and he's smiling a crooked smile. "You're a good cook."

"Thank you. I have help of course. I'll introduce you some other time."

"So, this choice, do I get it freely? Or do I just have to accept one or the other as a consolation prize?"

"People know."

"If you mean the Ernies don't worry."

"If you come back people will know more than we want them to know."

"So, we're talking about the Alien Relocation Program?"

"Would you mind?"

"Yes."

"They were afraid of that."

"So, are we talking about this being my last meal?"

"Oh my, no Jozeph! They don't want to harm you. Both the Council and the Board are considering perhaps relocating you to a different place. As a gift of thanks. I'm just negotiating the deal but I need to know what you want to do first."

"So now you're my agent?"

"Is that so terrible?"

"How different?"

"Have you considered other planets? Say Milicalazarra?"

"Yeah, right. How's that spelled?"

"Seriously."

"If there's a better place, than why are you all here?"

"Because you're here and not there."

"In part because we defecate and decay."

"Yes."

"It's a thought. But I don't think so. My life sucks, but it's biologically mine. I hope. So I'll ride it out. If you don't mind."

"It's the girl, then?"

"Claire? If not, someday another. I'm not done with my life. I've got things I want to put on paper. Things I am meant to say. Maybe even earthling kids someday, who knows. I have a father, a dog, and at least a few friends."

"Yes, you do. I hope you consider me as one."

"Of course. But I'm human. I belong on Earth."

"Yes, you are. A very lucky one."

"Besides, sex with Aliens isn't my bowl of grits."

"How do you know?"

"I know."

"For sure?"

"What are you saying?"

"And you've never even been blown by an Alien?"

"Of course not."

"How do you know?"

"Gray, if I have, I don't want to know."

"In the front seat of your Corvair? The Fall you bartended at Charlie's? That waitress, remember her name? Before the shooting."

"Tina? The double-breasted blond? That was you?"

"I'm good, no?"

"You rotten Alien bastard. You blew me?"

"Do you honestly think a girl built like that, with those looks, would just offer to get you off in the middle of Beverly Hills because she thinks you're a groovy bartender? Someone you worked with? A very nice country girl like Tina?"

"Well...."

"Relax, Cappy. She didn't remember a thing."

"Yeah, I got that."

"You seemed hurt by her."

"I felt used. Afterwards, she just got out. At work she never acknowledged that it happened."

"Tina's fine, in case you're wondering. With three gorgeous children and happily married to a man I found for her in Colorado. He works on satellites. Breasts firm as ever. Hers, I mean."

"You bastard. You still use her?"

"Sometimes she just feels like being naughty. And believe me, he's a lucky man for it."

"One more thing I've learned from you Aliens I can live without."

"You're not the only human who's been with one of us. We're everywhere. In every crowded room. We're on every busy street. Look around, play the odds. Aliens are here amongst all of you. They're more apt to be telling you what to do than not since they look upon you as simple minded Beings at the lower end of the evolutionary pool. But things are coming to a head."

"Don't I know."I look over at a curtained wall when the wind behind it abruptly ruffles it against the marble flooring. It's probably from a ventilating arrow loop funneling air down a small passage. "Is that a garderobe?"

"What, the shithouse? Of course, do you need to use it?"

"That's what I need right now, you watching me take a dump in a hole cut into a slab of stone. Hanging my privates over a cesspit of god knows what or how far below."

"Nothing I haven't seen you do in the woods before."

"Comforting."

"There's no stopping you humans from evolving on us anymore. Your ability and desire to fornicate is uncontrollable."

"So I've heard, from the Mook."

"Watch what you say to him. Regardless of what you think, the Mook follows his own path. He's neither good nor evil."

"A go betweener."

"A true intergalactic mercenary if ever there were one."

"He said my offspring were safe."

"For now. But things are changing quickly. Your Earth Watch high-resolution satellites are getting very close to detecting Earth's darkest truth. That you are not alone. By the way, would you mind not yelling that in public again?"

"I was feeling put upon."

"A far cry from what you'll feel if you keep it up."

"I'm almost over it."

"The Council and the Board, you know, they've had to stop deployment on some of your most sophisticated satellites. Amazing what a little defected chip can cause."

"You married Tina off to an Alien Clone?"

"Like her, just a human we borrow from time to time. He has no idea he's doing these things. Unlike you, he has no choice."

"Then I choose to stay me on Earth and finish the crazy life I started."

"Then I'll see you around."

"I'm open for suggestions on where to go from here."

"Good. I want you involved and helping me. Let Jetty think he's in the clear. When you hear from us, we want you to call him again on that phone Mooky gave you this time. Just keep telling him you're still dead."

"I get to haunt him?"

"Do you mind?"

"Mind? Can I do it now?!"

"No, we need to take care of McGuiness the right way. Give him a decent out. Make him a great mystery like they did Amelia Earhart."

"Will we ever find her?"

"Let's just say she made a different choice."

"So McGuiness must die a human death."

"And Jetty is just the man to take the fall for it."

"I can't wait to see this. Let me visit him."

"If you'd like, Cappy."

"Are you kidding? I'm the writer of canceled sitcom past?"

"Unfortunately, Jetty will be overcome with delusions. But not until I'm done with him."

How fun is that? I have no rebuttal, so I continue to eat. Gray gets up and leaves the room. I drop a pea, and look down to find that I'm sitting here naked. Holy breezeway, Dogman!

"You bastard, Gray!" The moist salty sea air suddenly engulfs me and I shiver.

His voice drifts back to me from down the echoing corridor. "Relax, I'm dead. Your clothes are being washed. So that you show back up in them. As your new powerful agent, I didn't want your upcoming work to stink."

"Hello?" My voice trails away. Alien bastard.

"Oh, relax. He's gone," a familiar female voice says.

Oh, my past. Run and hide, Jozeph, run and hide!

57

I turn and standing behind me is Stacey Carson, the redhead who tried to steal Bubba and kill me. The good news is she's unarmed and without Bubba. Instead, she has the barking cocker spaniel.

"What are you doing here?" I start to choke on my mutton, and she comes to me and whacks me good on the bare back and I spit it out. "Dame that hurt."

"It's better if you chew it."

"I thought you and the dog were feeding Alien babies through test tubes."

"Why would we?"

"Mooky told me."

"That creep. Watch out for him. Gray took us from him and brought us here."

The cocker spaniel comes over and licks my fingers where I spit up into my hand. He's so excited to see me he actually pees on the stone floor. Apparently, something cocker spaniels do inherently. Moving over to eat the mutton projectile I shot onto the tapestry rug below my feet. The tapestry appears to be from a series of seven tapestries dating from 1495-1505 from a culture in the Southern Netherlands. I hadn't seen one, and never on a floor, since touring the Metropolitan Museum of Art in New York City. I know of them from reading my collection of garage sale art books. This tapestry shows a group of noblemen and hunters in pursuit of a unicorn. I'm actually transfixed as much as I'm horrified that this spooky dog is lapping up what came out of my throat off such a magnificent piece of art. He looks up at me. I'm now his forever pal.

"Isn't this place the coolest?

"Dank, actually."

"It's warmer in the other rooms."

"So, you're human? And he, this dog, does he… you know?"

"Why wouldn't I be human, and yes the dog gets these things, side affects Gray calls them? And he licks and pees."

"Stacey, you haven't even learned the dog's name?"

"God, will you shut up about the dog? How about a drink?"

"Please. What's his name?"

"Dog. Grab your plate. The bar's in the next room."I pick up my plate, hold my napkin politely over my nakedness, and follow her perfect figure across the room and out. Dog follows my perfect plate of food. I can't believe that she's still alive. And this dog isn't dead. So I don't. If she offers me sex, I'll know she's Jerry. I'm even reluctant to pet the dog. I surely won't bend over to pick anything up.

"I know what you're thinking.

"I doubt it."

"Still weird I see. I went through the same thing. But I was given the same choice by Gray. I negotiated to stay here until I let them send me elsewhere."

"Like Milicalazarra?"

"Yes. Come with me."

"I think not."

"Please? You can bring that little fur ball, if you like. Or this butt-licker."

"My dog likes it on Earth. So do I. You have my permission to blip away and leave us to our earthliness."

"There are other humans there, famous too. Lots of them whose limelight were fading. Jerry collected and recruited them to replace themselves here."

"Let their clones do the final fade."

"We'll live a long-long time, and age must slower than here on Earth. Please, if I don't go, I have to go up there. And I don't know what that means, but it doesn't sound good."

I stop in the arch of the door to take in the next room. It's a huge room full of four matching pool tables and accessories with a fireplace large enough to put a brass quartet inside. There's also a life size solid gold statue. And what seems to be an authentic Michelangelo painting on the ceiling above me. From the look outside the open arched doors leading to the expansive terracotta tile veranda we're now somehow back in the hills of Sherman Oaks. Even the air is different, dry, dusty and hot, lacking that expensive Bel Air breeze I get at Mystery Towers.

"Is that?"

"Nearly solid gold. Except it's got one of Jerry's people inside that he inhabited long ago. Don't touch it. There's a creepy guy taking care of this place who insists the dust stays on it. I think I saw him peeing on it in a tearful drunken fit. "

"Whatever. Did we just change location somehow?"

"Yes, the view from every window is of wherever Jerry wants you to feel you are."

"Are we actually there?"

"I don't know."

"Are you for real, or a clone?"

She looks at me with an honest quizzical look on her face.

"What are you insinuating?"

"Nothing. You've been here ever since?"

"Yes. It's only been like four or five months. Hasn't it?"

I think it over. "It seems like another lifetime.

"What's the matter?"

"Nothing. You look great. Who else is here, and just where is here, if you don't mind me asking?"

"Here is here. People come and go. Lots of dinner parties. Look at this bar. I think this wood is from an actual Roman ship or something. I was really drunk when told. You'll find it helps in this place."

"What can I get you?" I move behind the bar, in part to hide myself and place my dinner between us.

"I'm set, help yourself. I had Gray put you in my room."

"That's nice. But I don't think so."

"You're not gonna start that old stuff again, are you?"

"Look, Stacey, I'm thrilled to see you again. Truly glad you're not feeding Aliens. But I'm out of here as soon as I put some clothes on."

"I've got them hanging up."

I pull a frock like thing off a chair and wrap it around my hips. I make my way over to the fireplace. It burst into flames, and I bask in its warmth. Dog comes and sits beside me, panting, maybe hoping I'll choke up some goodies. I scratch behind its ears. "So, was I in Scotland in the other room, and now back in Sherman Oaks in here? Is that how it works?"

"She doesn't know, Picasso. You're nowhere and everywhere. It's dimensional, and hardly worth discussing now."

I turn and McGuiness is standing there with my clothes.

"You ready?"

"But you said he could stay?" Stacey says.

He comes to her, wraps his arm around her thin waist, and pulls her close to him under his arm. He holds out my clothes with his other hand and I put them back on.

"We'll get you new shoes and there's fresh underwear."

"Thanks, these sandals will do." I wiggle my two sizes of big toes. "One size kicks all."

"Are you sure you don't want to stay and have a little fun?"

"If it wouldn't be too rude, Gray, I'll just go."

"I told you he wouldn't stay," Stacey says. She's angry. "He'd rather sleep with his little dog, anyway."

"Some humans take it personal when you try to kill them."

"Oh, shut up."

"Shall we?"

"Please."

And just like that. Blip!

58

"Have you ever been to the planet Milicalazarra?"

Ernie Burnstein looks up from his zipper, stopping just outside his private john.

"The intergalactic shuttle bus and large breasted redheaded tour guide is waiting."

"How did you get in here?" He looks at his office door, then to his windows. All closed and presumably locked. I can see that his imagination is locking onto my appearing and disappearing from his SUV last night because his eyes narrow in a drain of brain brownout. His eyes shift back to now, and his office door.

"Don't call those two goons of yours just yet."

Ernie moves to his desk and sits. He's got a black eye not covered very well by cheap makeup. I keep my distance. Just in case I missed a gun when I went through his desk waiting for him to finish peeing. "Where did you go last night?" He sees that his desk was riffled through.

"Scotland."

"Crazy bastard. I'm serious."

"If you won't believe me, why ask."

"I got pistol whipped by an irate actress last night because of your little disappearing act."

"Claire did that to you?"

"She went totally berserk on me. I have thirty stitches behind my left ear. Look."

"Pass. Is it ten a.m. yet?"

"Why? Oh, listen, I don't think it's gonna work out on that movie deal, Picasso. Sorry."

"Why?"

"Claire has made it perfectly clear that after taping these four remaining episodes she wants nothing more to do with Burn Productions."

"Because of what's happened to me?"

"You and that dog of yours. She thinks I nabbed him. That Jetty has something to do with your leg showing up in the river. She's threatening to go to the police with a complaint and to the press if either of us contacts her outside of the show."

"See? No matter what you say, you sound like you're lying."

"Well, I don't believe in ghost. So whatever you are, go back to Krakow, or Scotland or wherever that place is you mentioned and just leave me alone."

"It's not that simple, Ern."

"Yes it is. We got no deal without Claire. And who are you to be making deals if you are dead?"

"I'm not dead, Ern. I'm here in the flesh. And if you don't get those papers out of your desk like you promised, I'll blacken that other eye of yours. And introduce you to Jerry, my Alien agent."

I move over to his desk to make sure he's not pulling any fast ones. He looks up at me with that 'okay, I've got a gun, but I can't get to it' guilty look. "Okay, say you are here, and you and The Magical Man did make it out of that trunk, I still can't sign the papers."

"If you're worried about Jetty, don't."

"Has he seen you?"

"Not yet. You want to invite him over for a settee?"

"No. Look, you saw who dug that hole last night. I don't make the decisions around here without his approval. I even had to lie to him and tell him your dog was Clair's dog to get him on the show. It's been that way. I took a lot of heat for that misunderstanding. So I owe you nothing is how I see it."

"Just get the paperwork together, Ern. Let me worry about Jetty and his New Jersey Cow Association."

I can see Ernie's mind working again. He's so transparent now that his life is on the line. Maybe making these Hollywood types feel that their life depends on doing business with me is the key element I've been missing all this time. Who needs just a threat of an agent when you can use the threat of Alien debauchery, too? If the Big Fish don't need my talents to survive in this town, what good am I to them? Ernie leans forward like we're in a crowded room or something. He's suddenly on my side of the game. A concept that makes my skin scramble away from him. "You get Jetty off my back for good. I'll cut you an iron clad three picture deal."

"You want me to whack Jetty for you?"

"Ssshhhhhh! I didn't say that. I mean, you know, scare him away. Say boooo, or whatever it is you plan to do to him. I know you ain't dumb enough to whack him. Are you?"

"When I come back, I want those papers filled out. A one picture deal. I direct, your son produces and Claire stars and coproduces. I also get final cut. No Gray, no Jetty. No guns, no mob. Got me?"

"Or what?"

"Or you go down with Jetty in killing me."

"But you said you weren't dead."

"As far as you know, I'm still in that chest with McGuiness."

"Are you?"

"Don't have those papers signed and find out." I walk over to his bathroom and close the door. I can hear him get up from his desk, run to his office door, and fling it open.

"You stupid bastards! He's here!"

"Who's here?" Cyber Thug asks.

"Picasso! He's in my bathroom."

"Now boss...." Scare Face says.

"Get your hands off me, you moron!"

"Calm down, boss."

"You're both fired, do you hear me, fired! Now get that bastard out of my bathroom, out of my office, and off this lot!"

I can imagine what the secretarial pool is thinking. Surely, Ern the Burn has blown a cranium circuit board.

"Look, boss, the guy's dead! They're getting' rid of the leg tomorrow! You're payin' for it. Remember?"

"I don't know how he got past these doors. Or why he's not dead. But snap too, and get him out of my bathroom! What are you girls looking at? Call security!"

Maybe they're all waiting to see if I kill him this time. Too bad I have to disappoint them again. Men! No wonder there's so many lesbians in this town. If women can't depend on male suspected mass murdering-slash-sometimes filmmakers to kill their bosses to make room for their promotions, they'll just have to do it amongst themselves!

Excited footsteps come my way. I can't wait around to see how this all ends. Just in case, I don't flush the toilet and leave last night's digested Alien cooked dinner for all to scrutinize. The door flings open. But I Blip away before anyone fills it. I only wish that I could get a look at their reactions when they get a big whiff of my after dinner mint. It would be as satisfying at least as it was in leaving it. If anyone gets photos, Skype me.

59

It's not easy being dead. Carrying on with a normal life is getting tiresome to avoid. I need hot coffee real bad and I'm mentally dying to read the LA Times about my first person past tense Hollywood demise. So logically, in light of what's been happening to me, I find myself outside a coffee shop on Ventura in Studio City. The last time I was here, Mooky was shooting at Stacey, Bubba and I in full escape clause. It ended with a crash and gruesome dissipating Alien murder thrown in to buffer the false allegations. Things look back to normal if not remodeled. Good, those scraping chairs where killing me. A dark shadow appears quickly. I'm not alone. Still. Damn.

"What do you think?"

"I think I was hoping I'd get a moment of solitude to read the newspaper." I move to an open table and sit down along the glass panel Mooky shot out just months before.

"You will, white boy." Mooky sits joining me, adjusting his sunglasses as he smiles. He's got the paper. My best friend.

I look west up Ventura Boulevard. Apparently the torrential rains are gone for now, and our three days of clear skies are upon us... before the roofers get back to tarring our lungs to death. "Just stopped by to deliver you a vehicle."

"Really, where?"

"It's out back." He unfolds the paper. "Here's keys, a blue ninety-nine Jimmy. Old and nondescript but in good shape. This card is for a room. You'll find what you need in the truck."

"You mean, I can't go home?"

"Not yet. Tomorrow, if things work out."

"I understand I'm being cremated tomorrow."

"You want to go?"

"Can I?"

"We'll see, but there's someone we want you to go see first."

"Who?"

"There's a guy in a hospital, a friend of yours who you should talk to."

"J.J.?"

"Yeah. He plans on doin' somethin' that might get in our way of finishing this according to Jerry. So you've got to stop him. He's being released in about an hour. Your friend Erin is picking him up. If we get involved things change."

"They beat him pretty bad."

"Yeah. He's a little unstable, so go easy."

"What do I tell him and Erin if she beats me there?"

"Tell them you got it all worked out. They won't have to lift a finger in getting revenge. And give him this."

"What's this?"

"Cash to go rest somewhere or we take him. Make sure he understands it's better this way."

"How much?"

"Enough to get him out of that hole you let him live in."

"Am I controlling these Blips? Am I doing this on my own?"

"Have you some kind of cool other-worldly-power that allows you to be superhuman and Blip anywhere you want to go, X-Men style?"

"Fine, be sarcastic. Do I?"

"No. We're analyzing your thought process and making the best move for you."

"Really. Analyze this."

"Watch it, Picasso. You need me way more than I need you."

"Hey, guess who I saw?"

"Our little diamond friend.

"And the barking dog, too."

"Too bad you didn't fall for that."

"What do you mean?"

"Nothing. Keep the phone with you. It's in the truck. "He gets up. "Remember they think you're dead. So don't freak them out. And don't tell them anything that's real or we'll have to take them. I can't guarantee their safety if that happens."

"May I?" I reach out for the paper.

"What?"

"The paper. Can I read it?"

"You can have it, but you better go. Erin is leaving work right about now. So grab your joe to go and get moving."

"Can't you just Blip me there?"

"You're gonna need the truck." He starts walking around the corner.

Damn, I get up and go after him. "Mooky, why?" But I know he's not there, and I'm right. Damn him. I look down at the headlines and nothing about me is in them, so I go in to get my joe to go.

Halfway over Beverly Glen I'm still wondering what is about to happen. Why such an old truck, why not a new one? But this Jimmy isn't half bad. My pop still drives one, the two-door version. I like the four-door I'm in better. At the top of Sherman Oaks, I look in the center console and yes the phone is there. And so is a selection of CDs. I give it a look through and come up with the best of Creedence Clearwater Revival. Aliens may be creepy but they know their tunes. Or at least whatever human they took this truck from has good taste of the oldies. I shove the CD in and groove to sixties on the way down between Beverly Hills and Bel Air.

At Westwood Boulevard I start wondering why I didn't ask more specific question on where J.J. is staying. I pull over onto the side of the road and get on the cell phone to ask UCLA Medical where they have him. As I sit there Erin's Plum Explorer cruises by looking like she knows what she's doing. So

I pull back onto the street and follow her down into the underground parking. She has no idea that I'm alive, so why would she suspect that it's me following her? I'm calculating just how to approach this when I get the idea to call her on her car phone.

"Erin speaking."

"Erin, it's Jozeph."

"Who?"

"Jozeph. Look don't...."

"Oh, my god. Jozeph? Who is this?"

"It's me. Look, I'm three parking spots over in a blue Jimmy in the next row, facing you."

"This isn't funny, you sick pervert."

"Erin. Look, I need your help. I'm not dead. Erin?"

"Jozeph?"

"Erin, you have a three and a half inch tattoo on your right shoulder of the Cheshire Cat."

"Jozeph!? Where are you?"

"I... look to your left, three spots over, across from you."

I can see her looking through the windows of the cars. Then she looks up to find me looking at her. I wave. And she just drops out of the picture. Damn, she fainted. I'm feeling a little faint myself. But I get out of the Jimmy and move over to her Explorer. She's out cold. And her door is locked. So I knock. Cars are passing by and people who are getting out of them are looking at me. This isn't good. I knock harder.

"Erin?" Nothing. "Erin?" I rock the truck to get her to look up at me. It's working. Her eyes open. Not remembering why she's lying there. Her eyes lock on me looking down at her through the window and plop, she's out again. This is getting ridiculous.

"Can I be of help?"

Oh-oh. I turn around and a beefy female security guard is standing there. "Ah, my friend has fallen asleep."

The guard looks in. "Asleep, that woman looks out cold."

"She's a heavy sleeper. Narcoleptic. It's okay, I'll get her up."

"Driving a car? She on drugs? I got a Slim Jim in my car. We could pop the lock. Woman should not be driving a truck in that condition."

"I'll give it a go like this, thanks."

"You sure?"

"Positive."

The guard finally walks off. She's not as sure as I am though. I get the feeling she'll be back with the Slim Jim as soon as possible. So I rock the Explorer. Luckily the suspension on these things can be easily rocked if you've never tried. Erin looks up at me again. Her eyes blinking. Drool has formed at the corner of her mouth. She looks close to having an epileptic fit.

"Erin, it's me, Jozeph. Open the door."

Erin sits up. Apparently, she's figured that passing out isn't making me go away. She sits there looking at me. "Jozeph?"

"Yes, Erin, open the door."

"Not on your life."

"Look, we don't have time for this."

"What are you doing here?"

"Erin, that leg wasn't mine. I'm just hiding because there are people looking for me who wish that it were my leg." Yes, I'm lying to her.

"Oh, my god. You're alive then."

"Remember that time Bubba peed right on your entry rug? Remember, you had to throw it out?"

"What color was the rug?"

"White."

"What's Janet's dog's named?"

"Pookems and he lives with her ex-husband, Sammy. He's a scrawny, little white poodle, and not nearly as cute as Bubba."

The door lock pops and I step back to let Erin open the door on her own terms. She's still a little woozy from passing out. She steps from the truck and flings herself into my arms. "Oh, Jozeph, I'm so glad you're alive!"

How do you like that? I've been missed.

"I hope you have a good explanation or I'm gonna hate you in about two minutes when this starts to sink in."

"Look, let's go in and I'll explain everything to both of you."

"Oh, my god, J.J.! They hurt him bad. Broke his arm in five places. He may never be able to give anyone the bird again."

"Who, Jetty's guys?"

"Yes, those men with the mustaches, who claimed to be FBI. They came looking for an arm and head."

"Okay, not here, Erin. Let's go inside, before we're seen. Remember, I'm dead to everyone but you at the moment."

"You haven't told anyone?"

"Just you."

"You're not dead, and I'm the first to know?"

"Erin, you're the only one I can fully trust."

"I'm sure this will lead to no good, but thank you, Jozeph. You better call your father. He's on a plane in the morning."

"Pop is getting on a plane that's not taking him fishing?"

"Of course. He's your father. I called the numbers you had for him and made arrangements to get him here as soon as his friends could find him. It wasn't easy. He was on a fishing boat up near Mackinaw Island. On the Canadian side, and everyone else on the boat spoke only French."

"Really? He must have been working a fishing expedition."

"For some reason, they thought I was the entertainment, and kept asking me to send nude pictures."

"In my entire life Pop hasn't called me once. Now that I'm dead he's getting on a plane?"

"Will you shut up? He's very charming."

"Charming, he's got down. The calling part, he's not so good at. He probably thinks you plan to sleep with him."

"Shut up and give me another hug."

So we hug. And she hugs me so tight all my vertebras crack. Even my extra one. It feels intensely good to be alive again! Even under these extraordinary circumstances

60

J.J. unfortunately isn't feeling as groovy and full of Beatle love songs as I am. He's sitting there stewing in a wheelchair. He's waiting for Erin to take him home, so he can hatch some kind of harebrained revenge scheme. His face is severely bruised, still with a gauze turban wrapped around his shaved head. His arm is held aloft from his body by a rod that is attached to a cast around his chest. Damn, he looks more mummified than I'm supposed to be.

His past I'm not so sure of, but from the look on his crazed face, his future is easily bent on disaster. I don't know if any of his pent up anger is meant for me. When he sees me coming toward him with Erin smiling like a guilty circus clown, his face washes over with a mild confusion. He blinks several times to make sure he hasn't conjured me up by himself. "Picasso?"

"I found him in the garage," Erin says.

"Let's take this outside."I get behind the wheelchair and start to wheel. But J.J. clamps his feet down in a death-brake. He's not rolling anywhere with a dead guy until he knows what the is really happening.

"Who is this, Erin?"

"You know who he is."

"You lost little boy?" I ask him.

He lets his feet-brake go. I can almost smell the brake fluid surging through his brain. But he can't look back at me, so he looks at Erin.

" J.J., you forgot to answer, only my sheep."

"I'm thinking. I'm this close to committing mass murder and now I'm talking to the dead. Did I miss all the fun? Are we all dead? Did I kill the bad guys? Did I win? Am I front page of Variety at last?"

"No, J.J., it's really Jozeph. In the flesh."

"Guys, we need to go now. Or we'll all be front page."

"Excuse me?"

Too late. We turn to find a heavyset nurse with a clipboard. She gives us a look of suffering from a wedgie. "Who wants to sign?" She holds out the paperwork. Someone else is having a bad day. Imagine that.

Erin looks at me. Why not? So, I take the clipboard and sign very clearly, Jozeph Picasso.

"Thank you," grumpy says. "I'll push him out."

"Just get me to the door. I'm good from there," J.J. says.

But the nurse isn't answering. She's looking down at her clipboard again. "Is this some kind of sick joke?" She looks at me, then to J.J. and back to me, then to Erin. She's calculating. She knows who Jozeph Picasso is, and knows he's still dead.

"What's the matter?"I venture to ask.

"We have Mr. Picasso's remains in our morgue, and the press won't leave us alone about it. I don't find your sick joke remotely funny. That pour man is mutilated, lost and dead."

"He's a different Jozeph Picasso," Erin says, hitting me.

Grumpy looks closely at me, and then looks even closer. Her eyes widen in more disbelief than anger. "Are you...?"

"See you around."

"Security!"

Damn, that was a stupid prank. Erin and I push on J.J.'s chair and like that we're on the run-n-roll. We head out of the hospital and back into the underground parking lot. The beefy security guard remembers us right away. She's pointing fingers at Erin's Plum Explorer wanting to head us off at the parking spot. So this is what Mooky meant. The security guard runs for the truck. But we have other plans. I'm not sure why we're running. Last I heard it wasn't against the law to be alive after being declared dead. But who's got time to explain all this. "To the Jimmy mobile, Dogman."

This move surprisingly fakes them all out. While they all clamor around Erin's truck, we make it around to the next row and jump into my Jimmy. Getting J.J. in is a better trick and a half. Where's The Magical Man when you need him? I have to give up on the back seat and roll him on his side through the back hatch. Only, in backing up I don't quite see the security's motorized cart pulling up behind me trying to block me in. With a big kerplunk I tip it over and push it aside. The guy driving is so surprised that he just hangs on for dear life. But the cart does its job because I can only go one way and that is down further into the parking lot. Damn! "Buckle up!" New foot to the floor!

"Look out!"Bam! I smack a Toyota pulling out of a parking spot. This move spins us around until my taillights strike a cement pole. This crushes the back of my brand new old Jimmy. Now I know why this Aliens-on-a-budget gift-ride is a used truck.

J.J. sits up in back, digging the action ride. I'm now facing the right way to get out of here. I don't wait around to sign any more autographs and beat hello back up the ramp. The guards are all waving and waiting for me to sign my death warrant. But instead I wave back on the way by. Luckily none of them are packing. They see that I'm not planning on stopping to pay the fee so they raise the arm just in time for me to make it under. We are back up the exit ramp, nearly leaving the ground at the top. The wee-ha part suddenly turns into the uneven stony exterior drive of toothy jitters as I make it back to Westwood Boulevard and hang my given right and leave.

61

"Wow!"

"You liked that?"

"Can we get on the freeway and have a car chase before they kill us? I want to at least die on national TV news, if I can't make a living at it."

"Sorry, J.J., we don't have time to die right now."

"You never let me have any fun. It could be a real clever career move for both of us."

"The ending of."

Erin's gripping the riot bar on the dash. Her knuckles look about to pop into kernels. "Can we slow down now?!"

"Good, idea."

"You didn't by any chance bring cigarettes or a joint?"

"No, but you're welcome to stick your head outside the truck and suck in some diesel fumes if it'll make you feel better."

"Can I?"

"Anyone hurt?"

"Are we talking hurt before or after getting in this thing?"

"After." I look at Erin. She's still gripping the panic handle. "You still glad I'm back?"

"I'm debating that as we drive 'cause I might've wet myself."

"Hey, what's this? You get me something?"He holds up the package Mooky gave to me.

"That's your waving goodbye present."

"What's in here?"

"Money for your trouble."

"Cash? How much?"

"I don't know. It didn't come from me."

"Those bastards think they can buy me off. Screw them. Take me to Jetty's house. I'll shove this down his throat!"

"It's not from him. It's from a friend, or friends who care that you take a nice relaxing vacation. In a latitude far-far away, and heal your wounds, not your ego." I make a right on to Veteran as J.J. thinks this over.

"This tax free?"

"Yes."

"Wait, don't I get money?"Erin seems disappointed.

"Maybe you'll get beaten next time."

"So, I don't have to leave town?"

"They didn't mention you, just him. They fear he's nuts."

"Mixed-up and assaulted. Holy-mother of ducks! There's got to be fifty grand here! What the..?! What the heck is this, Picasso?""

"Damn, I want a vacation. I need a vacation. I deserve a vacation. I can be nuts. I can be peanut butter in a Jiffy for half that much," Erin says.

"It's more of the same stuff I couldn't tell you guys about."

"This is sexist not giving me shut up money? My mouth is as big as his, easily. And I'm female, I gossip all day. See, women are always paid less than their male counterparts, even in hush money."

"Since when did we become counterparts?"

"When we became his friends and you started getting paid for it.

"J.J., give her some."

"They broke my arm not my brain. Hey, there's a plane ticket in here to Tahiti. Wait a minute. One way."

"J.J., what time is that flight?"

"In about two hours. I can't go like this, I'll be miserable."

"Listen, J.J., I don't know how to put this. But they want you out of the picture for now. I'm afraid if you don't take the flight you'll end up on another flight to places that'll make you even more miserable."

"Why?"

"What have you been thinking for the past couple of days?"

"Anger, revenge, murder, violence, the usual getting even with Hollywood stuff. Why?"

"I think they want you to take a chill pill."

"They again. How do they know what I'm thinking?"

"I can't tell you."

"What's about to happen, Jozeph?" Erin finally eases her grip on the dash to wipe her brow and flex her fingers.

"I don't know for sure, but I think they want to make sure J.J. doesn't get in the way of their plans."

"That punk's friends deserve what I have in store for them."

"They'll end up with a whole lot worse if you let others hand out the punishment on this one. You'll get to do it on the next beating, I promise."

"They're whacking Jetty, and the other two mustache guys?"

"I don't know for sure. I do know that Jetty and his boys still think I'm dead. That's part of the plan."

"What do we do now? I mean me, if I'm staying around LA?" Erin asks.

"You don't have to lift a finger is how it was put to me. I've got a local hotel room for us to camp out in."

"You mean you and me?"Erin looks at me like I might have made an inadvertent indecent proposal. Finally.

"They only gave me one key. So I'm assuming there's only one room. If you want, you can come and crash for the night."

"Can I watch?"

"No, you've got a plane to catch."

"But I don't want to go some place hot and sweaty where I'll get sand and surely itch like a dog under this thing."

"Fine, give me the package."

"It's got my name on it."

"It's a package deal. Money and trip. Or stay and suffer the less than boring consequences."

"Let's see, travel and get the money and suffer, or stay home without the money and suffer."

"That's all I know."

"Am I traveling alone?"

"Not a clue. But if I know these guys, it'll be twisted if you aren't."

"Damn, just what the witch doctor ordered. To the airport, Boss-a-nova."

I don't have time to park, so I pull up to drop J.J. off in front of the baggage handler. Of which he has none. But standing there in all her glory is the double-breasted Hollywood redhead, Stacey Carson. She's got enough expensive baggage for the both of them. And a wheelchair. "Oh-oh."

"What?"

"Take a look at your traveling partner."

"Isn't that... wait a minute. That's the stupid broad who tried to kill us!"

"Maybe she's not waiting for you," Erin proposes.

"Yeah, maybe she's holding a J.J. sign up for another victim. There's got to be hundreds of them in this town."

"It's your call."

"But she stole Bubba, hit me, and tried to kill the two of you." Erin reminds us.

"People change."

"Usually for the worse in this town."

"Maybe she went to violent woman rehab and came out a salt of the earth. But I doubt it with a look like that on her face," J.J. says, getting a clear look at her. "Wait, are her tits bigger?"

"J.J., I'm still here."

"Well?"

"Just go."

I get out and open the back for him. Getting mad J.J. in was easier than getting excited J.J. out. We don't break any of his cast so I'm counting both our blessings. By the time I have him on the curb Stacey is standing there with the chair waiting.

"It's about time."

"We didn't know we were coming until just moments ago."

"Neither did I, but I'm here on time."

"J.J.?"

"I'll handle this. Listen red, I'm not in the mood for bullshit from you or anyone else from this day forward. If you're coming with me, you best learn how to like it. Untie that knot you got up your shorts, or I'll untie it for you. You got me straight?!"

"I was...."

"She's not going. Erin, you want to go with?"

"Fine! I'll be nice. It's either you or them, and I'm just tired of hanging around that old place, with that dog."

"What old place?"

"I can't tell you. If I do they'll have to kill you. And me."

"Picasso, what should I do?"

"Buy condoms. Last I heard she had this bladder thingy."

"You bastards. I made that up."

"Good. Picasso, if you're still alive tomorrow, will you start my truck once in a while?"

"Sure, have a nice trip."

"Let's go, Stella."

"I got your Stella, buddy."

Erin rolls down the window. "J.J., please call us when you get there. Make sure, okay."

"Why not, the phones are usually by the bed."J.J. gives Stacey the big fisheye.

Stacey pushes him toward the skycap and the mound of luggage. She looks back at me, her eyes sad. Maybe she's not coming back. Maybe J.J. is, maybe they'll make it to Tahiti, maybe Milicalazarra. It's hard to tell from that one look.

"J.J.?"

"It's okay, Picasso. Whatever happens next happens. I know something weird is up. No worries. I'll see you again. Goodbye, Erin. Look after him."

"I will."Erin wipes a tear from her eye.

J.J. turns away from us as Stacey steers the chair towards the door. Their luggage is being pulled away by a skycap. "How come your tits look bigger?"J.J. asks her.

"It's the bra."

"Too bad."

"Shut up."

"Mush."

"What's in the package?"

"A very expensive time."

"How expensive?"

"I'll tell you under the sheets of our cabana."

Stacey looks back at me again as they hit the opening doors. I give her the thumbs up. She narrows her eyes at me. But she's in, and she knows I'm out. And that's the way it will be from now on.

I get back into the Jimmy and drive off. In the mirror I can see J.J. waving his ticket at a skycap with his good arm.

"Is he coming back?"

"I really don't know."

"Where are we staying?"

"Erin...."

"Don't worry. We're friends, right?"

"Best friends, last I looked."

"Good. Because I got news for you. I plan on getting laid tonight."

"Really, with anyone I know?"

"You've met him, but sometimes I have my doubts if you really know what a great guy he is. Despite what everyone else in this town thinks of the stiff."

"Oh, well, let me put this in perspective. If you turn around and find me suddenly not there, don't take it as a rejection, because I have no control in these matters."

"You mean mentally or physically?"

"Both."

"You know, you're just weird enough to make this all worthwhile."

"You haven't seen anything yet."

"Yes I have. Only this time, I'm planning on some live action because we never know when you'll be declared dead again."

Wait until she gets a load of my one hairy butt cheek, over sized right foot, and unwanted tattoo. If weird turns Erin on, I've got quite the night planned for her.

62

The light on the situation is always altered once you get into the hotel room, and you've come to the moment of putting out or shoving off. Of all places they've booked me a non-smoking suite in Studio City's legendary Lodge Hotel on Ventura Boulevard, in the heart of San Fernando Valley. It says so right there on the menu.

After dinner in the Café, just outside the pool area, we made it to the bar and downed two vodkas and tonics to ease our burdens. It didn't work. Both of us are avoiding the inevitable situation of spending the night in the same bed. Or one of us cub-scouting on the couch. To mate or not to mate, that is the question hovering like fog on a crowded tarmac, beautiful yet dangerous to land in. We hesitate like seagulls hydroplaning on a jet stream, just at the peak of flapping our wings in flight. It passes unsaid, which to me is just as well. It's been so long, I fear I'll need training wheels to keep me up.

Later, there wasn't much on TV so we just kind of sat around for awhile waiting for the sleeping arrangement conversation to naturally arrive. That was about five minutes ago. Two of us, one bed, and the couch ain't much of a ride. Since then, Erin's been in the shower, and I sit here waiting my turn. I feel as though my life is in some kind of limbo, a writer's purgatory of not being able to finish my work. Knowing that I'll never get any sleep until I do. Being a natural born writer is a killer obsessive thing because most of the time while a writer writes he's thinking of sex, and most of the time while he's having sex he's thinking of writing. If this isn't prevalent amongst women writers as well, than how lucky they must be to feel an absolute contentment within their creative world.

Because personally, I find that there is a fine line between masturbation and writing on spec. No matter how hard I try to touch reality with my work, I really haven't accomplished anything until someone else enjoys my efforts. How cheap it must feel to be a well paid hired left hand. What writer in this town hasn't been jerked around trying to make some visionary like Ernie's fantasy come true?

"I'll be out in a minute."

"No rush."

"You can come in if you want."

"I'll wait. I like to fog up my own mirrors and write funny words."

"Me, too." Erin comes out with a towel wrapped around her from her armpit to just below her pubes. Another towel is wrapped around her head to dry her hair. "Anything on?"

"We can order a movie."

"Something good? Or something bad?"

"Your call. Did you save me a towel?"

"Of course."

"Then I'll be right out."

"I'll be right here."

I go into the bathroom to find the words YOUR MOVE written on the mirror in steam. I write IF ONLY. I turn on the shower to find a bathtub with the hanging curtains that always makes me wish I never traveled. But if nothing else, I need a shower so I look down to kick off my sandals and....

Blip!

63

I'm standing in a dimly lit dome Mediterranean mural covered foyer. It's full of knockoff Italian art with a live overflowing olive tree as its center attraction. A white marble staircase that Julius Cesar would've been proud of being stabbed on twists up nearly a hundred steps to a balcony overlooking the foyer. It leads into the rooms upstairs. Nice. Someone has some bucks.

An unfamiliar grand piano composition drifts in through a corner archway. It's not overly good but live. The fingering is more progressively sad than anything else. Maybe it's due to the waste of superior piano lessons on someone with no ear for original fine music. I follow it slowly because I'm not exactly sure where I am but I've got a hunch. Hunches are sometimes all one has to go on in these kinds of absurd Alien games.

Sitting behind an ivory-white Steinway is Jetty DiGarbo. I can tell he's feeling blue because his fingers are experiencing the inner turmoil. What a shame that in such a monumental moment, he would have so little originality to express. This is probably as close to emoting true natural emotions besides uncontrollable rage that he's ever had.

If he were a real actor, which he is not, he'd know he's having an emotional breakthrough in his career over all this. And perhaps not hate me so much. If I know Jetty, and I at least think I do, he's just wallowing in a pool of self-pity because he's drunk and bimboless for the night.

Blip, I find myself at the bar. I'm feeling a tad blue myself. Nice, Jetty still drinks Johnny Walker Black. He's got himself a glass. I grab a glass and the bottle and head over to where he sits. His plush white carpet helps to hide my steps. He doesn't look up until I'm reaching out with the bottle and refilling his glass. Only he doesn't freak like I would if the guy I buried alive just poured me a drink.

"Mind if I join you?"

"Go away, Picasso. I mean it."

"I can't, Jetty."

"Then tell me how you got out of that box."

"So you spoke with Ernie."

"He made me come over and look at a pile he claims you left in his toilet."

"That convinced you that it was me?"

"No. But MacAroy and Tucker came over and took a look. They told us what you'd done to them with the sodas in their car seats."

"They still think it's funny?"

"Yeah, we all got a big chuckle out of it."

"It's all about the laughs, isn't it, Jetty."

"What do you want, Picasso?"

"My life back. But I'm not calling the shots."

"No, you're not." He pulls a 44 magnum I probably should've suspected deep down he would have waiting for me, and points it at my chest. "I am." He pumps four deafening slugs into my chest! Blam! Blam! Blam! Blam! If you've ever been shot point blank by a bum actor then you know what I'm talking about. If not, wait, with the down turn of the economy maybe you'll get your turn someday. At this proximally the bullets must have passed right through me because I can hear glass shatter all over the bar area. That should leave a mess. Good. I plan to bleed all over his place.

I'm waiting for my legs to buckle underneath me, only they don't. I'm not feeling anything other than the Scotch burning my gut. Jetty is looking at me as though he's seen a ghost. He looks down at his smoking gun, then back up to me. I'm nearly as confused as he is until I remember Mooky showing up as a hologram. I look down, there are no holes in my chest, no blood, and I'm still feeling groovy. If I'm not here, how could I be holding this glass of Scotch and feeling it in my system? Does it really matter? If Mooky could poke my eyes while a hologram, can I poke Jetty? It's worth finding out. So I poke him good. What a crybaby. He starts howling like a hound dog on a burning stick.

"You prick. I wear contacts."

"What do you expect? Kisses? You shot me."

"You're not even hurt. You're ah, you're... what are you?"

"I'm a hologram, Jetty."

"A what?"

"A hologram."

"You're not a ghost?"

"This isn't Christmas, Mr. Scrooge. You're not about to see your mistakes paraded by with chained wails and get a second chance through me."

"Damn, this hurts. What do you want from me, then?"

"I have no idea why they sent me here. But it better be good because I was about to have sex for the first time in two years."

"Two years, really?"

"Being an out of work Hollywood writer-slash-murderer sucks with the ladies."

"Yeah, working directors get all the killer snatch anyway. Just so you know the next time you meet a chick in a bar you want to bed. Don't tell her you're writing a script. She'll know you're desperate for attention and will expect you to ask her to read something stupid in bed. Don't tell her you produce either. She'll expect high end money and/or a job and will jerk you around until you fork either over. Even then she'll walk all over you. I know all about that one."

"Claire's been playing you, huh."

"Stupid bitch. I couldn't get her alone long enough to put a decent move on her. Believe me I tried. I even created a show for her. So I had a legit reason to hang with her. That pooch of yours, and the dike she hangs out with keep gettin' in the way."

"The pleasant little PA. I've learned to love?"

"Yeah, Debbie, I couldn't shake her."

"At least you gave getting in her pants one hundred percent. That should be good for something considering your track record with the ladies on both costs."

"You can forget about it, Picasso. I know what you're trying to make Ernie do. We won't be signin' a contract with you to direct, write, or wipe the smirk off your face with. I don't care who wants to be in it. Or who you say your friends are."

"You're just sore because I won't let you change my dialogue."

"Without McGuiness there's no way that script will get off the ground."

"And you made sure of that."

"You bet I did."

"Do you know what you've done?"

"I killed a freak who was waxing some dumb kid when I found him. A guy who was in my way of the woman I want to marry and have kids with. Just like you and your dog."

"You hurt Bubba and I swear...."

"Forget about it, it's over. She's leavin' the show, walkin out on us, so your dog's not a problem anymore. You still are. Whatever you are."

"I'm not your problem, Jetty. McGuiness is."

"Screw him."

"I get the feeling it's gonna be the other way around."

"I suppose he's not dead, either."

"No, he's dead all right. The Alien who created him isn't."

"Don't start with that again. We're God's people. There are no Aliens."

"Do you have any other explanations to why I'm here?"

"Look, there's lots of unexplainable natural things goin' down on this planet that I ain't got a clue about. What does it prove?"

"That you're ignorant?"

"Keep gettin' cute, Picasso."

"Where are your two Mustachio Twins?"

This seems to make him think. Bullets have been fired and no one's here to find out why. He looks back at his gun. "They must not have heard it."

"Even you're not that dumb, Jetty."

"Maybe you'd like to hurry up and tell me what it is you want."He pours himself another glass and drinks.

I just watch him because frankly I don't have a clue as to why they've sent me here. I'm sure I'm a precursor to worse news. But so what? He's not freaking out or doing any of the things I hoped he'd do. Maybe this is all in the big plan. And I'm just too close to see it.

He gets up and walks away. "Goodnight."

"Jetty."

He stops and turns back to me. "Go away, Picasso. Nobody wants you in this town. Just go far away. Go back to Detroit. But leave this town."

"And leave it to dishonest bums like you?"

"Look, I may never get nominated for an Oscar. But I've made my mark in this business. I'm immortal as long as this stinkin' town exists. I'm very rich, I'm famous, and I've done everything I wanted to do. Screwed who I wanted. When I wanted. I even screwed you, Picasso. I got you fired from Charlie's. Told them I wouldn't spend money while you worked there. So they canned you on Christmas Eve. Mary Christmas by the way."

"Yeah, you've screwed everyone. Except Claire Davis. She's on to you. She knows what a shithead you are. You'll never get to make love to her. Even if you do get her in bed. You may fool yourself into thinking you have everything, Jetty. In the end you still don't have anyone to share it with. No one to pass all this wonderful life onto. Even your brother is dead. You'll soon be forgotten with no one to care that you've gone."

"Shut up. I've got my star on Hollywood Boulevard. And you, what have you done? Nothin'. You're a nobody. A bum hack, a murderer in the eyes of tinsel town. So buzz off. If I die tonight, I'll have lived a life you will never own."

"A life of punching out little guys in bars? Of humiliating anyone and everyone who gets in your way? Cutting off heads and burying other filmmakers alive because you can't have the girl you want? You call that making it? Well, I got news for you, Jetty. I call that pathetic. You're mayor of loser town."

"You think any of this is real, Picasso? This is as fake as you standing there now. Reality is what the public's mind perceives of it. To the world I'm a god. And you, you're nothin' but pond scum. The low of lows. You can't even make it at your own chosen profession. You ain't but an out of work hack. A filmmaker who hasn't made a thing worth watching. As far as I know, you're still locked in some Magical Man's trick box with a dead queer magician. Buried in some Sun Valley drainage ditch. You were nothin' when I met you, suckin' up chump change off the bar. And you're still nothin', livin' off your little piss head poodle that ain't even yours. It's your ex-girlfriend's. You'll have nothin' to live on when she comes back for him. If you ain't dead, I'll make sure of it."

"That's low, Jetty, even for you. My mother was a bartender. Both my grandfathers where bar owners. It's a respectable occupation."

"Not when you got dreams of doin' somethin' else, pal. Somethin' you ain't ever gonna be. You're a never was in this town." And he leaves me there with those words. A never was ringing in my head. The dirty rotten bastard.

I can't wait a hundred years for his walk-of-fame star to decay. I want to go after him and pulverize him right now. When I take the first step toward avenging my self-esteem....

64

Blip! Oh, no! I'm back in Gray's chained and padlocked trunk... and possibly six feet under. Alone and in the dark! "Jerry? Gray?! Somebody! Help me, somebody! "Why is this happening? Why am I back in the Magical Man's magic trunk? Where is Jerry? Where is Gray? Whose trick is this? What is that sound? Thumping? Shovels! They're digging me up?! Someone is digging me up! What do I say? What do I tell them? Who's doing the digging? What is about to happen to me? How long have I been here? Gees, there's a lot of questions left to be answered when being buried alive. Even more if you're still alive when they're digging you back up.

The thump of shovels on your tomb is never as loud as it is when you're still breathing. They've stopped! I can only hear muffled voices. Like maybe they've stepped away taking a cigarette break before finishing. Great! I finally quit smoking, and cigarettes have reached into my grave to kill me anyway! I got better news. So I start yelling. "Hey, hurry up! Hey, I'm still in here!"Everything goes quiet outside. "Heeeellpppp!!!

"Did you hear that?" It's Mike. Of Mike and MacAroy.

"Yeah. Sounded like it came from in there." So, Mac's here, too. How comforting to think they, Frick and Frack, are concerned that I might live to tell a true Hollywood Murder Mystery. Wouldn't A&E love to hear from me? I don't know for sure what got them here. But my bet is that I wasn't the only visitor from his jerk off past that Jetty got last night.

"Someone get a doctor over here. I think we got a live one."

"Didn't he say he cut him up?"

"Well, dig you dumb asses!"That a boy, Mike. Pretend you weren't here from the beginning of this mess.

"What's the matter?" I don't know this voice.

"Someone's still alive in there, Captain," a digger says.

"That's impossible. It's been buried for over two days."

"Hey, you dumb shits. While you're debating if I'm still alive, I'm dying to get out of here!"

"Shit! That came from down inside. Dig him out. Hurry up. Faster. Use your hands if you have to!"

"The mud keeps slipping back in the hole, Captain."

"Get that truck over here. Now."

I can hear a truck pull up. Maybe an ambulance. Who cares? "Get me out of here, Captain!"

"Loop a strap around the chain. Do it. Now!"

I don't know this Captain, but I want to have his babies. Then a sudden jerk and the trunk is pulled out of the hole. It slides about ten feet. I'd start kicking but I'm bent over, face against the floor with my knees up in my belly. I can hear the chains around my tomb being played with.

"Shoot it off."

Now wait. Whose...?

"Stand back," Mike yells.

"No, don't let that bastard..."Blam, blam, blam!

"You stupid bastard, you shot into the trunk."

"It was an accident," he tells them. "A ricochet."

"I saw it. Bounced right off the lock." Good old MacAroy.

I can see light and feel fresh air. I'm not feeling any pain. But, maybe I'm still just a hologram. Maybe...."

Jiggle, jiggle, and squeak. The trunk opens. "He's bleeding. You shot him bad, Mike," the Captain says.

I guess I'm really here in the flesh and blood. I try to say something but my brain and body don't seem to be reacting together anymore. Am I really dying? Finally!

"There's a whole body here," a digger says. "It's Picasso."

"Where's The Magical Man. Where's Gray McGuiness?"

"Maybe we dug in the wrong place."

"We got Jozeph Picasso here! And he, wait a minute, he's got both legs," the other digger yells.

"He does? Shit, he does? Then whose leg are they crematin'?" Mike sounds so sincere.

"Hell if I know," Mac says back to him.

I want to look up and join in on all the talking but I can't.

"Get him out," Captain says. "Mike, give me your gun."

"What? Why?"

"Just do. You're on suspension as of now. You two, Mac."

"I didn't shoot him on purpose. How would I know who was even in there."

"I don't know what you know. But I do know this... you just put your butt in a sling. I should've done this when you two shot those guys up a Jetty's place this morning."

"Shit. They come at us with guns, Captain."

"Don't they all. Take them both out of my sight. Now, you take it easy, Mr. Picasso. We got you an ambulance. We're taking you to St. Joseph's. Mr. Picasso? Can you hear me?"

Yes, but can I answer? No, I can't. The last sounds I remember is being put into the back of the truck. On an IV. I look over at one of the emergency guys and he winks at me.

"Don't worry, Jozeph. It's over. You're in good hands." He says this to me but his lips aren't moving.

"Jerry?" If I can hear his thoughts he can hear mine.

"Always love to play doctor. Would you like a prostate exam while I'm here?"

"Take me home, Jerry."

"Yours or mine?"

"I just want to see my dog."

"It's time to put a little Hollywood agent backspin on this sordid story. You ready?"

"You spin, Jerry. I'm sleeping."

65

When I wake up again, I'm sitting up in my bed with extra pillows keeping me from falling over. I put my eyes on the watercolor painting across the way to let them focus. All I can see is the frame and a shinning of the glass. All the color is hidden in the gloom of night. Voices come up the hall from the living room. Familiar voices I think, but female. I move my arms and they work. Not bad so far. Eyes and arms. I can live with that. My toes wiggle. My knees bend and I move my toes to the edge of the bed and plunge them down to my carpet. Not bad at all.

Wow, head rush. I flush over on my back, the world whooshing over top of me like long wet hair. Wow! Take another hit. What was that? I sit back up. Man, what do they got me on? "Let's try this again, Jozeph."Hey, I'm talking to myself. Imagine crazy old me, jabbering away to myself. What a phenomena? Crazy Jozeph Picasso speaks... to himself, again.

I make it to my feet. I'm determined to find out who's in my living room. I can now hear the colored balls from my table scatter as I near the two restrooms at the end of the hall. I want my dog. I need to use the john but not nearly bad enough to stop me from finding out who's here. Through the kitchen I can see a perfect female bottom bending over my table in just a hint of a skirt. Pink panties. At least in this light. Hey, I'm focusing now. Okay, so far I'm still in the pink. The bottom takes her shot and stands up and it's Claire. Claire Davis, the witty comedian, budding superstar, in a mini with pink panties? The Claire Davis is in my apartment in a mini bending over my table giving me a glimpse of daylight. Okay, fine, I'm dead, but I'm not in hell, yet. I make it past the refrigerator and click the light off as I go. I'm dead, but as far as I know I'm stilling paying the bills around here. The change of light turns Claire's head as I enter into my poolroom-slash-dining room. Claire smiles warmly. She wants me. The other two hot women playing pool with her want me too. I can tell. This is so sad.

"Jerry, you are pathetic?"

"Jozeph?"

"Give me a break, Jerry. You're not doing this to me again. Now get out. All of you, get out."

"Jozeph?! What are you doing?"

"Do I look like I woke up in a Magic Man's portmanteau? Now put Claire back where you found her and stop messing around, Jerry!"

"Jozeph? We stopped by to drop off your dog, like your note said. Come here, Bubba. We were waiting for you to wake up."

Bubba looks up from the couch. "Great, Dogman's awake and still crazy. Let me sleep." He puts his head down and goes back to wherever he was.

All three girls have beers. There are three other empty beers sitting on the counter scattered amongst the refuge of three carry out Italian food containers. "How do you feel?

"Confused?"

"Everything's okay, Jozeph. Beer's are in the fridge, and there's pasta and bread left."

I look back at the fridge. It's got to be Jerry. He's got Claire Davis here. I don't know what's happened, but it ain't gonna happen if it didn't already. I know Jerry digs me. He knows I dig Claire Davis but this doesn't make it okay. Not even bringing the other girls in to watch or whatever.

"Jerry, can I speak to you over here." I move into the kitchen, out of sight of the other two girls and motion him to bring Claire's scrumptious body to me. She comes over. Spike heels, mini, nearly a see through white cotton blouse tied at the waist. Her belly button smiling up at me. She looks much like she's using the pool stick as a weapon, but I'm not dangerous. So what's wrong with this picture?

"Who's Jerry?'

"You are, Jerry. Stop this."

"Stop what? What's the matter with you?"

"Okay fine, you blew me once in a parking lot, but it ain't happening again."

Smack! Can you believe it? She... he... It hits me. "Jozeph, snap out of it. You're scaring me."

I look at Claire. She's scared. But she's an actress, a working one, so what does any of this tell me? Damn, that hurts! "What is going on?"

"You tell me? First you're dead. Then you're not dead. Then I get this note from you to bring over your dog. When we get here, the doors open and you're babbling in your sleep like some crazy castaway."

"I never wrote you a note."

"Well, someone had one delivered."

"Jerry...."

She raises her hand again.

"Not you, someone I know. Jerry must've contacted you."

"People are looking for you. You're all over the news. They went to dig up the dead body of Gray McGuiness and instead they found Jozeph Picasso, alive."

"They don't call him The Magical Man for nothing."

"Don't you get it? I mean the police, the News Channels, Erin, they're all calling here wanting to know where you are."

"And?"

She hands me a note written in my handwriting. "You wrote that, right? That is your handwriting to bring you Bubba?"

"Yes. It's mine. It's just that. What day is it?"

"Jozeph. You were found in a box this morning. They were expecting to find McGuiness' mutilated body, but instead they found you in one piece. You were shot by that cop, Mike Tucker. Who by the way, is under investigation. That other one, MacAroy, too. An ambulance was seen driving you off. Two men were in that truck. The truck was found abandoned not far from where they dug you up. Now, do you want to tell me what happened? What happened to them? How did you get here? Where is the body of McGuiness? I need to know before I talk to anyone else about this."

"I told you, he's The Magical Man. You'll have to ask him."

"That's not going to cut it, Jozeph. What's going on?"

"Claire. Remember I said there were things I couldn't tell you about? Things that were better left unsaid? Better left unknown by either of us?"

"I thought it was just bullshit. But yes, I remember."

"Well, this is more of that bullshit."

"This and That?"

"A little more of That than This."

"So, now what?"

"A mini? You in a mini?"

"We were on our way out."

"Where?"

"Come with us."

"I don't know."

"You'll like it."

"Jerry?"

"I thought we got rid of him."

"I think it's time you girls left."

"Come play. There's an afterhours club I want to show you."

"Take her home, Jerry. Or you are never welcomed back."

"One night, come on." The other two girls enter. Jerry's got good taste. But I'm not going there. Not tonight. Not like this.

"To her home. Take these two lovelies and put them back where you found them. Or I start telling the truth about Gray McGuiness and just how his last and greatest disappearing trick really worked as soon as everyone finds me again."

"Can't blame a girl for trying."

"Or an Alien It. You were testing me, right?"

"Come on, girls."Claire stops to face me head on. The two girls right there behind her. More than any man rightfully deserves. "Mr. Picasso is indisposed for the evening. And may live to see another."

"He's not coming with?"

"Ah, I never slept with a real dead guy."

"Not tonight. Thank you, ladies. I promise to die again." I wave goodbye.

Like that they go out the door. I think. I didn't actually see the light from the hall or hear a door. Just around the corner and gone. That was close. He almost had me there. Claire in a mini. The thought does tend to linger. But I'm home, and I've got my dog. Bubba!? "Bubba?"

Bubba comes around the corner. He heads to his water dish. Slurp-slurp-slurp. He looks up at me. "You're pathetic, Dogman. I would've licked them all silly and I don't even have balls."

"Yeah, but I'm alive, and home, with all my... or at least four working limbs and I've got my dog back. And that ain't half bad. I look at the clock. It's much too late for a mini skirt. Ah, I mean a martini, but I'm having one just the same. I go to my wet bar and pull out the vodka. I look at the bottle. Amanda, Gray's Russian friend, made her last drink from this same bottle. The one I ended up drinking and finding myself out at the beach with the head of McGuiness. To the drain with that.

Okay, all is okay. Underneath the sink I've got some good stuff, my expensive stash, VOX from the Netherlands. Eighty Proof. And this is all the proof I need to know I'm home. After putting the left over pasta into the microwave I take my drink to the overstuffed burgundy chair, plop down in front of my new fifty-two inch flat screen and grab the remote. I've got a lot of questions. Some that may even be answered by the boob tube. I flick from channel to channel.

I'm up close and everywhere. I'm the pun of the moment. I'm the gold coin lost at sea. I'm the needle in every haystack. But no one knows where I am. Yet, here I am safe and sound in Mystery Towers. Home alone with my dog. I get up and turn off all the lights. And go over to my computer and turn it on. I get on the Internet to checkup on my Lions. The NFL Draft is coming up. I check my e-mails and I must have at least three hundred messages. Facebook and LinkedIn are jammed.

I open a few e-mails to find out that they are cyber condolences. To the cyber world I'm dead. To the real world I'm missing. And to the Space Travelers Advisory Board and Alien Security Council I'm just playing hard to get. What's an unemployed filmmaker to do in this Alien Biz? I don't have a clue, so I pet my poodle. And Bubba, he's all for it. "Pet away, Dogman. Then take me for a dump and drag."

Oh, I long for the real world of Picasso-land. But somehow I get the feeling that The Mystery Towers Magical Tour has just left the station. The moon passes overhead. Clouds scurrying by underneath it. No cars driving by boom music. No voices below. No neighborhood honking. I hear only the wind in the trees outside. Like that, I track the moonlight through my pine trees growing strong in front of my office's tower window.

The light is very subtle and calming to the envied human psyche. It's very peaceful to the soul clinging to my bones for dear life. The wispy sent of pine needles and sap fills the void of smog in the breeze. I could get use to this. Just me and my dog. Unfortunately I know it can't last. The true gloom that hangs over every human on Earth, no matter what life we live, is the only truth of all life, that this life is destined to come to a sad end. Maybe if the Aliens took this into account like Jerry does, maybe they wouldn't strive to be so much like us.

66

Early the next morning I realize the dented GMC Jimmy given to me by the Mook is parked downstairs in my parking spot. The keys are in it under the floor mat. My guess is that Erin got tired of waiting for me to come out of the shower and drove it home. She is probably now at work. So I go around walking Bubba to the empty lot behind my place and let him do his doody dance. I pick it up and make my way back down to the trash. The chute is as clogged as it can get. With much grumbling I unplug it and get rained on by kitty litter. Some things will never.... I stop myself right there. Because, yes they can. They can change if I put some effort into changing them. If nothing else, these past few days have proven that. Shit changes as often as the tide trying to wash you out of a beach house while gripping a dead clone's head. And who'd know better than I?

So I take Bubba back upstairs. I let him into the manager's apartment, my home, room 308. I make my way to my supply cabinet in the kitchen and pull out some good strong packaging tape. I go back out into the hall and move over to the garbage chute. I don't know why I didn't think of this. Sometimes you miss even the brightest of lights and get hit by the train. But it comes to me in my morning after of newfound glory. The world isn't all bad. The world isn't doomed because we are not alone. The world will not end if we humans disappear from it. The world will go on. And in time repopulate itself with someone or something else. Hopefully that special something will be more sophisticated and less destructive than the type of humans that have rented from me in the past. If nothing else, like all Earth's creatures, we are evolving. Like early man before us, the caveman and the tree dweller man will always be deep within our natural psyches and genes. For some, closer to the surface than in others. Obviously it is, from what I've seen thus far.

But now, after Jerry has led us out of our caves and trees, and has stopped zapping the other Aliens. The others visiting this planet still fear that we will soon evolve into knowing that they are here with us. They are using us to create Alien friendly environments that they can live in and on. At the same time, they are feeding upon us. Drinking us, cloning us, using us, and researching a way to enhance our blood so that they can use it to live here like one of us. They are willing to do anything to us to help them stay here in paradise forever. Earth, the Heaven of our Solar System. If we humans would simply admit we were already here, how different history would be, for good or bad.

Even under their supervision we have grown another vertebra. We have already allowed parts of our unused brains to be activated by increasing nerve flow and blood supply. Mooky and Jerry haven't told me this. In fact they'll contradict it again I'm sure if I bring it up. But I've got a hunch it's started. I'm sure the results haven't been good. Or we'd all know about it. Yet we might if we look closely at the supposedly insane. In time there will be the first to survive the mutation if they allow it to happen. Or if they can't stop it from happening naturally because it's happening simultaneously everywhere across the human races.

I've known about my unused vertebrae for years, but thought nothing of it. My chiropractor said it wasn't uncommon when I asked about it. Ask your chiropractor. Maybe he or she doesn't understand why either. Maybe they are one of them. Look at your x-rays. Why does the medical field not want to dignify the close examining of the spine by the masses? What are they, who are they, and why are they afraid of what we'll find? Signs of evolution in our skeletons, or nerves, our blood flow? Are we really evolving into something else by simply breeding amongst ourselves? To some other higher form of human life? Are they really trying to stop it? I don't know. It's possible in the light of what I've been told.

Turn around and there are thousands of us. And if we breed together, it will accelerate the change. How many times has this evolutionary development come about? If the Aliens are breeding us, guiding us, have they stopped certain DNA from interacting? Are they keeping us from evolving naturally? Is the spaceman really keeping the rest of us down? I don't know. NFL-NBA anyone?

If all of us find out they're here, will we experience another Dark Age to erase the memory or will it be a sudden brimstone and fire from the heavens like Sodom and Gomorrah? Will the switch be pulled from our power grids? Is there a reason we are so dependent on ground based power other than to continue to heat up the earth? Can they flip a simple switch and actually stop all mass computer communications with our satellites? Are we the inmates and they the guards to some kind of earthbound prison? Are we the next Atlantis? The Mayans? The Greeks, the Romans? Too advanced in our knowledge for our own good? Will we force them to reset man's evolutionary clock back thousands of years for what they consider our own safety? Could they, would they, should they do that to us? I don't know.

They are here because we process waste, fornicate and decay. We don't know they are here because they have evolved beyond those mundane things. We decay and make reusable soil. They dissipate and produce what, gasses? We have fossil fuel. They have intercellular technology that allows them to travel about at will. And there's portal humps, another change about to take place in us. Genius bumps we call them. Cop a feel. It's your head.

Even if this is all years away, a generation or two or four, they seem worried. So maybe they know they can't stop us from finding out. Perhaps they don't measure time in Earth linear years. So the future is possibly much closer to them than to us, running in simultaneous dimensions. Maybe it's too late to stop us this time because of that. It's impossible to stop humans from having sex. We have sex everywhere across the globe. Today, we are adding nearly 80 million people to the earth's population each year. Whereas for most of human history, up to around 10 thousand years ago Earth's human population remained stabilized at around 8 to 10 million. But now, worldwide, our children are running wild at school and at parties. Paying college institutions to drink and do drugs on video. Perhaps we are at the age of a new Sodom and Gomorrah after all. We're dogs in heat who play piano.

Same sex copulation surely puts a stop to a lot of very sophisticated human bloodlines. Same sex marriage is slowly becoming accepted here in the US. It even helped put an end to the Spartans in the big picture of things.

Have they evolved? Have they been altered so they no longer have the urge to propagate for a reason? I don't know. Will they, like frogs find a way? Like the Northern Salmon, learn how to change their sex to breed? Is that in our future? I don't want to know. I do know we are evolving, and evolving faster and faster. With every generation, we get bigger, stronger, and if not all of us smarter, at least more technically advanced.

If the Aliens really know our future, as well as they know our past, they must surely fear they can't control us any longer. Partly due to Jerry wanting to enjoy and save us from them, he becomes us. But because the others do fear our enlightenment, The Magical Man is now gone forever. Gray saved his greatest Magical Man Trick for his final exit. The big surprising climax Jerry wished for Gray McGuiness' illustrious career. The last magic box trick, the exchange of a murdered dismembered Adonis for a dead to the creative world filmmaker. Me, Jozeph Picasso. Perhaps, who knows, saving my soul for a rainy day?

Despite everything that has happened. I've become the It Man. A Human Bagman to the Space Travelers' Advisory board. I'm but a runner for the Alien Security Council, whose remaining right leg at that very same moment was being bemoaned on the other side of the hill at UCLA. If anyone still has any doubts of who we humans really are, eat meat with your bare hands next time. See if it brings out the primitive animal. Only, I kind of liked Blipping around, and as soon as I figure out how to do it by myself... you know I will be Blippin'.

I'd like to Blip myself into something less taxing than these next few days to come. But today is the beginning of my new tomorrow. I am no longer allowing anyone to dump on me. No man or woman is dumping anything on me again. I'm a survivor. And survivors don't allow it.

By the time I'm done thinking all this, I've managed to tape the arms of the garbage chute door hinges together on all three floors. It's now impossible to pull the doors open. The putrid garbage smell is locked inside and under the building where it belongs forever. I can evolve that! When I get back upstairs and in front of my computer I will compose a nice terse letter to all concerned to inform them that the garbage chute crises is over. They have lost their privilege to torment me with their garbage forevermore. We, as an apartment community, have evolved beyond raining waste down on Jozeph Picasso.

The freedom of such an action has given me wind in my sail. I drive my now dented up Jimmy down to my local coffee shop in downtown Studio City. I perch myself on a stool by the window with my hot cup of joe and a stack of local newspapers. Not surprising, my picture is plastered on the front cover of the LA Times, the Daily News, and nationally in USA Today.

Being still missing is quite amusing, since no one called my number while I was awake and I checked three times to make sure it was working. Was Jerry having my calls held? Maybe. But not once this morning has anyone come to my door. If I am dead and walking amongst the living as but a shadow of my former self, it's okay by me.

In the meantime, I read the account of how Jetty DiGarbo called 911 in a fit of drunken hysteria, and confessed tearfully to the killing of Gray McGuiness in the throes of jealousy. And how he had dismembered Gray and buried him, with the help of others, who remain unnamed, in Gray's Magical Chest at the edge of an earthen water storage canal in Sun Valley. Then somehow Jetty flung himself from the top of the stairs onto his white marble foyer floor. He landed at the foot of his beloved olive tree grown in his Bel Air mansion to end his own life. But the story does not end there. Damn, I've got a four page story in the LA Times. The world knows who I am. I'm suddenly a new kind of mental real estate. Great. I'll paraphrase. Wow, you miss a lot when you get buried alive.

Because, after digging up Gray's Magical Chest, an alive, though uncommunicative, Jozeph Picasso was surprisingly found inside the chest, alone, with both attached legs. Before opening the box Mr. Picasso was accidentally shot in the back by a Detective Mike Tucker. Now he and Sergeant Leonard MacAroy are on leave of duty pending investigation that will include the shooting of two of Jetty's employees outside his front door after the 911 call.

The story continues onto the back page... saying that the real surprise came when shortly after being driven away, Jozeph Picasso once again became a missing person. The empty ambulance was found abandoned at Sherman Way and Whitsett Avenue in North Hollywood. No drivers or ambulance workers were found. None were reported missing or stolen, leaving local authorities to believe that Jozeph Picasso was abducted by underworld friends of Jetty DiGarbo. If they only knew how over worldly wrong they could be.

At least there is no further mentioning of me being a suspected mass murdererererer. The fact that my leg had already been cremated and that I was found to have two attached legs is simply explained by way of a possible misidentification of the found leg as being mine. Perhaps the leg was wearing my boot because I gave my clothing away to Goodwill. A simple matter that was brought up by a Mr. Ernie Burnstein Jr. who made the suggestion on national camera. That could have indeed been the case when checking Goodwill records. Picasso often gave to Goodwill his own clothing and those he'd collected left from tenants of Mystery Towers. How bad could the guy be? Hey, it says it right here in black and white. Dead and/or missing I'm not so bad a guy. How's that for a spin. Alive I was barely worth knowing unless you cared to stop by Earth long enough to screw up my life. I'm almost touched by the positive press.

As I sit here I'm waiting for a visitor. One that I'm sure will be quite surprised to see me in the flesh once again. I made three calls on my cell phone while driving here. One to Erin to let her know I'm still living. She cried. And wasn't one bit mad about not getting laid last night. One call to Claire to make sure she made it home all right from her experience of being taken over by His Jerryness. She seemed very hung over and didn't quite understand what had come over her last night. She thinks she may have experienced her first lesbian encounter because she woke up in bed with two gorgeously strange women. I didn't mention Jerry to her because she seemed to be okay with being partially out of the closet to me. She made an appointment with her therapist just in case.

Who am I to argue? She felt bad about Jetty offing himself so publicly. Not ashamed to have rebuffed him in his desires for her. She felt his actions where entirely of his own doing, manifested in his sordid mind. Even in his public confession of what he'd done to the Magical Man because of his love for her.

My third call wasn't strictly business but could financially change my life forever. I look up and see his smiling face and know that someone truly inside the business is glad to see I've made it back. Even if he does shave his head and wears pants that expose his rich little abused butt.

"Jozeph?"

"Sit down, kid. Jesus, pull up your pants."

"Is it really you?"

"Yes."

"I can't believe it's really you."

"It's really me. Does Daddy have my contract?"

"We both signed it together right after you called. This is so cool. You are so hot right now." He tries to give me a hug. What can I do? I protect my coffee.

"Just stay over there."

"Shit, sorry. It's just that... I still can't believe what just happened to us, man. Remember what I said, you know, about life being out there, man. More out than in, man? Well, dude you are so flyin' out-out there. You know, you never were in, so you're so out now, man, you're blazing."

"So, we be makin' a movie? Because if you try to kiss me again, I'm gonna punch you."

"*Crazy Kind Of Love*, man. We locked in. It's all comin' together as we speak. Damn we gotta start thinkin' about casting. I can't wait to cast the hot chick opposite Claire. Dude, there's some real hot women in this town. This is so amazingly bad. You are one messed up dude, man."

"You have no idea, Junior. And please, pretend you grew up in Beverly Hills around me."

"What? Why?"

"Nothing, never mind, just be your rich ghetto self, Jun."

"Cool, Dogman, you wanna get high?"

"Not with you."

"Be that way. You gotta make me one promise, though."

"At this point, what good are promises in this business?"

"Yeah, but anyway. If at any point in the shoot, you feel we are, you know, like not alone. I don't want to know."

"You mean...?"

"Yeah. I'm done. I don't know what McGuiness really was. And I don't really care either. I'm a producer and a rich kid with stitches where the sun don't shine. That's far out there enough for me right now. Whatever you're into, you're into, just count me out. Okay? I don't want to go that far out again. I don't want to end up a jumpin' Jetty with a face full of foyer stone."

"Done. You got a pen?"

"Here, keep it. Just sign here, and here. Both copies. You heard the 911 tapes from Jetty last night?"

"Not yet."

"It was him. Gray. He was there. Doing like he done me."

"Sure, Junior. Just leave me these and I'll read them over."

"They're standard."

"If there's one thing I found out about this town it's that nothing is standard. I'll have my new agent look them over."

"Whatever. Remember. Nothing's a go if Claire drops out. And you've got to convince her to come back to the show. We'll need it to launch the shoot."

"I think I could arrange that. After last night I'm sure she's a changed woman."

"You did her?"

"Of course not."

"Good, and there's just one little clause my dad put in there. Something about taking a dump in his private bathroom."

"That's out?"

"Next time he'll have you shot."

"Whatever. Twenty-five mil?"

"That's what we're hoping on. Congratulations, Mr. Jozeph Picasso. You're a real writer/director. You're a genuine working Hollywood filmmaker, man. You're a somebody. You're in, man. You're a bankable, dude, and we're going places together."

With that he gets up, the baggy pants producer, shakes my hand, and leaves me watching him through the windows strut down the street.

I look around and suddenly the world is looking back. I'm supposedly dead, or gone, or missing, yet here I am, sitting in a coffee shop with my first big time movie deal in hand. I'm directing a script that I wrote with Claire Davis staring, with a solid twenty-five million dollar budget. Not huge, but big enough for me. "What has the world come to?"

"Don't ask."

Damn.

"I bet you're feeling pretty good about yourself, huh mister Hollywood big shot filmmaker."

"I was."

"It ain't over, Picasso. Know that."

"It's over as far as I'm concerned."

"We'll see."

"Stay away from me, Mook. Hologram or otherwise."

"Hey, watch it, white boy. We be walkin' in the same circle of light, pal. If they need you again, you won't have a say in the matter."

"Circle this."

"I didn't put you back in that box, remember that."

"Okay. What do you want?"

"I just came in for a cup of joe."

"Bullshit."

"And to read the papers, see if they mentioned my name."

"Very funny."

"You see how it works?"

"No one knows Mook the go betweener."

"That's your job, to take the heat for us. So, I give you about five minutes before your life hits the fan."

"I got news for you, Mooky. Not around me. Not anymore. No one gives me any trouble. Not knowing what I know now."

"Cool. As long as you keep it to yourself, I'm cool with that. Just let me know if you need any help. I'm always right here, just use that phone."

"Enjoy."

"Got any new tattoos?"

"Shut up and read."

"You still want the bird?"

"Caw? Where is he?"

"Sitting on your truck. He likes you."

"Is he a real bird or something you guys genetically made?"

Mooky just sips his coffee and reads.

"Well?"

"Some things you don't need to know, Picasso."

Corrections, some things I don't want to know.

"Maybe next time you witness a crime, you'll just tell the truth."

"We do what we do to get by, Mook. It's human nature."

"Your momma tell you that?"

"Found out the hard way. It's all about the Alien Biz."

"Got that straight."

"As the crow flies."

ALIEN MOBSTER

Jozeph Picasso's

Alien Trilogy Act 3
Filmmaking Adventures

When face to face with yourself
the trick is in which life you live.

Jozeph Picasso

PROLOGUE

Given the gravity of the moment, I hope this isn't my final confession for the horrible things they make me do on their behalf.

I'm not one to fear death and what may come beyond it. However, it always worries me when crossing a track in time the only thing the mind conjures is "Should've seen the train coming."But the plain truth is, this is no illusion. This ending moment is happening right now. The caboose of this event is passing on top of my chest, tearing me to shreds.

I, Jozeph Picasso, Alien Mobster, do humbly admit my violent despicable actions are being controlled by Aliens.

Karl J. Niemiec

Only, it's not working out so well.

The scent of burnt Java-Logs from designer Frazer Park Mountain log cabins stifles the air. I'm covered to my eyelids in frozen snow-slush, staring up at foreboding night clouds above the trees. Their rims glow wild from a fool's moon.

Mother Nature is freeze-drying me with her steady icy flake onslaught, kindly mummifying me before I'm eaten by an Alien enhanced werewolf. Yes, I hear the words rattle around in my skull. It's a true Humanimalia crime study unfolding before me.

You bastard, Mook. How could you leave me in these mountains alone to kill a cold-bloodedly monster-strong, hairy, wolf-like man-thing? With a set of gnarly white teeth and claws so full of razor sharp nails, that they allow him to scale anything at will, bounding like a cartoon villain from tree to tree. A real Alien werewolf! Just thinking it congregates images of my childhood watching old Universal B Movies. Me shivering in endless back-lake hotel rooms waiting for Pop to come off the ice so we could trade what he caught for other foods. But this is no movie. This is as real as a horror-able life gets. I'm fighting for my life in immense bloodletting pain with a thing so supernatural and scary I actually soiled myself.

Add freezing to my misery since my ski jacket is half torn away. I'm freezing to death because I missed it. I missed with the only Alien enhanced laser guided silver bullet shot I took before he bit my arm in two and took the gun from me. Missed slightly I should say, because I hit the bastard good. I just missed his heart by that much. Not a bad shot considering I was on the run, slipping and sliding, nearly shooting over my shoulder. The bullet passed right through him without hitting his heart and killing him. Hit or miss, it's a matter of inches that can make or take one's career in this town. In my case, it's my newfound fandangle showbiz life.

This werewolf has me dead to right. I've lost this round fair and square. I'm a lunar eclipse as humans go. I'm about to pass into never-happeness. Because the unfortunate part is that Dr. James Elwartowski, aka Alien Werewolf from another solar

302

system, has already bitten me. It grabbed a great big chunk out of my right arm, breaking the bone just above the elbow. Now the shattered arm is pinned behind me completely useless in my moment of needing to flap my arms and flee. The only two chances I've got of not bleeding to death are if I freeze to death first, or if the good doctor finds me in time to finish the deadly deed by eating me alive.

One thing for sure, I won't underestimate anyone again and won't run if I miss. I'll stand my ground next time and take what I've got coming. Especially, if I'm still in the middle of directing my first Hollywood movie with the Hollywood starlet I think I'm in love with. Next time, I won't allow my clone to get all the glory of spending New Years Eve with her in a romantic Connecticut rental home, all alone, accept for her two lesbian coworkers and my cuddly dog.

I won't let what's happening to me happen to me silently again if given the chance. I won't become one of their button men hidden from the human world. What I take from this moment is simple. If I live long enough for them to ever call upon me again. And I'm talking about the Alien Mob. I'll end it quickly by killing myself publicly. Instead of living the secret lies they make for me. This is the last time I'll ever let this happen to me. From now on, nobody lives my life but me. Even if it is my own Alien enhanced identical clone.

Damn, I'm dying again. I can feel it coming on now, creeping up from my toes.

"Mook, where are you? Caw, help me!" Nothing....then....

About the Author

To find a life worth writing about I stuck my thumb out at 19 to explore America and beyond. It's been quite an adventure since and I'm still writing the crest to wherever it's taking me. There are many things I would've done differently if I'd known better. Rides I would've taken advantage of, roads I wouldn't have taken. But I am the writer I am today because I did what I had to do to survive. Looking back, I'm lucky to be alive many times over, and I've witnessed and held in my hands strangers and loved ones who didn't make it on the way. I'm grateful I had the freedom to meet the people I've met, and the nerve to make those choices to create a family while it was happening. I see my life as half full, with many goals still to accomplish, and I'm a better man because of the life I've lived thus far. Jozeph Picasso Alien Adventures are based on those personal stories. Though many of the adventures in these stories are real and happened to me just as I wrote them, the characters in them have been altered to protect the innocent and have been twisted together into a sci-fi tale to fit within these pages.

Many Blessings.

Karl J. Niemiec

www.ingramcontent.com/pod-product-compliance
Lightning Source LLC
Chambersburg PA
CBHW061129200626
46817CB00016B/519